GOLDEN FAE

THE WORLD OF FAE
BOOK 8

TERRY SPEAR

PUBLISHED BY:

Wilde Ink Publishing

Golden Fae

Copyright © 2016 by Terry Spear

Cover by Terry Spear

Discover more about Terry Spear at:

http://www.terryspear.com/

ABOUT THE BOOK

How does the golden fae get into big time trouble with one fiery dragon? When playing with fire...

All the golden fae wanted to do was to pick mushrooms for her mother—in the forbidden dragon fae territory, but Kayla sees dragons practicing for their games, and she gets caught at it. She loses her locket that she needs to have when she comes of age in just a couple of weeks so she can keep her magic as a lavender grower for the golden fae. Only now, one highly annoying dragon shifter fae has got it, and she will do anything to get it back.

Alton can't believe it when the golden fae arrives at his friend's castle wearing the dragon fae aura now! But he has a mission to go on, save a human and a dragon fae in the human world, and Kayla ends up there offering to help—anything to get him to give her locket back to her. Only a fae seer shoots him with an iron bolt, and Kayla risks everything, trying to get him and the captured maid safely back home again.

Now he will do almost anything to learn the mysterious golden fae's secrets and protect her from his own kind at all costs.

To Cat Belkovsky for loving my fae world! May you always have good fortune and enjoy their antics even if the fae visit you to play tricks on you.

PROLOGUE

Unable to resist watching them despite how dangerous the notion was, Kayla saw two dragons practicing for the dragon games, one brown and the other a blue as brilliant as the sky until he disappeared against the blueness like a chameleon. The two dragons shot flames at each other as if in a swordfight. Despite knowing better, she raced through the woods, when she shouldn't have even been there, but the dragon fae woods next to the river dividing their territory from the golden fae's had the best mushrooms she'd ever found, right on this side. She couldn't resist them either. And no one ever came here to this side of the river. So why should they go to waste? Her mother, Tasha, loved them. And as much as her mother was always doing for her, she loved to prepare them for her in lots of different dishes.

Not that Kayla ever admitted that's where she'd gotten them from. Her mother would have been horrified.

All Kayla had to do was fae transport over to the riverbank, dash into the cover of the woods, search for the mushrooms, then transport right back home. No problem. She never got caught, never had seen any dragon fae in the area, so she wasn't worried about it. Only this time, she saw the dragons practicing for the dragon games, something she'd never seen and never would be able to observe, not as a golden fae when her kind and the dragon fae shifters were arch competitors for gold in any form.

Curiosity got the best of her, and she dropped her sack of mushrooms in the dark piney woods and headed for the clearing just ahead where she could get a better glimpse of the dragons. She saw them then diving around each other, flying together, splitting off, and circling. She wondered if it was a kind of dance.

Her eyes widened. A mating dance? Ohmigoddess, how cool!

She was hidden in the understory of the pine trees, bright green ferns as tall as a man giving her sufficient cover, but then she couldn't see the dragons as they headed for the sun. Only the brown one was visible as a pinprick in the sky. She moved closer to the edge of the bracken, squinting against the glare of the sun, hand over her brow, shading her eyes.

First, she saw nothing. Not even the pinprick of brown in the sky any longer. Disappointed that they'd left the area, she still remained there, hoping to catch another glimpse of them. That was when she saw a spot in the sky morph into the form of a dragon—the blue dragon. He was still mostly camouflaged by the sky, but he was growing closer, more vivid blue, and he was...

He was headed her way! Her heartbeat tripped.

All the gold she was wearing must have caught a bit of sunlight and broadcasted that a golden fae was standing next to the understory of the piney woods. No longer hidden by them. But standing there for the whole dragon fae world to see.

Her heart pounding erratically, she thought she could just transport from there, but when she tried, she didn't go anywhere at all. That had to mean iron ore was in the soil here. She started pulling off her gold earrings and necklaces, her headdress and throwing them in the ferns behind her. Like the golden fae, the dragon shifters could smell gold. He would go for that before he came for her.

At least she hoped.

But when she tossed one of her necklaces, the chain of the locket she always wore tangled with it and both fell behind her. She turned to go back for it, but she heard the dragon's wings flapping up and down, drawing way too close. He roared and she dashed off, hoping that he wouldn't find that necklace as it had fallen between the fronds and was somewhere on the muddy ground. Her boots squished in the mud, leaving footprints, but she was also leaving a fae dust trail behind.

She reached her bag of mushrooms, grabbed it, not wanting the dragon to know why she'd been over here, or she would never be able to return, and told herself to transport. And nothing happened. She tried again, thinking that she was so scared she'd messed it up somehow, which was impossible. But she just stood there, not going anywhere when she'd transported to the riverbank multiple times before, with no trouble at all. She dove beneath a ledge of speckled granite rock and prayed to every god and goddess there was that the dragon wouldn't find her before she could swim across the river.

No, not swim across just yet. As soon as she was certain he was gone, she would return for the locket, hoping beyond hope it was still there.

ALTON HADN'T BELIEVED anything could steal his concentration while he'd practiced with Olaf as they did their maneuvers, flying around each other, trying to take the advantage, trying to best each other as they knew they would have to do in the dragon games. They had nearly finished their practice because Olaf had a job to do, though as competitive as Alton was, as soon as Olaf took off, he'd had every intention on practicing further on his own. Until he caught sight of the glint of gold in the bracken, and a girl wearing it.

As soon as she realized he was coming for her, she dashed into the shelter of the bracken, but he tore after her, intent on seeing who she was, his dragon practice all but forgotten.

He couldn't believe it when he found a trail of jewelry left behind as if telling him the way to go. But he knew she thought to stop him in his tracks while he gathered up all the gold. He could have come back for it, but then he would have reached her too quickly, and he didn't want to end the hunt too soon.

Who was he kidding? Dragons lived for treasure, and he couldn't ignore any ring, necklace, or bracelet she had tossed away in her haste. She knew his kind too well.

He finally reached a stone ledge and looked out across the churning river, her fae dust ending right here. She had to have swum across at this point. Disappointed now that he hadn't caught up to her, he considered his next move. He would set all the jewelry down in the middle of the open field on a big stone and see if she came for it while he practiced more of his maneuvers up above.

If she was a golden fae, maybe she would risk coming back for it, but this time he wouldn't collect just her gold. He smiled darkly at the thought.

KAYLA RETURNED to the fronds at the edge of the clearing, careful not to allow anyone to catch sight of her and saw a dragon circling high up above, only this one was purple scaled. But what caught her eye next was her jewelry piled up on a slab of stone as if saying, "Come and get me if you can."

Where was the blue dragon? She glanced quickly around, worried he was hiding in the trees while the other kept guard over her jewelry. Knowing waiting for the dragon to leave was futile, she had to look again through the fronds, found the imprint of her locket in the mud, but the locket was gone.

ALTON CIRCLED for the longest time, got tired of waiting for the girl to show up, and dove down to grab the jewelry. As soon as he did, a falcon fae dove toward him, trying to chase him off like he'd seen a tenacious smaller bird try to chase off a larger bird of prey. But he was a dragon! Not a bird of prey, and she was a falcon fae, a girl equipped with falcon wings that enabled her to fly. He seized the gold jewelry and was intent on returning to his castle when the falcon fae attacked him again. With one burst of flame, he could incinerate her for attempting to steal *his* gold!

She had to be deranged. With his teeth, he managed to grab hold of her locket, and tore it from her neck. Served her right to fight him for the gold the fae had left behind for him.

She screeched at him, and he flew home, his powerful wings carrying him farther away from where she was. Then he transported to his castle gate and entered, shutting it behind him.

As a dragon, he didn't leave a fae trail dust, so she wouldn't have any idea where he'd gone. Served her right. He smiled and would add the treasure to his as soon as he had a moment to do so. Who would ever have thought a day practicing for the games could lead to a treasure hunt too?

1

"I have a week to find the golden locket," Kayla said, as she and her friend, Tanya, headed for the river that divided the land of the dragon fae kingdom of Morcalon and a small corner of the golden fae territory. "Or my life is forfeit."

Tanya was a dream-weaver fae, her red-blond hair often worn in curls on top of her head, pink flowers in half a circle around her hair this time, green eyes that hinted at a world of secrets. She and her parents were the only ones of their kind living in the golden fae kingdom. She and Tanya got along great, loved to hang out in the human world when they could both get away, loved to go to the movies and the beaches there. Unlike Kayla, Tanya cared nothing for jewelry or any kind of metal ornamentation. She was strictly a flower girl, and she often wore silky, dreamy-looking gowns, which suited her dream-weaver fae persona.

Kayla focused on her problem though. She was still furious with herself for getting into the predicament she had when she'd left the locket behind and a dragon fae shifter had taken it. She didn't have a clue as to which one. A blue one. Sure. But there were probably tons of blue dragons in the dragon fae kingdom. When she'd returned to the place where she had lost the locket, all she'd found were his huge dragon footprints, and she'd followed them to the edge of the woods. She'd heard a dragon's wings flapping and expected to see him flying off. Except the dragon was the prettiest shade of violet. She hadn't heard of a dragon changing colors, but the one who had come after her had definitely been blue. So had another come to see what was going on? She'd never heard of a dragon that color before though.

What had happened to the blue dragon then?

"You don't know for sure which dragon took it, right? You can't go asking them. You can't go traipsing around their territory, nor are they allowed into yours. They hide their stacks of treasure and even if you did learn which one did it, you would have to discover where it's hidden. And then you would have to get past his traps or guards or whatever keeps people from trying to abscond with it. If he or she caught you trying to steal it back, no matter that it was yours in the first place, you would be toast."

All valid points and Kayla hated to admit her friend was right. "It was mine. If I take it back, I'm only reclaiming *my* treasure." More than that. It was a right of passage for her kind. Kayla had to hold it in her possession until she turned of age in two weeks! The magic in the locket would be bonded with her forever after that. Without it, she was lost. Her fields of lavender wouldn't bloom and flourish in the spring, which was just two weeks away! And she would be excommunicated from her homeland.

"They won't see it that way. Maybe if you can bargain for it…"

"They won't bargain. They hoard their gold, just like the golden fae do." Kayla forged through the fronds behind her.

"Yeah, and if you were able to speak with one on neutral territory, he would think that you were trying to steal from him."

Kayla let out her breath in an annoyed huff. "Don't you think I know that? It doesn't really matter anyway. If I get caught trying to steal back my locket, I'm dead. If I don't have it when my time is up, I'm dead. Lavender is like gold to our people. And the queen will have my head if I don't have my locket at the celebration and the flowers never come back. No lavender for tea, breads, rice, chicken, for scenting our clothes, for the dye that—added to roses, a little mint, and some lemon juice—creates the beautiful, bright pink cloth that our queen loves for her gowns and curtains more than any other color in the world, and everything else she uses it for. If only my mother could grow the lavender, but she can't." Not to mention the medium, violet-colored flowers were Kayla's heritage and she loved them and loved working with them. Who could say they toiled all day in fields of lavender and came out smelling like... lavender?

"How do you know it was a dragon shifter who stole it if you didn't see him do it?"

"I found the imprint of the locket in the mud. And right next to it, big dragon footprints. Now, if I could match up the dragon footprints, I would have it made. Well, not that I could easily get my locket back, but at least I would know who took it."

"Then the dragon came onto our lands when he wasn't supposed to. You can appeal to the queen for restitution."

Kayla didn't respond. How could she tell her friend she had been picking mushrooms and then had seen some dragons practicing for their dragon competitions flying high above the treetops on *their* side of the river and fascinated, she headed into the pines to watch? She would never have had the opportunity to otherwise. But also, she should never have been over there in the first place, collecting mushrooms.

She was certain the gold had bought her time when she'd dumped all the jewelry she'd been wearing. The dragon couldn't give up the opportunity to take home her beautiful gold treasures. If only the chain of her locket hadn't tangled with her other necklaces, though valuable, *they* were replaceable.

Before she could run back and retrieve the locket from the mud where it had settled—courtesy of the rainstorm they'd had the night before—one of the dragons had nearly reached her. And in truth, as she'd hidden beneath the ledge, she'd heard his claws tapping on the top of the rock ledge as if telling her he knew she was hiding beneath it. Her skin had chilled at the sound. Had he smelled the gold she'd been wearing on her face, arms, and hands? Had he been making her sweat for having been on their lands?

But he didn't do anything more than taunt her because he already had her gold?

What could she do but return later and find the dragon had stepped on her locket, pressing it into the mud underneath one of the ferns. She'd seen an imprint of her family's crest, a sword and flowers, and two large dragon clawed feet standing on either side of it where he'd placed his feet after stepping on the locket.

"You were on *this* side of the river, weren't you?" Tanya's green eyes were wide in disbelief, as if suddenly figuring out the truth.

"I might have been on the other side."

"Kayla! You know it is forbidden. So if you dropped the locket over there, it's finders keepers and you don't have a prayer at claiming ownership. If you ever did. I can't believe this. You can't even go to the council and ask to have them send a missive to the dragon fae queen, stating a dragon fae shifter had come onto our lands illegally when you'd accidentally lost your locket and the dragon stole it. Why didn't you tell me?"

"For this very reason!" Then Kayla explained exactly what had happened.

Tanya just keep shaking her head with condemnation. "I can't believe you've managed to live this long. Picking mushrooms over there? Don't we have any over here?"

"Not like those."

Tanya let out her breath. "What was it last winter that you risked your neck over while your garden was lying dormant? You traveled to Wolf Mountain to see if winged wolf shifters actually existed? What if they had and they'd killed you for invading their territory? Besides, you didn't even ask me if I wanted to go."

Kayla laughed. "Like you would have disobeyed your parents and gone with me."

"You could have asked. I didn't say I would have gone. But I might have. Now you will never know."

"I've been thinking about that. What if they do exist?"

"The wolf shifters?"

"Yeah. Just because I didn't see them doesn't mean they weren't there. Only that they didn't want me to see them."

"Just because the mountain is called Wolf Mountain, doesn't mean any wolves live there. I think you didn't see them because they don't exist." Tanya glanced back in the direction of their cottages. "Well, what colors were they?"

"What colors were what?"

"The dragons you saw practicing for the games. That would give you a clue as to which one it was."

"One was brown and the other blue. The blue one blended with the sky and was nearly invisible. I thought how hard it would be to shoot him with a bolt if he was soaring against the blue sky. And then, the oddest thing occurred. The blue dragon, who had followed me, was not the one I saw leaving the area. His scales were violet."

"I didn't think they could change colors."

"Neither did I."

"I didn't think there was such a thing as a purple dragon either."

Neither did Kayla.

Once they reached the white-capped river rushing over the smooth-faced boulders, Kayla and Tanya hid in the understory of the trees and ferns reaching six feet in height. It was perfect for hiding most men intent on spying on the enemy, for the enemy was the dragon fae shifter kind. That was the trouble when two kinds of fae wanted the same thing—gold, and tons of it.

Their kinds were very much different from each other. Not only did the dragon shifter fae turn into dragons at whim, but they hoarded their gold and kept it hidden away; whereas, the golden fae were exactly who they appeared to be. Fae who loved their gold and showed it off at all times.

Except for now. Kayla had learned her lesson and was completely unadorned, wearing no gold in any shape or form so that the sun's rays couldn't reflect off the shiny metal and give her away. Kayla felt naked without her gold, uncomfortable, maybe reminiscent of discarding her jewelry the last time and losing the locket.

Not wearing the gold didn't mean another fae couldn't recognize them if they saw her or Tanya. Her golden aura couldn't be disguised unless she bribed a fae who had the ability to cloak someone's aura or her own. But a falcon fae they knew could do such a thing. Sigrid loved knowing secrets and holding them against those who wanted her services. So unless Kayla was desperate, which she would be if she couldn't manage this on her own, she refused to use the falcon fae's services.

Tanya had only come along to ensure that Kayla would not cross the river and get herself into more dangerous waters. Kayla knew her friend was irritated with her for not telling her everything from the beginning.

"I don't see any dragon fae. You can't cross the river. I said I would go with you this far, but that's it, Kayla. Do I need to remind you that your uncle met his end doing just what you're thinking of doing? Playing with fire will get you worse than burned. You'll be dead. Incinerated. Ashes. The dragon fae don't play around when it comes to protecting their gold. You're just lucky they didn't torch you right then and there, and instead, stopped to get your gold."

"It's my locket and if I don't get it back, I'm dead anyway."

Tanya let out her breath. "There is that." She stared at Kayla for a moment, then shook her head. "You look so...plain."

"So do you." Kayla's kind were always covered in gold—headdresses, earrings, necklaces, even flakes of gold on their face and hands—more, if they were at a party. Even when they went to the world of humans. Why not? Some of them wore blue or pink or purple hair. So what was a little gold ornamentation for the fae? The humans thought the golden fae were cool. Or weird. Sometimes the golden fae started a new trend. Not that the humans knew what they were.

Tanya frowned at her. "I always look like this."

"I know, I just mean…oh, forget it." Kayla had offered gold to her friend to dress her up a bit, but Tanya had always declined, preferring the more natural, unadorned look. Except for her hair, and she loved fresh flowers in her hair.

"Someone is coming." Tanya crouched lower.

Kayla moved closer to the edge of the river on their side, though they needn't have hidden. They were perfectly within their rights to be here.

Tanya grabbed her arm, nearly giving Kayla a seizure. "What?" she whispered harshly. "We are on *our* side of the river!"

"And if they see you, then they will begin patrolling over there if they believe one of our kind is even thinking of crossing the river. Or maybe even because of knowing that one of our kind *did* get caught over there."

"I *didn't* get caught."

"Well, nearly. And you left all kinds of evidence behind that said you'd been over there. They might even be patrolling the area right now."

"What if I pretend to be drowning in the river and one rescues me? Then I'll be on their side of the river, and—"

"And if they don't rescue you? Besides, you won't be able to tell if they're dragon shifters or just plain dragon fae. Unless they shift, and if they do, they could just drop you right back over here.

They're not going to keep you on their side. If they don't just get rid of you."

Tanya had a point. Kayla stiffened as a girl and boy came into view, both about her and Kayla's age—the boy wearing human clothes—jeans, a T-shirt, sneakers as if he was planning to go to the human world and wanted to fit in. He stopped at the water's edge and looked in Tanya and Kayla's direction. Her skin chilled. But she reminded herself she could be here. She was on the golden fae land and well-hidden anyway.

Dark eyes as brown as the dragon she'd seen flying in the sky with the blue one the other day, appeared to look straight at her. Yet, she knew he couldn't see her. She didn't think.

The wind swept his curly, dark brown hair about his face, and she had to admit he was cute in a roguish-looking way.

The girl had short black hair when most of the fae women wore their hair long. She was dressed in a black leather corset, leggings, and a sword was sheathed at her waist.

Kayla's heart practically stopped when she realized who she was. "Ena," she said under her breath.

Tanya nodded. "Dragon shifter fae. A fae tracker, deadly assassin, your worst nightmare."

"Alton," Ena said, arms folded across her waist, looking annoyed, "Brett and I always had a connection. I can't explain why I fell for him, but I did. So get over it."

"He was human. Your prisoner."

"And he turned out to be one of us. Kind of."

Alton snorted.

"What about Aideen? She's fun to be with, cute, and looking for a mate."

Kayla raised her brows. Ena, the darkest dragon shifter, was giving dating advice to another dragon shifter? She smiled. She just bet he would love to know golden fae were listening in on their conversation that looked to be private otherwise. *Not.*

Alton rolled his eyes.

Ena laughed. "Now *you* are copying that annoying mannerism that Brett uses."

"I ought to have killed him when I'd had the chance."

"Ah, you can't tell me you don't like him now."

"The annoying phantom dragon has a way of growing on you."

"Really, I've got to go. You'll find another woman you will truly love. Several are interested in you."

"Shifters? Dragon fae, yes. But who wants a mate who can't fly with you? Can't compete in shifter games? Doesn't have a hoard of gold to call her own?"

"Maybe you should return to the colony where you're from. Where Brett was from. Maybe you'll meet someone new there."

"*Whatever*. I don't need your sympathy. I just wanted to say I think you made a mistake."

"No you don't. As much as you would like to believe I should have married you, you don't really believe it. Besides, I hear the shifter games have opened up to dragons from all over. Polish your scales and be ready. What color are they today?"

"Silver, like they have been for a couple of days." Alton smiled. "Silver scales beat gold any day."

"I don't know. I swear I blink, and they've changed color again. Are you sure they're not tied with your mood?"

Kayla's mouth dropped open. Had Alton been the one then who had been blue and then violet?

"If you call me a mood dragon again—"

The sound of flapping caught everyone's attention and in the fading sunlight, Kayla looked up to see a golden-scaled dragon flying overhead, then dive down, land next to the dragon fae, and shift into a brown-haired boy, his eyes blue like the sea.

So that was who Alton was comparing himself to. The golden dragon mated to Ena.

"Brett," Alton acknowledged, folding his arms.

"Alton." Brett turned his attention to Ena. "We're late. Your brother fixed his first dinner for us in celebration of our union, and he's going to be torqued off."

"I'm coming. Are you going to be all right, Alton?"

"Why wouldn't I be?" Then Alton smiled darkly. "Next week, I'll be beating the tail off your mate."

Brett laughed. "As much as I'm still trying to learn how to control my wings and tail, I wouldn't doubt it. Come on, Ena. I don't want your brother thinking your marrying me was a bad idea. I believe I'm finally getting on his good side. A little, anyway."

Then they said goodbye and Ena shifted into an olive green-scaled dragon, Brett into his golden scales, and they both flew off.

Kayla couldn't help but want to see if Alton would shift. She'd never seen a silver-scaled dragon before. Tanya was barely breathing too as she watched to see what would happen next. What Kayla didn't expect was for Alton to shift and his scales were a shimmery violet. He stared at the water for a moment, looking at the color of his scales, then shook his head.

She suspected he hadn't expected to see them that color. Just like she hadn't. They were beautiful though. All shades of purple were her favorite colors.

She thought Alton would fly off then like the others had done. Instead, he shifted back and said under his breath, "By the goddess, what has happened to me?" He ran his hands through his hair, then turned and stalked off down the rocky bank alongside the river.

Kayla almost felt sorry for him. Curious as to what he would do next, she hurried to follow him, remaining hidden in the ferns, though she was disturbing them as she brushed against them. So was the breeze, and she hoped if he saw the movement, he would only think it was because of the light wind.

Tanya followed right after her, and Kayla wished she wouldn't. With two of them moving in the ferns, they had double the chance to catch the dragon fae's notice. She turned and motioned for her friend to stay back, wishing she would just go home.

Her friend shook her head at her, stubbornly resisting the idea when she hadn't even wanted to be here in the first place. Normally, Tanya just had no sense of adventure.

Then a shadow loomed above them, and they looked up to see the violet dragon hovering overhead, his wings flapping to spread the fern fronds wider so he could see who or what was making all the movement in the bracken.

Not to be intimidated, though he was totally intimidating as big as he was, and with the knowledge that his fire could be the end of her, not to mention his wicked claws and teeth could tear a fae to pieces, she rose to her feet and placed her hands on her hips. "You are on *our* side of the river."

He merely smiled, showing off a mouth full of dangerously-menacing teeth as if amused, or maybe to show that he didn't care if he was in the golden fae air space or not.

She only smiled back, her teeth very small and not in the least bit dangerous. Tanya stood by her, but she wasn't smiling at all. In a word, she looked: terrified.

"By the way, I love your colorful scales. I wouldn't worry about what anyone else might think of them. Be yourself."

He roared, shooting a flame across the sky in a display of anger.

Tanya sliced a glower at Kayla, her expression saying Kayla shouldn't say anything to antagonize the dragon, who had shown an obvious dislike of his scales shifting colors. Without a word, Tanya blurred and disappeared, using her fae transport and leaving Kayla behind.

At the same time, Kayla ducked a bit from the fiery dragon display, not wanting to show she was afraid of him, but she did have a healthy respect for fire. If he scorched her hair, she was reporting him. No playing nice with the irritated dragon, who *was* in their air space.

She was sure his annoyance about his changing scale color was because he seemed to have no control over it. Maybe not so much that he didn't like this particular version. She could imagine if her hair just suddenly decided to switch to a different pigment at whim. She wouldn't like it either. No choice, no say when, just suddenly it changed.

His fire dried and heated the air and made her want to fan herself, which she resisted. She didn't want him to know that what he was doing affected her in any way.

But she didn't expect his next move. He grabbed her shoulders with his talons and flew off with her! She swallowed the scream on the tip of her tongue and thought to fae transport right out of there and leave him holding empty air. But when she tried, nothing happened! As if she hadn't tried at all!

She tried again, closed her eyes, and concentrated this time, though she'd never had to do so before to fae transport, telling herself she wanted to be sitting in her lavender fields, weeding them like she was supposed to do before the blooms began to arrive. The weeds always shot up way beforehand. But no, she had to run off and antagonize a dragon. Not that she had thought that was how her trip to the river would have ended up. She'd had the notion in mind that she would cross the river and return to the place where she'd lost her necklace and see if the dragon had dropped it when he was carrying so many other gold pieces of jewelry she had left behind. Not that they mattered like the locket did.

"Let me go!" she screamed. He let her go just as she had commanded, and instantly, she realized her folly as soon as she spoke the words.

She was falling to the ocean below, the scream caught in her throat as she again told herself to fae transport. When she couldn't, the ocean spray soaked her clothes. Her heart beating spastically, she braced for impact.

To her shock, dragon talons grasped her by the arms and carried her upward, away from the water. She should have felt some elation, but she didn't. She was still thinking about how she had nearly plunged into the ocean, until she focused on what he was doing with her now. She wouldn't make the mistake of telling him to let her go again, no matter how much she wanted to.

Infuriating dragon. He had no right trying to terrorize her like this.

Then he flew her over to the beach and deposited her on the warm sand. She fell to her knees, unable to quit shaking and her legs had just plain given out. No matter how much she hadn't wanted to look like she was shaken from the whole experience, she couldn't force herself to pretend otherwise. He settled beside her, studying her, his dark brown eyes curious.

She rose shakily to her feet, felt a large seashell beside her foot, grabbed it up, and threw it at him. The conch shell hit him squarely on his scaly chest, and his eyes widened in surprise. She liked when she could unsettle him as much as he had her.

"You had no right taking me from my realm!"

He shifted into his fae form, looking as cocky as the devil, folded his arms, and lifted a brow. "You had no right eavesdropping on us."

"We had every right if you're going to talk about anything just across the river from where my friend and I were getting ready to fish." She didn't know why she said that. She didn't owe him any explanation.

"Really? I saw no fishing poles. Unless you catch them with your claws."

"*You* are the one with claws." She was surprised he could grasp her with them like he did and not hurt her. She should have tried transporting herself home again right then and there, if she even could. She thought maybe his holding her had somehow stopped her from transporting.

But she'd never gotten this close to a dragon before, and she was curious about him. "So the Goth dragon stood you up for the golden dragon?" She wasn't sure why practically every word she said to him was meant to rub him the wrong way.

"What were you really doing at the river's edge? Not contemplating crossing the river to my side, were you? And causing some kind of mischief? You know how my kingdom feels about your kind entering our realm."

"Like you came over on our side?"

"The air space can't be controlled by anyone."

"Says you. Why do you wear human clothes? Are you going to their world?"

"Why didn't you try to transport when I first carried you off?"

She truly had thought it had something to do with his claws holding tight to her. She didn't know why it would be otherwise. She hadn't been able to transport since she'd lost the locket. *Ohmigoddess*. She had thought that if she couldn't find the locket in time, she would just transport somewhere else and go into hiding, well, except she would keep searching for the locket. Did that mean she couldn't now?

Her heart beating wildly and the palms of her hands sweating, she tried to leave the fae way again. Nothing. Happened.

Attempting to appear nonplussed by it in front of the dragon when she felt anything but, she shrugged. She wasn't about to tell him she couldn't transport.

"You like to live dangerously then?" he asked.

Sometimes, but flying through the air on a collision course with the ocean was not exactly her idea of living dangerously. Trying some new ice cream, or hair color, yes. Tracking down her locket was going to be dangerous enough.

He suddenly frowned. "You are a golden fae. I can see your aura. But you aren't wearing any gold at all. I have never heard of one of your kind being out and about who was not adorned from the top of her head to the tip of her toes in gold. Were you afraid your gold would catch the rays of the sun and tip us off that you were hiding in the bracken and spying on us? That's it, isn't it?" He smiled, then furrowed his brow at her again. "Tell me why you were there, or I will leave you here to perish."

"Where is here?" If it wasn't too far from home, she would just walk.

"No Man's Land is that way." He motioned in the opposite direction of the beach. "If you climb up that cliff and make it to the other side, you would be in the hawk fae territory. But the creatures that live in those caves in the cliffs would make a meal of you, either when you're attempting to climb the cliffs out of here, or if you remain on the beach for the night."

"So why did you bring me here?"

"To get the truth out of you."

"But I could just fae transport."

"Then why didn't you before? Unless you couldn't. Now that you are here, you have no ability."

Great. Even so, she didn't trust him and tried to transport again. Nothing happened. "Why? Do you?"

"No. Not me either. Iron ore is beneath the soil and the ocean so that even taking a boat away from here will not help you to escape by fae transport. So tell me, what were you and your friend up to?"

"If I tell you, will you return me home?"

"To the place I found you, yes."

"Okay. But you won't believe me."

"Try me."

"I have every intention of stealing your gold."

A lton nearly laughed at the golden fae's claim that she intended to steal his gold, but he wasn't certain she was just jesting about it. What if she seriously believed she could abscond with his treasure? A fae who couldn't even transport places? Not a chance.

"What name do you go by so that I will know it when I find my stockpile of treasure is gone?"

"Kayla."

"Pure and beloved." Alton laughed. "Somehow, I can't see you as pure, as in innocent, not as mischievous as you appear. Beloved? Your mother, of course, would think so."

"And Alton means old town. Why would anyone call you by such a name?"

"I was of the old town, the last dragon shifter born there before my parents moved to Morcalon, and we lived among the dragon fae there. Though the colony moved elsewhere and still remains."

"I have always lived in the countryside outside my village with my mother."

"Sisters? Brothers?"

"None. You?"

"None. Well, Kayla, I will return you to your side of the river, and then I will double my guards to ensure my treasure remains safe. So I should thank you for telling me your plans." He paused before he shifted. "Do you even know where I keep my treasure?"

"No. If you tell me, I would be grateful though."

He smiled, then frowned. "Why *my* gold? Why not Ena's or—"

"Brett's? He is mated to Ena. It's much easier to steal from one dragon than two."

"You do know what we do to anyone who tries to steal our gold, do you not?"

"Yes. Actually, if you could spare one small gold locket, I would leave the rest of your treasures alone."

"And what would I get for it?"

"My undying gratitude."

Alton shook his head. "A golden fae would never give up her treasure, just as a dragon wouldn't." He'd always thought they were an odd sort of fae. Showing off all that wealth was bound to encourage thieves to attempt to steal from them. Better to keep it hidden away.

Then he shifted and carried Kayla to the river, half a mile from where he'd found her. He couldn't chance that her friend had gone for help and her people were searching for her near where he had taken her.

He shifted into his fae form to say, "Happy hunting." Then he shifted back into his dragon form, still not believing his scales were the color of violets again, flew into the woods across the river, and shifted again.

He thought back to the lass, her hair the color of gold, her olive-green eyes with a hint of gold still capturing his imagination. He wondered what she would look like covered in gold. Would he, a dragon and hoarder of gold, want to keep her with his pile of treasure?

He couldn't imagine what was going on regarding his scales, but he couldn't show them off when they were every color of the rainbow and more. He would be the laughingstock of his people if they saw they were now violet.

He considered the golden fae again. They were devious like most of the fae were, and he wondered what Kayla and her friend had truly been up to. He pondered why she couldn't seem to transport on her own like the other fae had done.

Then he saw his advisor, who was also his butler and financial manager, Ferdinand, riding out to find him, when Alton was just getting ready to fae transport.

"What is the matter now?" Alton asked.

"The queen has an assignment of great urgency for you. Mark Creston, that human friend of Brett's, has gone into the human world and not returned. Ena and Brett are searching for him as we speak, but the queen wishes you to go as well. At once."

Alton might not have any control over the changing color of his scales, but at least he could still fae transport. "Who took him there?" The human couldn't have transported himself.

"According to Ena, one of her people took Mark to the human world because he wanted to see his dying foster mother. Somehow, Muriel and he became separated. He has no real family there any longer, so he really has no other place to go."

"Yet, he has gone somewhere, so it seems." Alton didn't care for humans living in their world. They belonged in their own home world. They couldn't fae transport and their injuries didn't heal as quickly as their own. They were nothing but trouble. "So where were they exactly?"

"As far as we know, the school that Ena had to go to in search of the queen's daughter where she'd gone to school herself."

"All right. I'm on my way." At least if the queen ordered it, the pay would be good, courtesy of Brett's saving her life so she would do anything for him that he asked, within reason. Alton just hoped they would find Mark quickly. He loved lots of things about the human world—ice cream shops, their clothes, but school wasn't one of them. Too many rules.

At least he was already dressed like one. He loved their jeans and sneakers and T-shirts too. He appeared next to a set of school lockers, not caring whether he startled anyone with his sudden appearance or not. He was almost disappointed to see the halls were empty as the students must have been in classes.

Then he heard footfalls and saw Ena come around a corner. "Alton. I'm so glad you're here."

"Where's Brett?"

"He's looking on the second floor of the school."

"Any sign of Mark?"

"No. It's not easy finding a human who isn't attending the school any longer. He doesn't leave a fae trail like us either."

"You don't think Mark has hooked up with fae seers, do you?" Alton knew Mark was a fae seer himself and what if he fell into the same old habits? See the fae? Terminate the fae?

"Only if he was forced to go."

The bell rang and the halls filled with students, some heading for the cafeteria. Some heading outside to get lunch somewhere else.

"I'm going outside and watching that door and see if he leaves the building," Alton said.

Ena nodded. "I'll check the cafeteria."

Before they left, they saw Brett coming down the stairs, talking to a blond-haired girl.

Alton folded his arms and smiled. "Your eyes are glowing gold, Ena. You wouldn't be jealous, would you? You wouldn't have to be worried about me if I was talking to a human girl."

"Ha! I'm going to the cafeteria." Ena turned and stalked off but caught Brett's eye.

Brett quickly ended the conversation, but then he saw Alton and hurried to talk to him. "Thanks for coming. I know how much you're not fond of humans so I really appreciate that you're here."

"Mark helped us out a few times. Old girlfriend?" Alton really thought Brett was just trying to learn if the girl had seen Mark. So he was totally surprised when Brett responded to his question in the affirmative.

"Yeah. Did Ena see?"

"Yeah." Alton wanted to feel smug about it, but he shouldn't have because he was friends with Brett now. Okay, so he felt wholly smug about it. He smirked.

"Talk to you later." Frowning, Brett hurried after Ena.

So much for Brett looking for his friend.

Guess the job was all Alton's. Then he saw a girl with chestnut colored hair, her back to him, but her petite build and her gold jewelry made him think of Kayla. No way would she be here. Curiosity got the better of him and he stalked off to catch up to her.

"Where have you been all this time?" Tanya asked, looking ready to slug Kayla for scaring her as she joined her at the river's edge. "I've been to your cottage so many times, trying to avoid your mother seeing me and wondering where you'd gone to. Tasha would have known something was wrong. I was getting ready to call the guard. But I knew you would kill me, given the reason we were at the edge of the river in the first place. I thought you had transported right behind me. Then you didn't appear, and I didn't know where you'd gone to. I went back and your fae dust trail just disappeared! I thought the dragon had taken you hostage. But I was certain he wouldn't have. So I returned to where we'd been and saw the dragon fly across the river from our side, only a half a mile south of there. I chanced transporting here and sure enough, there you were."

"He wanted to know why we were spying on him."

"What? He shifted? Talked to you?"

"Yes. I told him I intended to steal his gold."

Tanya's jaw dropped. "You...didn't."

"I did. He wouldn't have believed it. I asked him for one locket then. I wanted to see his reaction. If he'd been the one who had picked up the locket and my other gold that one day, I figured he would look smug, or surprised, maybe thinking that I had been the one who had dropped it, or something."

"So how did he react?"

Kayla let out her breath and began to walk home. "He just smiled darkly and asked what he would get for it."

"What did you say?" Tanya asked, her eyes wide.

"That he would earn my undying gratitude. He didn't believe I would stop at wanting just my locket."

"I can't believe you really talked to one. Do you think he's the one who took your gold?"

"I think so. From what he and Ena were talking about, his scales keep changing color on him, so I think it was him. Maybe if he was flying around this area, his gold is even hidden around there."

"Or the other dragon's gold was? But you said they were practicing for the dragon games. If he was even one of them that you saw that day. I doubt two dragons would be in the same area if one had his gold hidden around there. Whatever possessed you to hang around and talk to him?"

"Okay, listen. For whatever reason, I can't fae transport. It must have to do with not having my locket. The whole thing is tied in, I guess. I had every intention of leaving, but I couldn't."

"Ohmigoddess, that's awful."

"Tell me about it. If Mom expects me to fae travel somewhere, I won't be able to. And then she'll probably know why."

"I would never have left you behind if I'd known that. Why didn't you tell me?"

"I didn't know. I haven't needed to fae transport until the big, bad dragon was in our airspace. Well, when I was on the other side of the river too, I had lost the ability, but I hadn't connected the dots."

"You need to tell your mom that you've lost your locket. She might even have a good idea as to what to do."

"Are you kidding? She would be worried sick that I'll be excommunicated once the day arrives. I need to keep this secret until I can locate the locket and straighten this out."

"Will it reverse the effect of the magic? If you locate it after the fact?"

"I don't know. I hope I can locate it before I have to find out the answer to that question. I had thought to transport somewhere else until I could find the locket so that our people wouldn't ever know."

"But they will. Spring will be here, and your flowers won't be. So what are you going to do?"

"Befriend a dragon. The only one I know for now. He didn't incinerate me for telling him I was going to steal his gold."

"That's because he didn't take you seriously! If you actually tried to do it, he would take care of you, permanently. Forget worrying about the locket." Tanya frowned at her. "I know that look. That you're even considering it makes me think you've lost your mind along with your transporting ability."

"I'm going to ask Sigrid to hide my fae aura. Or disguise it with another fae aura."

"You. Can't. That witch will make you do something for her that you'll soon regret."

"I can't think of any other way to handle this."

"If you do it, then what?"

"I don't know. Ask around and see if anyone has seen a gold locket I lost in the woods?"

"In dragon fae territory? Now I *know* you've got to be nuts."

Kayla didn't believe she had any other choice. "You've got a cousin living in the human world. We could go see her like we've done in the past. Mom won't mind because I'll only be gone a few days."

"When are you seeing Sigrid?"

"*Now*, first thing. I need to do this now and I guess ask Sigrid if she can fix it so I can have control over the aura or Mom would see that my aura is hidden or that it has turned into some other fae kind."

"Okay."

"You could meet me after I see Sigrid."

"No. I'm going with you. I want to see what the fae wants of you in payment for giving you this 'gift.'"

"You're not talking me out of it." Even though Kayla didn't want to involve Tanya, she'd had to tell her what she planned to do in case anything went wrong. But her locket wasn't going to just appear out of the blue, and she had to risk trying to get hold of it any way that she could.

"People rely on her power for gain and then she uses the knowledge to blackmail them," Tanya warned.

"How do you know for certain?" Kayla had heard the rumors too but that didn't mean any of it was true.

"Just stuff I've heard tell. Just like you've heard it too, I'm certain."

"What can be worse than the mess I'm in now? Once I have the locket, if I can get it, it won't matter the lengths to which I had to go to get it back. If I can't, I won't be living here any longer. So see? She couldn't hurt me anyway."

"Kayla, what you did had all to do with being a curious fae. You broke our law and the dragon fae's, but you didn't do it to hurt anyone. And you only hurt yourself. I still think you should come clean with your mom about this." Tanya glanced at her and frowned. "I know that determined look on your face means you're not going to change your mind. Fine. What do you want me to do?"

"Pretend we're going to the human world for a few days. That will be our cover story."

"You don't want me to fae transport you to the other side of the river?"

"If you don't mind." Swimming across had been treacherous enough the few times she had done it since she had lost her ability to transport.

"I don't know what you intend to do. Run around their land asking dragons who was in the woods that day?"

"Yeah. As long as they don't realize I'm a golden fae, I might be able to find out who has it. Maybe I can still bargain with him. What have I got to lose?"

"Your life?" Tanya was silent for a few minutes. "All right, but I could see this all going so wrong." She glanced over at Kayla again. "You've been missing your locket for a week?"

"I've been searching for it all this time."

"Across the river?"

"Yes, across the river. For a whole week. The problem is the dragon took off and flew away, so no footprints leading home."

"How did you get across to the other side?"

"I swam."

Tanya gaped at her, then shook her head. "You could have drowned, and you should have just asked me to take you over there once you knew you couldn't transport over there and back on your own."

"I just kept thinking I was having trouble because there was iron ore somewhere in the area. I've never heard of the locket controlling that aspect of a fae's abilities. Besides, you wouldn't have agreed to take me over there, for my own good, right?" Tanya never disobeyed any laws, as far as Kayla knew.

"I can't believe you hadn't told me before this. I'm your best friend!"

"I know. Why do you think I didn't tell you? I didn't want to get you involved. I didn't want you to be hurt."

Tanya chewed her lower lip like she always did when she was thinking about a problem and trying to come up with a solution. "Did he leave a fae dust trail?"

"No. I assume they do only when they're in fae form. When they're dragons, there is none."

"Well, did you see fae dust where your jewelry was when he shifted into fae form?"

"No. The dragon must have just taken the gold in his talons and flown off with it."

Frowning deeply, Tanya didn't look like she wanted to go along with this plan if she had any choice. "I'll wait for you here at the fork in the path to Sigrid's cottage."

"Okay."

Kayla rushed home to tell her mother the news. She practically sprinted on the path through her lavender fields to the entrance of their walled-in garden. She pushed open the wooden gate and shut it, then hurried up the path, hoping her mom wouldn't ask her a million questions and delay her. She opened the front door.

"Mom?" she called out as she walked inside the four-room cottage, everything neat and clean as usual. Dried lilac and lavender flower displays covered the shelves in the main room of the cottage where they entertained guests and buyers of their floral products. They had a barn out back where all their flowers hung from the rafters and dried, and jars of jellies, potpourri, teas, and dyes were stored out there too. They would run out within the month though. Which was fine because they would have fresh spring flowers to replenish their supplies. Well, at least Kayla's mom would. At this rate, Kayla wasn't sure about her lavender flowers.

The place was quiet, and she realized no one was home. What did her mom say she was going to do? She couldn't remember. Visit the tea shop in the village to sell more orders of their teas they would soon harvest? She groaned at the thought.

Heart thundering, Kayla rushed back outside, thinking she needed to weed the five acres of lavender she owned. But she didn't have time. Purple-crowned fairy wrens with their purple heads, black masks, blue tails and blue and gray feathers fluttered about the green stalks of lavender as if they knew she had something to do with the flowers returning soon.

Now, if only she could use Sigrid's services to remove all the weeds from her garden so Kayla wouldn't have to do it manually. She would have to take her weed-wacking wand and touch each weed to eradicate them as soon as she returned home from her mission, locket secure around her neck. The problem was she couldn't just wave the wand and have the weeds magically disappear. She had to touch each weed and the shock went through every root, frying them. That was the end of the weed, but it took time.

She figured she had six hours before sunset. If her mom saw all the work she had done on her garden, surely she would say it was all right to go to the human's world for a few days.

But her mom hadn't started on her own fields of lilac, and if she didn't, that meant Kayla had more time to do it. No sense in weeding the garden if it wasn't going to be a garden any longer, and she realized just how sad that made her feel, as if she'd lost one of her best friends in the world.

3

"Hey, Kayla," Alton said to the blond-haired girl in the high school where he was searching for Mark. Alton wasn't even thinking about the fact she had no gold aura until she turned around, a brow lifting. "Sorry, I thought you were someone else."

The girl smiled, showing off a mouth full of braces.

Not Kayla.

"No problem." Then she waited as if she had to be released, and he nodded.

And turned then for the door to the outside. The halls were nearly clear now so anyone going out to lunch was already gone. And he'd missed the opportunity to see if Mark had left the building. Alton wondered where Ena's maid had gone. He realized her fae dust led straight out this door, and he walked outside. A storm was gathering, jagged lightning forking down to the earth some distance away, and sheets of it rippling across the darkening clouds. Thunder boomed off in the distance.

The air smelled heavy of rain and the winds were blowing tall trees back and forth. The wind had blown the maid's fairy dust trail everywhere and there was no tracking it now. Then to Alton's astonishment, he saw Mark sitting at a picnic table speaking with a blond-haired girl out in a park-like setting across from the school grounds. He was wearing blue jeans, sneakers, and a T-shirt, typical human attire. The girl was too. She was vibrant and smiling, waving her hands around as she talked, strands of her long blond hair caught up in the wind, twisting this way and that. Mark was watching her intensely as if deeply absorbed in whatever she was telling him. An old girlfriend? Was that why he really had wanted to return here?

It seemed wrong somehow. If Mark was her boyfriend, he would have appeared more...Alton didn't know, smiling, maybe? But Mark didn't look that way. He appeared tense, his gaze unwavering from hers.

That was when Alton heard movement behind him. Instinctively, he transported, knowing in retrospect, he shouldn't have just disappeared in front of people, if anyone was about. But the human world could be dangerous for their kind if fae seers were about. Since Mark was one of them, had he grown bored of living with the fae and had returned to again trap them?

Alton transported to the roof of the school, and crouching down, he looked to see who had come out of the school behind him. Two big male teens carrying a fishing net. An iron mesh net meant to trap a fae and keep him or her from transporting. Alton had to warn Ena and Brett. They had to find her maid. But first, he was taking Mark out of there, who he suspected was being used to trap them. If he was innocent, Alton didn't want him being used as bait.

Was the blond-haired girl in on it? Thinking the fae could have bargaining power if the fae seers had taken the maid hostage, he'd grab both Mark and the girl. The problem was carrying both of them as a fae. The other problem was warning Ena and Brett. The solution was as bad as transporting in front of humans and allowing them to see his disappearing act. Or worse. Being a dragon in a world without dragons, except for the mythical kind, was bound to be captured on a few cell phones if anyone caught sight of him.

Alton prayed to every god and goddess known to the fae that he would not turn into a purple dragon.

He shifted, saw that his body was covered in shimmering silver scales, sighed with relief, and dove for the picnic table.

The two male fae seers were arguing with each other about what to do, when Alton flew in close to grab Mark and the girl.

Mark had been watching the two guys arguing, but he was the first to see Alton flying toward him, his green eyes widening. Though the way Alton was changing scale color at whim, he was certain Mark didn't know which of the dragon fae shifters he was. He didn't move, quickly averted his gaze so as not to alert the girl, and Alton was glad for it. As far as he believed, Mark wasn't in on the deception, but a victim of circumstance.

Alton grabbed the girl by her shoulder, the girl shrieking in terror. Alton did the same with Mark right after, hauling them both toward the roof of the school, but further back where someone standing on the ground couldn't see them. He hoped the girl was in on the whole thing then so he hadn't terrified her for nothing. Then he released them on the rooftop and shifted. The blond collapsed on the rooftop in a dead faint. Mark didn't go to her aid, which said a lot about what had gone on. She wasn't his friend.

"Where's Muriel?" Alton quickly asked.

"These clowns took her." Mark ran his hands through his light brown hair, frowning furiously.

"The girl is involved?"

"Yeah, their bubble-headed leader. Or at least that's what she wants everyone to think outside of her fae seer group. But she's leading this bunch. One of the guys recognized me as a fae seer and rumors had gone all over that I had become one of the fae. And since I was with Muriel, that seemed to prove the rumors true."

"Okay, keep her quiet," Alton said. "I've got to warn Ena and Brett."

"Don't get yourself caught. I don't want to be stuck here."

"Yeah, well you endangered Muriel, remember? You're still a human and can just move somewhere else and be safe from your kind. We'll talk later." Alton wanted to know why Mark had really wanted to return. He had put everyone in danger—not just Muriel.

Not visible to humans, Alton transported to the cafeteria where Ena and Brett had gone. He didn't see Brett, but he saw Ena talking to a guy, smiling, flirting with him. He'd never seen her act in such a way. He didn't like it. Even if she was mated to Brett. And even though he knew she was just trying to get information out of the guy.

She had the rare ability to hide her fae aura so that no one could see it. If the guy she was talking to could see the fae, if Alton just walked right up to her and started talking, the teen could think she was in league with one of them.

He couldn't delay though. He had to warn her. Instead of heading straight for her, he walked around, watching others, trying to ensure that no one else was observing him. Only the fae seers could see him when he was invisible to the humans.

The two guys who had been outside rushed into the cafeteria, the one on his phone. The one talking to Ena suddenly pulled his phone out of his pocket. "Yeah? Oh really?" He turned his attention from Ena and looked at the other two guys headed for him.

Alton transported from where he stood to a place right next to Ena. He grabbed her hand and before she could say anything, he transported her to the roof. Mark was crouched in front of the girl, tying part of his torn T-shirt around her wrists, her mouth already gagged. She was still out.

"Is she one of them?" Ena asked.

"Yeah, their leader," Mark said, standing, looking angry, but a little concerned too.

Maybe Alton's words had sunk in a bit. Maybe Mark was worried the fae might just abandon the human in his own world after what had happened. But Alton knew Ena wouldn't do that. Despite her reputation for acting harshly when the situation warranted it, she had a real soft spot for some of these humans.

"Where's Brett?" Ena asked.

"Not sure," Alton said.

"And Muriel?"

Alton shook his head. "One of us needs to take these two back home with us. We need more help to locate Muriel."

"You go. I'll find Brett. They can't see his or my aura."

"But they know what you look like. The way you're dressed." Alton liked the way Ena dressed, like a Goth in the human world, the same at home. But she stood out too much now if they thought she was one of the fae if she was going to reveal herself to question anyone.

"I can wait here with her and keep her quiet," Mark said. "I know neither of you want to leave Brett or Muriel behind. I don't want to either."

The lightning continued to flash, and Ena considered the girl's blue-gray rain jacket. "I'll wear that."

Mark quickly untied the girl's hands. Ena removed her jacket and then slipped it on. "Okay, I'm going back down."

"I'm taking them to your place and then I'll come back. If I can grab those guys who were carrying a net, I'll take care of them too." Alton shifted, then grasped Mark and the girl in his talons, and transported them to Ena and Brett's castle. He still couldn't get used to the notion that Brett was even part of the equation. Though he had to admit, the guy was a good fighter with his fists and had taught him a thing or two that might someday prove to be useful. If dragon fire wasn't a viable option, that was.

~

"MOM WASN'T HOME, and I left her a note," Kayla said to Tanya as she joined her at the junction of the path. "I've done it before, and she was all right with it." Kayla adjusted her backpack.

"Okay, if you think so." Tanya transported Kayla to Sigrid's cottage deep in the woods.

She was living alone now, after having lost both her parents and her grandmother, who was supposed to have been the one who had given Sigrid her powers. The girl wore black like Ena, had fairy wings, and yet not like those of the winged fae kind. Hers were feathers, browns and rust with white spots, and they actually could lift her unlike the other winged fae Kayla knew of.

Sigrid was not a golden fae, though she lived among them. She didn't care anything about gold or any other kind of jewelry. Some said she could shift into a falcon, but no one Kayla had talked to about it had ever actually seen Sigrid turn into one. She had straight dark brown hair, almost as black as the leather bodice she wore and the black form-fitting leggings and boots.

They didn't know where she'd come from, who her people were, but it was rumored they had killed one another off with their magic powers and somehow her grandmother had lived, hidden away with a baby daughter and a little boy who was orphaned. Eventually, the grandmother found her way to the golden fae's territory to live among them and raise the two children. When they grew up, her granddaughter and the boy married. And Sigrid was the result of their union.

Most of the golden fae really didn't care where she came from or who her people were, as long as her talents were useful and could help those who lived here. But there was always a price to pay when playing with magic. Even the queen had used Sigrid's powers, some said to have a child. But some said it was only rumored and not true at all.

Still, as they approached the cottage, Kayla wondered just what she was getting herself into.

Like most, the cottage was built of stone, with a little stone wall out front and a garden planted just inside of it to grow some of what she needed for cooking and potions. The wall protected the tender plants from the deer foraging in the forest.

"Are you as nervous as me when I'm not even asking her to do anything for me?" Tanya asked, wringing her hands.

"Why not?" Sigrid asked, climbing out of a tree.

Kayla and Tanya jumped a little and watched Sigrid drop the last few feet, her beautiful wings spread, making her land softly on the pine-needle covered ground. She was such an odd person that Kayla shouldn't have been surprised, yet she really hadn't expected the girl to be watching them, hidden in the tree. Had she been a falcon up there, and that's why they hadn't noticed her?

Tanya's face was colored in embarrassment. "Why wouldn't I ask you for anything? I don't need anything. That's why."

"Everyone needs something. Even you. But if you didn't come here to see me," Sigrid said, turning her dark brown eyes on Kayla, "then it must be you who is in need of my services."

Kayla didn't want to tell Sigrid what she had lost. She only wanted to ask Sigrid to help her hide her fae aura with that of another and lose the fae dust trail she would leave behind. But what if she could ask Sigrid if she could retrieve the locket for her? Or find it for her at the very least? It seemed silly to just want something that might not work, when she could ask for the one thing she really needed.

"You are missing your locket," Sigrid said. "Come into my cottage."

"How did she know?" Tanya whispered to Kayla, sounding just as shocked.

"You are not wearing the locket," Sigrid said as they entered the room.

By the gods, could she hear everything that was said from that distance? Falcons had sharp hearing, enough so they could hear a mouse running through the understory way below where the falcon was soaring. So maybe Sigrid could.

"My tunic could be hiding it," Kayla said, her eyes focused on Sigrid, challenging her to come up with another explanation for why she knew the truth.

"It could be, but you always wear it out. You're proud of it, and you want others to know how carefully you protect it. But not carefully enough, eh? So you have lost it to a dragon, and you want it back. How can I assist you?"

Kayla shut her gaping mouth. How did she know so much? Had she been watching them all along? Sitting in trees? Kayla wanted to ask if Sigrid could come with her. She didn't think Sigrid would do it. And Kayla had no intention of asking. So how did the words come out anyway?

"Could you go with me? To retrieve it?" Kayla felt Tanya's gaze boring into her. She knew her friend would be as shocked as she was for mentioning it.

Sigrid smiled. "Have some tea with me?"

The girl rarely offered anyone tea. She conducted her business with whoever needed something and then they were out of there. Kayla wasn't even sure if Sigrid ever invited anyone into her cottage, come to think of it.

"It would cost you more if I went with you, but I think you already know that." Sigrid poured the hot tea into three floral teacups.

Kayla didn't even know what it would cost her to just have her aura changed.

"Tell me your plan first." Sigrid motioned to a small table with a view of the gardens, then smiled as Kayla smelled the tea. *Lavender.*

Kayla hadn't known her mother had sold it to Sigrid.

"It's my favorite flavor of tea. I would hope you would get your locket back so that I may continue to buy your tea."

"But a dragon has it and I don't know which one."

"Maybe the one who carried you off? I followed the two of you for a while, but then he transported and vanished. I had work to do, so hoped he would bring you home okay. And he did."

Tanya's mouth gaped. "He flew *off* with you?"

"He wanted to know why we were spying on them. I told you. I said I intended to steal his gold."

Sigrid laughed. "I bet he loved to hear it."

"He didn't believe me, naturally."

"You didn't tell me he flew off with you." Tanya scowled.

"Sorry. Nothing happened."

"Except that you made a friend, kind of," Sigrid said.

"He threatened to leave me to perish!" Kayla said.

Tanya gasped. "You said nothing happened!"

"Okay, so that happened, but he did leave me safely back at the river. Do you know who would have stolen my locket?"

"You left it behind, did you not? Finders, keepers." Sigrid finished her tea and put her empty teacup on the table.

Kayla knew that. She didn't want to be reminded. She glanced at the way the cottage was decorated and thought it suited someone else. All lace curtains and pastels. Hand-painted bunnies on tables and chairs. But then again, just because Sigrid wore all black, didn't mean she liked to surround herself with the same color in her furnishings. Maybe this was the real her.

"My mother's decorations. Do you like them?"

"They're beautiful," Kayla said. She was much more into pastels than dark or bright colors. Except for the lavender. She loved the way it was so vivid and colorful. Mix it with pastels and it was the perfect combination.

"It reminds me of her. I wouldn't change a thing." Sigrid looked down at her empty teacup.

Kayla felt badly for her all at once. She must miss her mother. She hadn't ever thought someone who was so powerful would miss anyone. But why wouldn't she?

Sigrid quickly looked up, tears shimmering in her eyes. She quickly blinked them away. "Here is the deal. You obtain a bronze locket for me that has the symbol of a falcon engraved on it, and I will help you to reach the dragon fae kingdom in relative anonymity."

"The same dragon stole from *you*?" Kayla couldn't believe a dragon would risk...well, she didn't know what Sigrid was truly capable of. Maybe she couldn't put a hex on the dragon or strike him down with a lightning bolt.

"Yes. And if you want my help, you'll have to retrieve my locket for me. What say you?"

Kayla was shocked that the falcon fae would ask her to retrieve something for her also. From a dragon! "With all your powers, why don't you just go and get it yourself?" She didn't ask it in a smart-aleck way. She really did wonder why Sigrid would have to rely on anyone else to get her own locket back.

"If I could, I would. I'm much too busy." Sigrid motioned to the jars sitting on shelves on one wall. The potions were of a variety of colors, mostly pale green or amber in color. One said love potion on the gold label. The color of the liquid was lilac in color.

Kayla suspected that something was holding her back. Were their lockets similar in that Sigrid couldn't transport either? But then how could she still use her magic to create spells or help Kayla? Something else seemed to be going on. "But you don't know which dragon it was?"

"He had purple scales."

Alton?

～

"Why did you want to return to the human's world?" Alton asked Mark as he shifted after carrying both him and the girl back to Brett and Ena's castle for safekeeping.

"Muriel went to the human world to check on my foster mother and learned she was dying."

"I didn't think you had any family left."

"I didn't. I mean, she had taken care of me when she wasn't angry that I existed. I just wanted to see her one last time."

"She had her memory wiped. She wouldn't even know who you were."

"I know, all right? I just had to do it for me. For closure."

"So Muriel took you to the hospital? Your home? What?"

"The hospital. It's the one right across from the school. Three fae seers were checking on a friend at the hospital who had broken his leg during football practice. They saw me and not only knew me, but they saw Muriel too. She was invisible to humans, but they saw her plain as I can see you now. They grabbed us both and said they would kill her if I didn't cooperate. They knew I'd disappeared, but thought I was dead. I tried to convince them we want to work together, and that I'm living with you. Well not with *you*, but your kind. They said that was fine. You would come for me then."

"So where's Muriel?" Alton asked.

"I don't know. They took off with her in a pale blue pickup, and then Hannah stayed with me to ensure we were the bait."

Alton looked down at the blond-haired leader of the fae seers. "So, Hannah, where did they take Muriel?"

"Jump off a cliff. I'm not telling you nothing."

"Fine. Have it your way. Your friends probably won't even care if you don't ever return. You're in charge, right? So someone else will take charge instead."

"If I tell you, then what?"

"I'll let you live. I don't want to do it, but I will."

She shook her head.

"Fine. Have it your way." Alton shifted, grabbed her up, took a flying leap into the air and flapped toward the sun, then dropped her. The only way to prove he meant what he said was to show her he meant what he said.

She screamed as she fell toward the trees down below and Mark shouted, "But she can *help* us!"

Only if she was willing to help. Otherwise, she was useless to them. Hoping his demonstration helped to prove his point and didn't just give her a thrill like the humans enjoyed riding the tallest, fastest roller coaster rides with 400-feet drops, one with a record ten inversions—Alton knew because he'd been on them before—he dove down and picked her up in his talons before she hit the tops of the trees.

She'd fainted, which was a disappointment. He'd wanted her to feel just how terrifying it would be to fall from that height with no safety net involved, no brakes, nothing to keep her from impacting with the trees below her and tell him everything he wanted to know.

When he returned to Ena and Brett's castle, he dumped Hannah into the water fountain, a statue of a dragon in the center spewing water, instantly waking the human. She shrieked, scrambling to get up. At least the water was warm and clean. Satisfied he'd elicited some kind of response from the human, Alton set Mark down on the cobblestones, landed, and shifted.

The girl was spluttering and coughing, trying to regain her footing in the slippery fountain as Mark hurried to help her out of it. "Thanks for not dumping me in there too." Mark didn't say it in a nice way, more sarcastically. He knew Alton would have gladly dumped Mark in too for all the trouble he had caused—and it wasn't over yet—if it wasn't that Alton might have angered Brett, the queen's favorite dragon for now.

Alton stalked to the huge oak doors and knocked.

"Coming! Coming!" Ryker, Ena's butler, answered the door at

some length wearing all black as he felt a butler should. He frowned at the party, no maid, and no Ena or Brett.

Instead, Alton had brought a dripping wet female fae seer who was wringing out her blond hair and looking furiously at everyone while Mark escorted her to join Alton. At least Alton had recovered Mark from the human world. If that was any consolation.

"Lock this one up," Alton said, roughly hauling her by the arm into the main sitting hall, realizing afterward that she was dripping water all over the slate floor, when he saw the golden fae seated on one of the burgundy brocade couches drinking from a teacup. *Kayla.*

Except she wasn't wearing the aura of a golden fae this time, but a dragon fae's! She was dressed in dark brown clothes, the kind women wore for horse travel or for fighting, not for socializing, the skirts in layers so that when she moved, slim fitting breeches could be seen beneath them. She also wore brown suede boots for traveling, not impractical shoes meant for dancing or visiting, but something that she could wear to walk long distances through the woods.

Her eyes widened as soon as she saw him. He couldn't believe she was there and for a moment, he just gawked at her as if she were a ghost.

Was she here to steal Ena and Brett's gold instead of his own? Had she been speaking the truth about it? She couldn't even fae transport, unless that had all been a lie. It had to be.

"Chain this one to the rack in the dungeon," Alton said to Ryker. He just hoped Ryker wouldn't tell him Ena didn't have any torture devices in the dungeon or anywhere else. None of them did. Alton knew that, but he wanted to use any means to scare the fae seer into telling them what they needed to know. "She knows where Muriel is."

"In that case..." Ryker nodded.

A woman screamed from the dungeon that made a chill crawl up Alton's spine.

"It's currently in use. We'll have to confine her to a room until she can be tortured, but soon," Ryker promised, not missing a beat, his expression indomitable. "We have four more ahead of her, in fact."

Alton raised a brow at him, trying hard not to share a dark smile too.

Ryker shrugged. "It's been a good week."

Alton smirked. He knew Ena kept her gold in her dungeon. No room for prisoners. But her prisoners didn't need to know that. He wondered who was screaming in the dungeon to help with the charade though. Cook?

"I'll take her to a room," Mark said.

"No letting her go," Alton said, his brow furrowed.

"Like she has anywhere to go?" Mark sounded irritated that Alton would even assume he would help the girl escape. He took her arm and walked toward the hall to the chambers on the first floor.

Humans in the employ of the dragon shifters really needed to learn some manners. Alton turned his attention to the faux dragon fae next, taking great strides to reach her. She couldn't fae transport inside the castle to the outside, for the same reason other fae couldn't transport inside. Iron ore in the outer walls kept the castle secure. "What is she doing here?"

Before he could apprehend her, she quickly set the teacup on the rosewood table and rose from the couch.

"She is looking for a special locket that she lost in the forest," Ryker said. "She's hoping to learn if one of the shifters located it since all of you have such keen senses."

"She is, is she? Would she pay a lot of gold for its safe return?" Alton reached for her arm, but she slid away from him so that he missed taking hold of her. "Lock her in a cell until I can further question her."

"But—"

"Do as I say. She's not who she claims to be." But Alton didn't explain that she was a golden fae either. "I've got to return to help Brett and Ena find Muriel. Don't let this one flee no matter how she begs you to let her go."

"Well, I came in peace and friendship, and this is how you treat a fellow dragon fae?" Kayla haughtily asked.

"She is not one of us. Lock her up." He grabbed her arm then and handed her over to Ryker.

"And what about Mark?" Ryker asked, taking hold of Kayla's arm.

Alton noticed Kayla was only looking at him, not with concern or conceit, but with genuine interest. He couldn't figure her out.

"What if I could go with you and help out?" she asked.

"How could you possibly help out?"

"I can hide my fae aura from the humans."

"And what would you want in return?"

"A bronze locket with the symbol of a falcon on it. It's a friend's."

Alton studied her responses, hoping to see through her deceit. "I thought you were searching for a locket that belonged to you."

"I am. I want mine back too."

"If she could help," Ryker said, "wouldn't it behoove you to take her with you?"

Alton thought she would be more trouble than it was worth. Then again, he was curious about her and the real reason she wanted the lockets. "She couldn't help." He wasn't about to agree to anything he would regret later.

"What about Mark?" Ryker asked, his brow arched.

"He should be doing whatever job he was supposed to be doing instead of creating problems. I've got to go." Alton gave Kayla one last discerning look, noting she was not wearing any jewelry today

either, and headed outside where he could transport to the high
school in the human world. When he arrived there, he found it was
pouring rain and the school was closed now. He paused on the roof,
trying to decide where to go next.

"Okay, listen," Kayla explained to Ryker. He'd been so nice to her
until Alton showed up unexpectedly. She'd wanted to sink into the
sofa, hoping he wouldn't look her way, but nope, he had to catch
her drinking tea and that was the end of being totally unseen. She
hadn't ever thought she would end up running into him here. She'd
asked in the village and was staying far away from his castle for the
moment. But if he was returning to the human world, his castle
would be the perfect place to visit! "Alton is irritated with me
because I was mouthing off about his scales changing color
constantly. He has annoyed *me* in the past. I just figured it was time
for a little payback."

Ryker was still holding her arm and looking down at her, a glint
of humor in his eyes. Did that mean he liked it that she was giving
Alton a hard time? She wasn't pulling away because she was trying
to maintain her cool and pretend that she had no intention of
doing anything wrong.

"In fact, I told him that I thought his scales were beautiful when
they turned a lovely shade of violet."

That earned her a little smile. But then Ryker's serious face was
back in place, and a woman screamed from the dungeon again.

The high-pitched scream made Kayla's skin crawl. She wanted
to save the woman. She wanted to get out of here before she was
put on the rack! "Listen, since it sounds like Ena and Brett may
take a while longer to return, I'm going to check with Alton's friend
to see if he might have been the one to have found my locket. He
was practicing for the dragon games with Alton in the same vicini-

ty." She had to bluff her way through this, not knowing who the brown dragon was by name and hoped Ryker wouldn't catch her up on it.

"What about Alton?"

"I already asked him. He wouldn't say."

Ryker still hadn't let go of her arm, but he'd loosened his grip.

"You aren't going to let a dragon shifter, not of this household, tell you what to do, are you?" Kayla asked so sweetly, Ryker's smile returned. "I wouldn't, if I were you. He has no right telling you what to do as if you work for him. Bossy dragon shifter."

Ryker released her but eyed her warily.

"Thanks. I'll put in a good word for you with Ena, next time I see her."

"I'm sure that releasing you is a mistake, but anyone who would dare tell Alton that his scales are beautiful deserves to have a chance to do it again. If you are not who you claim to be, though, don't come back, and I won't have to incarcerate you like I've had to do with the fae seer. However," Ryker said, sounding like he was hatching a plan, "I do worry about Ena and Brett and her lady's maid, Muriel. If you could see to helping them, I would be sure to put in a good word for you regarding the lockets, if your deeds prove worthy."

"Could I ask you to do one other thing?"

"What's that?"

"Stop the torture down below?"

Ryker smiled, but the look was more dangerous than reassuring.

"If you do, I'll go," Kayla said.

"Agreed."

"Where do I need to go?"

Ryker told her the location in the human world and hating schools more than anything, Kayla told herself this was going to work. She was not going to get caught by any fae seer. She was going to do a good deed for the dragon fae shifters, and they would reward her by giving her the two lockets.

She hoped she wasn't fooling herself.

She thanked Ryker, trying not to overdo it, and headed outside. Then she transported to the human high school and was standing in the empty parking lot where lightning was streaking to the ground off in the distance, thunder followed in a huge cracking sound, and rain poured down from the heavens, soaking her. There was no sign of anyone—fae or human.

What now?

4

Alton couldn't believe that the golden fae had sneaked into Ena and Brett's castle, pretending to be a dragon fae. The power to switch fae auras was rare. He had to admit he admired Kayla's tenacity, and he wondered about the locket she was trying to locate. And the one also that he'd taken from the falcon fae.

The only reason he'd even taken it from the falcon fae was because she'd fought to steal the gold the golden fae had left behind. He was now certain Kayla was the one who had torn off her jewelry in the piney woods before she disappeared. That made him wonder why she hadn't changed her fae aura and pretended to be a dragon fae at the time. Why leave her gold behind?

What he hadn't expected was for a falcon fae to attack him out of nowhere. When he was a mighty dragon!

The locket had to mean a great deal to Kayla if she was risking her life trying to find it. The same if she was trying to locate the falcon fae's locket. The other fae had to be a good friend of hers, for the same reason, he realized, that she had attempted to steal the golden fae's locket from him. At the time, he had believed the falcon fae had just wanted the gold objects. What did he know? He didn't really know anything about them.

He had to look over his treasure again. He hadn't noticed anything unusual about the gold jewelry he had found in the woods. He had just grabbed all of it and after searching for the golden fae and not finding her, then fighting with the falcon fae, he had gone to the cave where he hid his treasure and dumped his find on one of his piles of gold and silver.

He had to know both the lockets' secrets and what it would be worth to Kayla for him to return them.

The dragons paid the merchants and their staffs well. They could afford to. Likewise, when their dragon services were needed, they could ask for a goodly sum, depending on the case. But they didn't give up their goods for generosity's sake. If he had her treasure, he would have to ask for something worthwhile in return. It was only good business. Dragons normally didn't give their gold away unless it was to someone they cared deeply about. He should have known when Ena gave jeweled weapons to Brett, she did so because she cared a lot about him, and it hadn't been just a means to give him a way to protect himself.

Alton transported into the school, heard someone polishing the floors and then saw one golden fae coming down the stairs. He stared at Kayla in disbelief. He couldn't believe it. Why was she here, of all places, when Ryker was supposed to have locked her away?

"What are you doing here?" he asked Kayla, his tone harsh.

"I came to help Ena and Brett and her maid."

"So you know them?"

She had the good sense to look a little nervous. Even though she was wearing the dragon fae aura still, he knew what she was. So there wasn't any sense in her trying to pull the wool over *his* eyes.

He doubted she knew either of them, unless she'd met them somewhere other than in the dragon fae kingdom.

She folded her arms. "I wanted to help. It seems we're wasting time here chatting."

"You want to help from the goodness of your heart? You thought if you helped me, I would give you something in return."

"I'm helping Ena and Brett," Kayla said defiantly.

Alton smiled in a dark way. "Good. Then *they* will owe you. How come Ryker let you go?" *The traitor.*

She narrowed her eyes. "I reminded him you had no right ordering him about. Not only that, but I told him about your stunning purple scales. I think he almost smiled when I told him how I'd mentioned to you how beautiful they were. He released me after that."

Alton could strangle her. No one knew, at least yet, that his scales had turned purple. So far, they'd been blue, silver, orange, and Ena's olive-green color when he'd been in the other dragon fae's presence. Only Kayla and that irascible falcon fae had seen him wearing purple scales. Then again, maybe Ryker hadn't believed her. Alton was certain that wouldn't be the case, or the butler wouldn't have released her.

"So what do you suggest we do?" As if the golden fae would have a clue about tracking down someone and rescuing him or her from fae seers. He was used to it as a dragon shifter. He often had dangerous missions to go on. That made him wonder what Kayla's job was back home. Was she even prepared to fight the fae seers?

"We follow the fae trail. The one I found upstairs," she said, waiting, as if to see what he thought of that.

KAYLA KNEW Alton didn't like that she was here, and what was worse, she didn't think she could really help, or that he would give her locket back if she did.

He nodded when he saw the fae dust scattered on the floor. "Brett was up here. He came here looking for Mark."

The problem was Kayla really didn't know whose fae dust was whose. Ena, Brett, and Muriel all lived in the same castle, and she'd seen all their fae dust there.

They heard someone coming up the stairs and both turned invisible to humans.

"Ena," Kayla said first when she saw her. Not that Ena would know who *she* was. Kayla remembered the dragon shifter from when she spoke with Alton at the river though. She was wearing a rain jacket that looked so out of character for the Goth-looking fae.

"Who is she? A girlfriend?" Ena asked, looking surprised, and actually happy about it from the way she was smiling, in a dark sort of way.

Alton snorted. "A golden fae interested in stealing your gold."

Ena scowled at him. "Be serious. We found the place where they're keeping Muriel, but I wanted to come back to see if you were here and could help." She smiled at Kayla. "We're glad he brought a friend to aid us."

Kayla cast Alton a superior look. Alton just gave her an evil look back, promising she would be sorry. She so wanted to needle Alton, mention something about his beautiful purple scales, and learn if Ena had seen them already.

But this was a dangerous business, and she kept her thoughts to herself.

"So where is Muriel?" Alton asked.

"A mausoleum."

"Now that's morbid," Alton said, and Kayla had to agree.

WHEN THEY ARRIVED at the cemetery, Kayla glanced at the oak-tree shaded grounds filled with headstones, a tall angel with her hands outspread as if the person buried here had been extra special, others that were old, some that had flowers in holders at their bases, some that had a flat granite marker on the ground. She and the other fae with her remained invisible to humans, though if fae seers were about, it wouldn't have mattered. At least in Alton's case. Thankfully, due to Sigrid's power, Kayla's was hidden. And Ena seemed to be able to hide her aura too from the fae seers.

They walked toward an older stone mausoleum, and Kayla saw Brett sitting atop it, waiting for them. Only he wasn't in his fae form but his golden dragon form, and he wasn't visible to the humans either. She assumed he was wearing his dragon scales in case any fae seers were about. Even though she was invisible to them, she still felt unsafe. Ena shifted into her dragon form, flew off, and perched next to Brett.

Alton let out his breath and considered the lock on the vault. "Anyone want to use their fire on this?"

"Go ahead and try," Kayla said, as if she was truly in on this with them. It was exciting to be working alongside dragons. She never imagined losing her locket would result in breaking into a mausoleum in the human world and working with the enemy to do so.

"Look what we have here," a boy called out.

Alton shifted, prepared to protect himself as bolts flew in his direction.

Kayla hit the ground because though they couldn't see her, the bolts bounced off the mausoleum door behind her.

Brett and Ena flew toward the shooters to the east, and Alton went after another to the north.

Three tall boys wearing jeans, T-shirts, and sneakers ran off, crossbows in hand, yelling. Heart beating furiously and her hands clammy with worry, Kayla bolted from the ground and reached the mausoleum door, then studied the combination lock. Leaning down, she lifted the lock and twisted it one way and then the other, listening carefully, stopping, twisting back again, hearing the clicks with her ultra-sensitive fae hearing. She'd never thought her hearing was that sensitive. Was it also a gift from Sigrid to help her bring the lockets home?

The lock clicked open, and Kayla pocketed it so no one could secure the door again. Then she opened the door. The hinges creaked all the way until it was wide enough that she could enter. She found a light switch and flipped it on. Spiderwebs hung from the top of the structure and the stairs leading down into the burial vault. Dust covering the stairs revealed several footprints. The place smelled musty from the dampness. She shivered from the chill in the building and the cold in her bones. This was the creepiest thing she'd ever done.

She climbed down the stairs calling out, "Muriel! Are you down there?"

No one answered. This could be a setup to capture whoever discovered Muriel was supposed to be down here. How had Brett and Ena known? Had the fae seers left them breadcrumbs to find their way here?

Kayla tried to fae transport out of the building, just to make sure she could in case she had to. She couldn't. She could transport within the mausoleum from the point at which she had been standing to the door, just not outside it. Her skin prickled with unease. The notion of being trapped down here made her heart pound even harder. "Muriel," she called out.

"It's a trap!" A woman screamed from somewhere in the bowels of the crypt.

Was it truly Muriel? Or someone pretending to be her? But then she wouldn't have warned Kayla that it was a trap, she figured.

Kayla had to help the woman however she could. She made her way cautiously toward where she had called out, trying not to make any sound as she stepped on the stone floor in case a fae seer was down here also and was listening for her movement. She had assumed the fae seers were on the outside of the mausoleum in a fight with the dragons up above. And that was who Muriel was talking about. But if one or two were down here, Kayla would deal with them however she could. If *she* had been locked down here, she would hope someone would have come to rescue her.

She saw her then, a girl a couple of years older than her dressed in a blue gown and boots, wearing iron manacles around her wrists and standing at the back of the mausoleum. Muriel saw Kayla then, but she quickly looked to her right where a boy was standing with a mesh net in his hands, intently watching the stairs.

Kayla transported to the other side of the crypt in case the guy had heard her footsteps. He rushed forward, unable to see her, but he must have heard her coming. He probably wasn't used to being around a fae he couldn't see.

At least she could observe him. He continued toward the stairs and Kayla hurried to see to Muriel. Her cheeks were wet and her eyes red from tears.

"Everyone's here to rescue you," Kayla whispered to her as she looked at the manacles. She couldn't get them off, but thankfully Muriel wasn't chained to anything in the crypt. "I'll transport you to the door. We have to walk outside, and I can transport you away from here."

Muriel quickly nodded. She was a dragon fae, a servant, so she couldn't be a shifter. She wasn't Kayla's enemy because she didn't hoard gold like the shifters did.

Kayla worried then when none of the dragons were rushing in to help save Muriel. What in the world had happened up above? It didn't bode well.

Kayla wrapped her arms around Muriel, who was shivering uncontrollably. Then she transported her to the doorway. Feeling nervous about going out into the night in the event fae seers were just waiting to throw a net on Muriel, Kayla saw the guy in the crypt was still searching for her.

"Ready?" Kayla whispered.

"Yes."

Kayla wanted to alert the dragons that she had rescued Muriel, but she was afraid if she hung around for any time at all, Muriel would end up in another dungeon of sorts and they might not find her the next time. Still, Kayla had to let them know because she didn't want any of them having to stay here any longer than they had to, believing Muriel was still a prisoner. She rushed outside with her, saw two boys running toward the open door to the mausoleum, one with a net and the other a crossbow. She quickly transported Muriel to the top of the crypt.

"Howard, are you all right down there?" the kid with the net called out.

"Yeah!"

The other kid readied his crossbow to shoot Muriel, and yelled out, "She's up there!"

Kayla transported her beyond the gate to the cemetery and called out, "Ena! Brett! I've got her!" She paused, waiting for a response. "We can't wait. We need to get you—" she said to Muriel.

A pained groan nearby caught her attention, and Kayla turned to see Alton in his fae form, lying on his back, his hand covering the place where a bolt had entered his side, blood trickling out. Kayla felt sick to her stomach. Where were Ena and Brett? Had they all been wounded, dying, or dead? Dread pooling in the pit of her stomach, she couldn't think of that now.

"I'll come back for him," Kayla whispered to Muriel.

"We can't leave him," Muriel pleaded.

"I'll leave you someplace safe a short distance from here. I'll come back for him." Kayla didn't have time to argue with her. The fae seers were sure to find Alton before long. She wrapped her arms around Muriel and carried her to the hospital rooftop. "Just stay down so that no one can see you up here. I'll be right back."

Kayla thought her heart was going to thump right out of her

chest as she transported back to help Alton, and prayed the fae seers hadn't found him yet. Teens were shouting near the crypt, everyone furious Muriel had gotten away. She grabbed Alton into her arms and when he cried out in pain, she winced.

"Over there!"

She quickly transported Alton to the rooftop where Muriel was.

"What about Ena? Brett?" Muriel asked, her voice laden with tears.

"I don't know. I know they would have helped if they could have. I need to get you both out of here."

"We can't leave them behind," Muriel insisted.

"I can get an army of dragon fae down here, right? To rescue them?" Kayla said.

"Take Alton first."

"I will. It will still take time," she said, tearing off a strip of her skirt and wrapping it around his wound. "If I take him to see Ryker, will he get help for him right away?"

"Yes."

"Okay. I'll be back as soon as I can." Kayla hated leaving Muriel here. Alton was a fighter, but so badly wounded she feared he would die. Muriel served as a lady's maid and didn't appear to be a fighter at all. And she was still manacled. "Stay low. I'll be back."

"Hurry."

"I will." Kayla wrapped her arms around Alton. He briefly opened his eyes and narrowed them, then closed them again. "You totally owe me my locket and everything else you took from me," she said as she carried him into the black void that was the way they transported from one place to another. Though holding onto someone this way made them lighter than they normally were, she still couldn't have managed to carry both him and Muriel.

"Muriel," he said under his breath, and groaned.

"I'm going back for her as soon as I leave you off at Ena and Brett's castle."

"Get her."

"No. You'll die on me and whoever inherits my treasure that's with yours won't feel obligated to give it back. And Sigrid's too. Since I've left poor Muriel behind, which puts her at risk again since she's wearing iron manacles and I couldn't remove them, you better not die on me. It's not just about my treasure and Sigrid's locket. It's about putting Muriel in danger when I could have taken her instead." She didn't know why she was talking so much. Maybe because she felt so rattled, so worried about leaving Muriel behind and so concerned that Alton wouldn't make it. Even though she wasn't exaggerating when she said she wanted her locket and Sigrid's back, she didn't want the arrogant dragon to die on her either.

"I thought you would be capable of dodging an archer with a crossbow. How did you ever manage to get hit anyway?" She didn't expect him to answer her.

He grunted.

"What happened to Brett and Ena?" She didn't want to hear they were dead. Or wounded even. But why else would they not have come back for them?

"They...flew off..." Alton coughed, and she was scared he would die right then and there because he'd tried to talk.

"Rest," she scolded. "It was a rhetorical question. You shouldn't be talking. You die on me and well, you don't want to know what I'll do to you then."

She swore he managed a half chuckle.

When she finally arrived at the castle, she had to lay Alton down on the doorstep and then banged and yelled at the ornate double doors.

"I'm coming. I'm coming," Ryker called out. But as soon as he opened the door, his face blanched.

"Take care of him. I'm going back for Muriel before anyone finds her. Brett and Ena were dodging bolts. I don't know what happened to them." She felt tears prick the back of her eyes. She now saw why the dragon shifters were paid so much money. She decided if she got her locket back, she would never complain about weeding her lavender fields ever again.

"I'll send reinforcements," Ryker said, then yelled for someone in the house to help him.

"To the Greenwood Memorial Cemetery. But be careful. Fae seers are armed with crossbows and iron bolts. I'll return with Muriel as soon as I can." She quickly squeezed Alton's hand, and said to Ryker, "He promised me my gold back, the locket most of all, and my friend's falcon locket also. Just in case he dies, I want you to be the witness."

She swore Alton lifted one corner of his mouth, but she didn't think it was a promise to give back her jewelry look. More like a darkly amused look.

Fae travel could be exhausting and by the time Kayla arrived back on the hospital rooftop, she was worn out. As soon as she saw Muriel lying down on top of the roof, her heart went out to her. She hoped she wasn't ill, and that instead, she was hugging the rooftop to limit her exposure to anyone around there.

"Are you ready?" Kayla asked.

"Shouldn't you go for Ena and Brett?"

"No. Ryker's sending reinforcements. Ready?"

Muriel nodded and Kayla gathered her in her arms. And like before, she chatted away as if Muriel wanted to hear her talk incessantly. "Are you okay?" she finally asked.

"Yes. Tired. Scared half to death. Mark wanted so badly to see his foster mother and he did. She died, not knowing him, but he felt better to know he saw her at the last. Then we were taken hostage by those three holy terrors, fae seers, every one of them. And then that girl..." Muriel shook her head.

"We have her in custody. If we have to, we can trade her for Brett and Ena."

"Then you would need more than that."

"Hopefully, the reinforcements sent will reach them and bring them home safely," Kayla said.

"Who are you? I don't remember seeing you before. You're not a dragon shifter, are you?"

"No. Alton has my locket, and I came to ask for it back. If you have any influence over him whatsoever, please do use it on him."

"Me?" Muriel snorted. "Not me. Ena is the only one who has. At least in the past. Now that she's married to Brett, maybe not."

Which meant Kayla had to rescue Ena. Or Brett. Since he was the love of her life. Well, and Ena too. If the reinforcements didn't pan out. "I'm Kayla, by the way."

"Muriel, Ena's lady's maid."

"Pleased to meet you, though I wish the circumstances had been better. I would love to lock the fae seers up in that crypt for a week and see how they like it."

"I would get rid of the key," Muriel said. "Why does Alton have your locket?"

"Complete misunderstanding. He thought I had left it for him to find while I was bathing in the river."

Muriel didn't say anything.

"I mean, swimming. I didn't want to lose my necklace and so I set it underneath a fern, figuring it would be safe. But you know dragon shifters. They have a nose for gold, and he smelled it and took off with it."

"I'm surprised he would even think of it if he saw you swimming."

"Well, he did. And I guess he just figured it was lying around, and he found it, so it was his. But it isn't. *His*."

"And now you want it back."

"I have to have it back. It's my heritage. Not only do I want it, I have to have it. I don't have a choice." Kayla wasn't sure why she had opened up to Muriel, not all the way, but telling her how important it was when she hadn't planned to tell anyone but the rogue who had it, if nothing else would work on him.

Maybe it was because she felt she and Muriel had escaped death at the hands of the fae seers, and they had something in common now.

"What are you going to do when we get back?" Muriel asked.

"Going back." As much as Kayla hated to, she felt it her duty to help Ena and Brett, unless the dragon fae made her stay there. She still felt if she helped Ena and her mate, she would be able to convince someone to influence Alton to give up the lockets.

As soon as she arrived at the castle with Muriel, Ryker took her in and one of the other maids hurried to remove her manacles.

"Where is Alton? Is he all right?" Kayla asked.

"The queen's physician is seeing to him," Ryker said.

"Did you send dragon shifters to look for Ena and Brett?"

"They have already left. Ena's brother wished a word with you though."

Kayla didn't like Ryker's serious expression. As if he knew who she was and she was in big trouble. Even if she had saved Alton and Muriel from the fae seers. Dragon fae weren't to be trusted.

She saw a black-haired guy dressed in a uniform decorated over the shoulders with royal gold cords, revealing he had some official capacity in the queen's household, moving toward her in an aggressive way. She was certain this wasn't a social call.

"Why don't you come with me?" he said, not in a way that was asking.

She heard heavy footsteps approaching behind her and whipped around to see four guards coming for her. Alton had told on her. The traitor!

Why? So he didn't have to give up her gold? She would never ever save his life again, if the need ever arose again.

She transported beyond the guards, dashed out the door, and

transported right out of there, swearing she would get even. *And* get her blasted locket back too!

5

Alton was in such a fog after the queen's physician had given him so many drugs for the pain where the bolt had been removed that he couldn't think straight.

"Where is she?" Alton asked Halloran, Ena's brother and Alton's best friend. Halloran was now Dragon at Arms, the highest position any dragon shifter could have. Though the queen had offered the position to Brett for his saving her life, despite having been wounded at the time. But he had asked that Ena's brother have the honor instead. Which had both shocked Halloran and pleased him.

Why had Brett done that? So he could stay close to Ena.

Would Alton have done the same for her? He doubted it. That was the most coveted position any dragon shifter could ever want and hadn't been filled for years under the old king's rule.

It had been three days since Alton had returned to their kingdom, and he was still forced to be on bedrest—per the queen's orders.

"My sister is fine. She and Brett had to take refuge in an abandoned warehouse for a time. Fae seers had surrounded the building, and Ena and Brett couldn't leave until reinforcements arrived. But we got them out before dawn the next day."

Halloran had said Ena would be Alton's mate, and Alton had planned on it, even though several dragons had been vying for the honor. That was until Brett showed up in her life. But Alton *wasn't* talking about Ena. The queen's physician had told Alton that Ena and Brett were safely back home. Alton wanted to know about the *golden fae*, though he'd been extra careful not to call her that. To everyone, she was a dragon fae, and he wanted to keep it that way.

"What about Kayla? The girl who brought me back? The physician said she returned Muriel safely also. Where is she?" Alton had worried—once he was able to really concentrate on anything much when he wasn't taking so many pain medications—that someone would wonder just where she'd come from. Even so, he'd expected her to be visiting him repeatedly, hounding him to get out of bed and return her locket to her. And her friend's also! Maybe even returning all the jewelry she'd left behind when she'd endangered her own life for him.

"The golden fae?" Halloran's brows furrowed.

Alton frowned just as much, his skin growing cold all at once. Had her aura slipped and suddenly she'd exposed herself for what she truly was to the dragon fae? Or had she mistakenly thought that since she'd helped both him and Muriel, she could reveal what she was and the dragon fae would make an exception in her case?

He didn't think she could be that naïve.

"She transported out of here as fast as she could. She knew what would happen to her once she was found out," Halloran said.

"She brought me back here." Alton wanted to punch whoever had made her leave. "Muriel too." As if Halloran hadn't known that. "She must have thought that would count for something." Even in his book it did.

"You're the one who told us what she was."

Alton wouldn't have! Not after what she'd done for him.

"You told Ryker she intended to steal Ena and Brett's gold. At the high school, you told Ena she was a golden fae. Though my sister hadn't believed it at first, not when Kayla helped save your neck and Muriel's. Good thing you told us. We wouldn't have had a clue otherwise."

"I told you?" Alton felt sick to his stomach. He couldn't believe it. Did she know he was the one who told on her? She would hate him forever when he had no intention of doing anything of the sort.

"You kept talking about her. Over and over again. You didn't make much sense half the time, but we pieced it all together. When I went to question her, she took off right away. It's unbelievable what one of their kind will pull just to get in our good graces, then wham, the next thing you know, the little thief has robbed you blind." Halloran leaned against the wall and pulled out a pad of paper and a pen. "I came to talk to you about the games. I need to know if you want me to pull your name off the list, or you think you can still take part in them."

Alton felt absolutely awful about Kayla. He'd wanted to thank her for saving his life. Oh, sure, he knew she was helping him so he would give back her locket, but in no way had he ever intended to tell anyone what she truly was after what she had done for him. He still wanted to know why the locket was so important to her. Family heirloom? He suspected that was it.

"Alton?"

"What?"

"The game?"

"I'll be there. In the games."

"It will be worth it just to see if your scales turn different colors again." Halloran grinned at him. "You're looking better. Doc said he would let you go this afternoon."

"How's Muriel?"

"Furious with you."

"Why now?"

"Because of the golden fae. She said you ought to be ashamed of yourself after all Kayla had done for the both of you. You owed her your life. But Muriel isn't a dragon shifter, so she has no understanding of the troubles we've had between our kinds."

"Where's Ena?" Alton tried to sit up in bed, but his side still hurt.

Halloran helped him and readjusted his pillows. "She's angry with you. For the same reason Muriel is, I suspect, though she wouldn't say for sure."

Alton didn't have to ask what Brett's viewpoint was on the matter. People mattered more to him than gold. Alton figured it was because he hadn't been born a dragon shifter. Or, at least hadn't known he was until a few months ago. That could put a different perspective on it. So Alton knew he would side with Ena on the issue.

"Don't worry. You did the right thing." Halloran started to leave but paused at the doorway. "Muriel said Kayla had been bathing when you grabbed her gold. You're more of a dragon than I could ever be. I wouldn't have given the gold any thought."

Bathing? No way had Kayla been bathing when he found her jewelry. She'd been running away.

"Wait, what about that fae seer? Hannah? What is to become of her?" Alton asked.

"Ena has petitioned the queen to allow her to keep the girl at her castle, like she did Brett, Mark, and Bryan Jessup. If Ena continues to take in fae seers, she's going to be overrun by humans." Halloran shook his head.

"Does Ena think the girl might be a fae?"

"Like Brett? Maybe. Mark and the other one haven't come into fae abilities, so who knows. All I know is that it's causing a bit of dissension. Their kind have killed our kind, and—"

"Our kind have killed theirs."

"Don't tell me you want her to stay too."

Alton scowled at him as he got out of bed to dress. "Be serious. How do you think I lost Ena to one?"

"Well, I didn't think so, but just checking. You don't have some feelings for this fae, do you? The golden one?"

"Hey, she saved my life. I at least owed her a thank you. She didn't have to risk her neck to go with me."

"Unless she wants something from you in return." Halloran lifted a brow. "Are you sure you didn't see her bathing?"

"WHAT ARE YOU GOING TO DO?" Tanya asked Kayla as she marched into the woods to Sigrid's cottage.

"I've got to ask Sigrid if there's something else I can do to disguise myself, and learn how I can take down a dragon shifter."

Tanya's eyes rounded. "You're kidding, of course. You don't seriously mean it."

"Yes, I mean it. I saved his life! And what does he do? Turns me over to the Dragon at Arms. I mean, who would do something like that to someone who saved his life? Have me thrown in the dungeon?"

"A dragon shifter fae who's afraid you're going to try and steal his gold."

"I can't steal it. I don't have a clue where it is."

"Then he's afraid you're going to ask him to give you the two lockets back, and he doesn't want to part with his gold."

"Now that's more like it."

Kayla couldn't believe how angry she was about it. The ring around her eyes had been glowing gold for three whole days. She was just glad her mom had left a note saying she'd gone on a trip to see her sister and hadn't waited for Kayla to get back. Then again, she hadn't waited to tell her mother either. Her mother must have figured Kayla wouldn't be home anyway. Which was a really good thing because how would she explain why her eyes were glowing otherwise?

"I still can't believe you went to rescue a fae and ended up rescuing an injured dragon who had taken your locket. I've never been in a mausoleum." Tanya shivered. "That must have been morbid."

"It was. Buried under the earth." Goosebumps rose all over Kayla's arms. "I want to go to the games."

"The dragon games? You've got to be kidding. Why? They didn't catch you and throw you in the dungeon, so you want to go back to see if they'll catch you this time?"

"No. Of course not. I want to see Alton."

"Why? He will only try to have you imprisoned again."

"That's why I need some kind of magic. I'm not going to just talk with him. He'll probably just take me to the dungeon himself. I need something that will—"

"Paralyze him?" Sigrid asked.

They looked behind them and saw Sigrid using her beautiful wings to float to the forest floor.

"Well, not paralyze him. Of course, if I did that, he couldn't lock me up or call the guards to have them do it. But I need the lockets. So I'll need to do something to him that will force him to give the lockets to me. I thought of a truth serum, but even if I asked him where his treasure is, it might be well-guarded. I need to...bind him to my will. Like a vampire would do."

"A vampire?" both Sigrid and Tanya asked at the same time.

"Don't you guys know anything about the humans' vampire lore? They mesmerize humans and make them do things for them."

Tanya smiled. "Wow, if I could have that power over Shane, I would do it in a heartbeat."

Sigrid laughed. "See? What did I tell you? Everyone wants something."

"What if someone else told on me and it wasn't Alton after all?"

Kayla couldn't help but grasp at straws, trying to make sense of why Alton would do something like that to her.

"Who else knew?" Tanya asked, sounding skeptical.

No one. That was the problem. Kayla slumped her shoulders in defeat. She'd really hoped to come up with another reason for his betrayal. A reasonable explanation. One that let him off the hook. "No one. Just Alton. It's just that I can't believe he would tell on me like that. Not after I saved him."

"To keep his gold safe? A dragon shifter would do anything." Tanya cast her a worried look. "Listen, it was a rotten thing to do. We've just got to figure a way around this. Assume, like we did in the first place, there's no helping their kind. You've just got to steal the gold back."

"Well...he was injured." Kayla remembered a time when she was zapping the weeds in her lavender fields and a bee landed on her hand. She'd shaken her hand to get him off, pulled the trigger on the wacker accidentally, and hit her foot. It burned right through her boot and scorched the top of her foot. Her mom had said Kayla had made some pretty weird remarks while she had been under the healer's care, all doped up.

"So?" Tanya and Sigrid said at the same time.

"Well, what if he was out of it because he was on pain medication? That can make you say some pretty strange things. Remember the time you broke your arm, Tanya? Sure, we heal faster than humans, but we still take some time to heal, and you were on some pretty heavy-duty pain medication. You said you were going ice skating, or something weird like that. It was the middle of summer. And you've never gone ice skating, ever."

"Telling the Dragon at Arms that you were a golden fae wasn't weird. It was the truth. Face it. The dragon turned on you as soon as you had transported Muriel safely back. Right?" Tanya said.

"Yeah, but he was probably under while they took out the bolt and repaired the damage to his muscles and stuff. By the time I returned, he might have been waking from the anesthesia and told them about me. Maybe he'd been asking to see me, and he mentioned the golden fae, letting it slip, but not meaning to." Kayla could see how that could happen and then he would have been perfectly innocent of ratting her out.

"Okay," Tanya said as they entered Sigrid's cottage. "Let's say for the sake of argument that in a drug-induced state, the dragon made the mistake of calling you what you really are. What do you propose to do at the dragon games? If Halloran, Ryker, Ena, Brett, Muriel, or any other of the dragon fae saw you at the games, you'll be hauled off and manacled in the dungeon. If you think Alton won't turn you in, how will you be able to get hold of him to speak with him alone? If that's what you're thinking of doing. At the games, he will more than likely be in a special place for dragon contestants, don't you agree? Ena, Brett, and Halloran will surely be with him to participate in the games."

Sigrid poured water into the tea kettle. "What about a love potion?"

"What?" both Tanya and Kayla said at the same time and looked at her like she was crazy.

"That would be a way to bind him to you. Hey, you were the one who brought it up. Vampire wills him to do your bidding."

"How in the world would she get it to him? Here, have a nice glass of water to quench your thirst after all that dragon gaming stuff. And oh, by the way, you don't know me as Kayla, the golden fae," Tanya said. "But you love me." She put her hands over her heart and sat down at the table as Sigrid made the tea. "And more than anything else in the world, in fact, you feel you will just die if you don't give me the two lockets I've asked for. I'll even help you look for them. And then, you'll remember nothing of this conversation or anything that you will do."

"He would remember all of it," Sigrid warned, pouring the tea into floral cups. "Once he snapped out of it and was no longer under the influence, he would remember everything he did and said."

"That would serve him right." Tanya took a sip of her tea. "Lavender. It's my favorite too."

"But how would I give it to him?" Kayla asked, getting interested.

"You could blow magical dust in his face. If the wind is blowing the wrong way or shifts, you could be the one doing anything he asks of you instead, though. You could give him the potion to drink. But would he trust you? That would be the other problem. Why would you be nice to him after what he did to you? You could shoot a dart at him, but you would have to hope no one caught you at it, or you could be incarcerated in the dungeon. Well, for any of the situations if you got caught."

"But then he would come to get me out because he would be under my influence," Kayla said, thinking this had real possibilities.

"Only if you had eye contact with him once he was under the influence. Otherwise, he could be under someone else's influence until it wore off." Sigrid sat down with them at the table.

Great. That wasn't what Kayla wanted to hear.

"She still has the problem with others seeing her and recognizing her," Tanya said.

"I can disguise her. She could be an old hag or a beautiful dragon fae. I can even turn her into a dragon shifter. Beware, if I do this, they might think you're there for the games, and you won't know anything about flying or breathing fire. It's something you would have to practice. And fast."

"Sounds too dangerous to me," Tanya said.

"It sounds absolutely perfect to me." It was the best plan ever. At least Kayla thought it could be. And she loved the idea of flying. "Can we do it now? So I can start practicing right away?"

"We can."

"What about when she's in her fae form? What will she look

like then?" Tanya asked. "She can't look like herself or wear her dragon scales all the time while she's there."

"If I make her too old, they won't believe she can be in the games, most likely. Too young, same thing. But if I make her the right age, and too beautiful, she may have all kinds of suitors. Dragon suitors."

"Wouldn't that be a laugh on them?" Kayla didn't believe she would have all kinds of dragons interested in her for a minute, but she got a kick out of the idea just the same.

"We can dye your hair a different color. You can wear human colored contact lenses. The kind that are just for looks, not to clear up vision problems. We can work on your makeup too. We can change what you wear to something that is completely different to give you a whole new appearance. The pretend you."

"You mean like wearing Goth clothes and makeup like Ena because I never wear anything like that."

"Exactly," Sigrid said. "I don't think I've had this much fun since I gave Morten the hiccups after he called me a witch. After two days, he finally apologized and begged me to stop it."

Both Tanya and Kayla stared at her in disbelief. What was she truly capable of?

"Don't tell me you wouldn't have done something to him if you had the power to do so," Sigrid said, sounding annoyed with them.

"Maybe worse," Kayla agreed, knowing Morten bullied every-one, given the chance.

"Hey, what if Sigrid turned you into a boy?" Tanya sounded thrilled with the notion she had come up with as if it was the best idea ever. "Not for real. Just in outward appearance," she quickly added when no one responded.

"Wouldn't work," both Sigrid and Kayla said.

"So you'll need to wear something really different if we're to disguise you properly. We need to cut your hair too. Instead of long and wavy, how about short and curly? You'll still be you, just a different version of you. After we've made all the changes, we'll take you to see your friends and see how many recognize you. If several do, even if they're going to know you better than Alton or the others who have only seen you once or twice, we'll get to work on making *certain* the majority have no clue it's you." Sigrid refilled her teacup.

"I'll do it," Kayla said, certain they could succeed. As far as the business of participating in the games, maybe not. She wasn't certain she could fool Alton since she had seen more of him. But everyone else? No problem.

"So what do we do first?" Tanya asked.

"First, we cut her hair, then color it." Sigrid quickly finished her tea. Then she rose from the table and collected the empty teacups.

Tanya helped her with cleaning the teacups. "Where?"

"Human world, where else? Most of us have long hair. We don't have hair stylists that can think innovatively." Sigrid took both their hands. "Do you know how to get us to Houston?" Both nodded. "Then take us there." She gave them the directions.

"Wait, but what about your wings? Can you hide them?" Kayla asked.

"Once I come of age." Sigrid grabbed a cloak. "Let's go."

THE BUILDINGS WERE TALLER, lots of glass windows, when they appeared behind a dumpster at the back of some buildings.

"Where are we?" Tanya asked, wrinkling her nose at the smell of garbage.

"Houston. And we have Le Chic Boutique Hair Styles." Sigrid led them around the back of the buildings to the front. All kinds of dress stores with all kinds of fashions were featured. And the hair salon was smack dab in the middle of them.

"We would probably have to have an appointment in a place

like this." Kayla stared in the windows at the people sitting inside, waiting their turn.

"Nah. Leave it to me." Sigrid pulled open the door.

A couple of customers looked her way. Sigrid eyed them, then smiled. She turned her attention to the stylists, their hair cut in every way imaginable, B.o.Bs, short curls, bowl cuts, long and pink.

"I'm not going with pink," Kayla said.

"No. It would make you stand out too much." Sigrid eyed a stylist who was just finishing up a client. As soon as she did, Sigrid was standing at the checkout counter, smiling at the stylist. "My friend here has an appointment with you. *Now*. For a short, curly hair style, big full bangs, and she wants to be a brunette."

The stylist was wearing a razor haircut, her black hair emphasizing her pixie face. Kayla thought she would make a suitable fae. The woman looked at the computer and Sigrid snapped her fingers to get her attention. "You're ready to turn her into a beauty. *Now*."

"Now," the woman and took Kayla right back to wash her hair. "You may take a seat—"

"We stay with her," Sigrid said.

"Of course."

Kayla wondered why Sigrid couldn't just go to the dragon fae kingdom herself as many abilities as she had. She could even transport her there. But then again, Sigrid had the problem with her wings and that was something she might not be able to hide.

Kayla was glad they were with her and hopeful she would look okay after all that the stylist did with her hair. When Kayla was having her hair dyed, a patron began to complain that she was supposed to be next. Sigrid drew the woman away from the other clients and spoke to her softly.

The woman laughed and said, "I can't believe I mixed up my days. Thanks." Then she walked out of the salon.

Kayla wished she could do what Sigrid could do. Having a

magical touch with plants didn't seem quite so useful. Not in this situation anyway.

After her hair was unwrapped, the stylist rinsed it out and patted it dry. As soon as she removed the blue towel, Kayla stared at her hair color. It was dark brown, nearly black, and even now, she didn't think she looked like herself. But before she could talk herself out of having her hair cut short, the stylist started to section it off and snip away.

She relaxed. She could do this. Her hair would grow back. Eventually.

When she was all done, she couldn't believe how lightweight her hair was or how bouncy and fun it felt.

"Much, much different," Tanya said, as they left the shop. "I'm your best friend, but believe me, if I saw you coming out of a shop, I wouldn't have realized it was you."

"Ready for clothes and makeup? So what do you think?" Sigrid motioned to a shop carrying 1960's fashions: mini-skirts, patent leather boots, opaque tights, head bands. "Or how about that. Circle skirts, saddle shoes, sweaters, white shirts."

Kayla laughed.

Then they saw a corset shop with old vintage clothes for Renaissance fairs and the like. Big plumed hats filled one window, beautiful embroidered corsets in another. "You could go with black. That's what Ena and I wear. Or you can do something different. Your favorite color," Sigrid said.

"Purple."

"Okay, so we go with everything purple. Maybe purple and black so you can wear high black boots and a pants skirt like we wear for traveling." Sigrid frowned. "Unless you've already worn anything like that around them."

"No. She was wearing brown. She always wears brown," Tanya said, sounding like that was the most boring color around.

"I do not. I've got all kinds of colors in my wardrobe."

"Let's get some purple corsets in a variety of shades so everyone will know her as the—" Sigrid said.

"Lavender dragon," Tanya said. "She has to have scales that color too when she shifts into a dragon."

They both looked at Kayla, but she turned her attention again to a black and violet colored corset that blended in with her lavender flowers. She would match Alton's dragon color, scale for scale if she had this color too.

"Maybe a different shade of purple for the scales," Kayla said. "So I don't look like I'm a matched pair with Alton."

"Come to think of it, without my locket, I'm not sure what color I can make you."

They entered the store, and Kayla glanced at Sigrid. "You're not going to charge me anything more because you've had to do so much extra stuff to help me get the lockets back, are you?"

"No. I want my locket back. We have to do whatever we can to get it back."

Kayla frowned at her. "You can't fae transport, can you?"

"No. I can give you the ability through my powers, but I can't do it myself until I have my locket back. And there are other spells I can't do either until I have it back."

"How did you lose it?"

Sigrid snorted. "I was being foolish."

"Hey, how are we going to pay for all this stuff?" Tanya modeled a blue corset over her clothes in front of a mirror.

"You don't need a do-over." Kayla gathered up four different corsets in her size—purple and white, purple and black, purple and lighter purple, purple and teal.

"I like this. I've never worn one. They're cute."

"We pay for it like we did the haircut." Sigrid spoke to the clerk, who wrapped up the purple corsets and the one blue one, and then they went to a store that sold cosmetics.

A woman applied the makeup to Kayla's face, no gold. Instead, she gave her cat-like eyes and shadowed them with violet.

"Do you have boots and pants-skirts that will go with these?" Sigrid asked.

"Yeah. I'm all set." She glanced over at Tanya who was still getting her face painted. "I don't want to bother with colored contact lenses. When we get back, can you turn me into a dragon, Sigrid?"

"Yes, but just be careful where you shoot your flames. They can be deadly."

"Right." Kayla glanced in the mirror at herself. She looked older, and she definitely didn't look like herself. She'd never worn anything wild like this. Surely, others wouldn't recognize her.

As if knowing what she was thinking, Sigrid said, "But first, we need to see if anyone recognizes you."

"Where to then?"

"Let's go to the village to 'shop.'" Tanya hopped off the stool she'd been sitting on to have her makeup applied.

"Okay, question. Do the two of you always hang out together?" Sigrid asked as they walked out of the store with a couple more sacks.

"Mostly." Kayla enjoyed Tanya's company. They were best friends so naturally they did a lot of things together.

"Then you can't for this experiment. If the two of you are always together, people who know you will still think you're Kayla. But if you're on your own, or hanging out with someone like me, they won't immediately believe you are."

"Good point." Kayla saw something behind Sigrid's comment though. She wondered if no one was her best friend. If she isolated herself from other fae because they treated her like she was a witch. Though Kayla and Tanya hadn't openly befriended her, and they had talked about how scary she could be, they hadn't shared what their

concerns about her were with others. And at least for now, while
Sigrid needed Kayla to retrieve her locket, Sigrid seemed like a nice
enough fae. "I would be thrilled if you would pal around with me."

Kayla didn't want Tanya to feel left out or that Sigrid was
suddenly going to take her place. Tanya did look glum about the
whole idea.

"You can observe us from far away." Kayla wanted Tanya to be a
part of this. She had been all along, and Kayla didn't want her to
feel unneeded.

"It's okay. I don't want to mess this up for you. It's really important that we learn if people we know will recognize you or not. I
really don't mind staying away." Tanya seemed eager to do what she
had to in order to help out, but at the same time, Kayla knew she
was disappointed that she wouldn't be right there with her the
whole time, watching reactions close up.

"You'll be my silent partner in this. I really need you to do it for
me. We can't really watch people's reactions. We have to act like we
belong there and just be ourselves. You'll be able to observe
everyone who encounters me. Hey, you could even ask others who I
am. Pretend you don't know me and see if they do."

"Oh, yeah, excellent idea!" Tanya's face was alight with excitement. The fae were known to play tricks on each other. Though in
this case, they had important but dangerous work to do. Still, as fae,
they couldn't help but be drawn to the deviousness of their plan.

"Let's go then." Tanya was so eager to leave the human world
and get started on this, she took hold of Sigrid's hand and this time
Kayla transported on her own. They met up at Kayla's cottage so
she could dress in her new clothes.

Kayla tried on her various pants-skirts with the corsets and
before she chickened out, she decided on the purple and teal with a
teal pants-skirt and brown boots. She had never worn anything so
risqué before, so she wanted to throw on a shirt or jacket or something, and then just have it open in the front.

"This is the new you, remember?" Tanya grinned. "I love it. You look so different. I swear if I hadn't watched the transformation, I would have to have looked twice to recognize you. Just be the new you and enjoy! This is so much fun, I think Sigrid and I should try it next."

Sigrid laughed. "They will always think that I'm a witch."

She was smiling when she said it, but Kayla didn't think she was really happy about it. And she decided right then and there, Sigrid was going to be their best friend too. Wasn't it better to have a 'witch' on their side than against them? Besides, she loved all Sigrid's suggestions and was having lots of fun with this, when she had been trying to handle this on her own—unsuccessfully. Kayla still wondered how Sigrid had lost her locket too. Maybe she would feel like opening up to them later, after she realized they wanted to be her friends and not just that they needed her for a job.

"Why don't we go first to the farmer's market?" Sigrid said. "I want to get some fresh tomatoes. They have fairy ice cones now too. Everyone goes there when it first opens."

"Sounds good to me." Kayla looked to see Tanya's take on it.

"I want one of the watermelon ones. I can even be there at the same time you all are, only I'll just pretend I don't know you."

"It's a big market so it should work." Sigrid held out her hand to Kayla.

Kayla took it and knew it must be bugging Sigrid that she couldn't go to places on her own like that, unless she walked, until she got her locket back. Just like it was for Kayla. "See you there. Well, but we'll pretend not to see you."

Tanya smiled. "This will be fun." And she sounded like she really meant it.

Kayla was glad. She took one last look in her bedroom mirror and her reflection showed her a person she didn't recognize. "Oh, what about my voice? Even if I don't look the same, won't people recognize my voice?"

"Try to change it when you talk. If that doesn't work, I might be able to do something to change it. I doubt anyone would recognize it who doesn't know you really well though."

"True. Ready? Let's go."

As soon as they transported to the farmer's market, Kayla saw two guys she knew talking to a girl she didn't get along with at the ice cone stand, Helena. Blond-haired, blue-eyed, she always had the guys' attentions. Darrel and Sebastian glanced in Kayla's direction, their eyes widening. Was it in recognition and because she looked so different? Or because she looked so different, and they didn't know her and they wondered who she was?

Helena turned to see what they were gawking at, and Kayla turned her attention away from them, remembering she wasn't supposed to act like she knew them. She hoped she hadn't already blown her cover.

6

Alton knew it was a dumb idea thinking Kayla would return to where she must have been spying on him while he had been practicing dragon games with Olaf before. And that was where she had left her jewelry behind. After the way he had told on her, even if he'd had no intention of doing so, he assumed she wouldn't come anywhere near the place. And yet, she'd seemed so desperate to get her locket back that he felt she wouldn't just give up.

Flying high above the clearing with the brown dragon, Alton kept searching the area for signs of her gold glittering in the sunlight as if she would come here wearing gold again and risk getting caught, but he saw no sign of her. Everyone was practicing their skills before the games, and he often practiced with Olaf here, so at least the dragon didn't wonder why Alton wanted to return here. For a second time, Olaf tried to fly with him in an upside-down arc and Alton nearly plummeted to the ground. He thought he saw a glint of gold, when it was only a yellow leaf fluttering in the breeze. Olaf alighted on the ground and shifted.

Alton joined him, thinking he wanted a break, but Olaf said,

"Listen, if you're still hurting and don't think you can make it in the games—"

"No, I'm fine. Really."

Olaf eyed him speculatively. "Then what? I've never seen you so...distracted. Normally you never are and that's why I like practicing with you. We were doing so well working as a team for that part of the games, I thought we would take first place for sure. But if you're really not up to this, we can plan on it for next year. If you're not feeling well, I don't want you to pretend you are for some stupid macho reason just to prove you can still participate and end up injuring yourself even worse."

"I'm fine, okay?" Truth of the matter was an ache throughout the area where the bolt had struck Alton still persisted and some of the diving and arching he was doing made him grit his teeth to fight the pain. But he would participate even if it nearly killed him.

Olaf frowned at him. "Then what is the matter?" He folded his arms and cocked his head. "Don't tell me it's about this Kayla. The golden fae. Halloran said you were angry he had intended to take her into custody. You said yourself she was planning to steal Ena and Brett's gold. So, what? You had a change of heart concerning her because she rescued you? Big mistake, bro."

"Yeah, well see how you would feel if someone, even if she was a golden fae, saved your hide and didn't have to. She had risked her own neck in doing so, in fact. So yeah, I had a change of heart. Why wouldn't I?"

Olaf looked around at the pine trees and bracken growing at the edge of the clearing. "Is this where she dropped her gold jewelry?"

Alton didn't want to tell him everything that had occurred, but he figured he wasn't going to be able to just pretend it didn't happen.

"Listen, I took something of hers, all right? So I want to give it back."

"You stole from her?"

"No, she left it behind."

"Then it's yours. Where did she leave it behind?"

"Here."

"Then it really is yours since she had no business being over here."

"She was watching us when we were working on our techniques for the games, curious, I guess. At the end of our practice, I saw her gold glittering. You flew home because you had a job to do, and I took off to check out what was sparkling in the fronds. I heard her fleeing, but I knew I would catch up to her, so I grabbed her jewelry first. She had a lot. I never observed her, just saw the fronds moving. By the time I reached the river, she'd vanished. So I assumed she'd transported home again. I couldn't understand why she hadn't done so in the first place though, instead of trying to slow me down by leaving her jewelry behind."

"There might be iron ore in some of the areas beneath the soil. On the other hand, you don't think it was a trick, do you? She was drawing you to the river's edge for some devious purpose?"

All fae kind were tricksters. Alton didn't know one who wasn't. Well, maybe Ena. He swore she lived to work, except for the relationship she had with Brett now. As far as he knew, he hadn't seen her play tricks on anyone ever. The rest of the fae? It was part of who they were.

"It was bizarre, I'll give you that. It could be that she was trying to lure me to the river's edge for some purpose, but something thwarted whatever devious plan she'd had in mind. Which is another reason I would like to know the truth. She only wants a locket back. I would think she would want all her gold if she's making such an effort to get her jewelry back."

"What if the locket has magical properties?"

"Or some sentimental value. Family heirloom, maybe."

"Did it look old?"

"That's the real problem. I didn't pay any real attention to any of the jewelry. I just tossed it on one of my piles of treasure and buried it with more after that. So I don't know what is hers, really."

"Sounds to me like you could bargain with her. Force her to pay you a lot of gold to obtain her locket."

He'd thought about it. He was a dragon after all. That was before she'd saved him. Well, maybe he'd thought about it even after that. Not that he'd wanted payment, but he wanted to know why in the world she didn't transport herself to safety when he was carrying her over the ocean and dropped her. If she couldn't transport, why was she able to do so to the human world? Had she lost her powers and now regained them?

And then she was able to change her aura and hide her fae dust, but she didn't when he went after her gold. Why? She could have just worn the dragon fae aura, and he would never have guessed she was anything but one of his people. Though the fact she was wearing so much gold paint on her face and hands would have clued him in that she wasn't what she appeared to be.

So she was a total mystery, and he wanted to know what he could about her. Before he handed over her locket.

Olaf snapped his fingers. "I've got a date. Need to run. Do you want to practice again tomorrow? Maybe another location so you can concentrate better?"

"Here, tomorrow, same time." Alton smiled. "Who's the date with?"

"Not saying. Next thing I know, you'll be asking her out like you did Ena."

"Ena was to be mine. Her brother and I had a deal."

Olaf laughed. "Ena has a mind of her own. See you later." Olaf shifted and flew into the sky, the sunlight reflecting off his brown scales edged in gold.

Olaf was right. Alton had to get his mind on the game. So why did he shift and take off for the golden fae territory and was flying over the golden fae countryside, well away from the castles belonging to the nobility where archers would be sure to attempt to take down the offending dragon?

How could he possibly hope to catch sight of Kayla anywhere in the areas he was soaring over? He saw a few blond-haired girls that were about her petite size, wearing brown tunics and pants-skirts, their necks and wrists and hands covered in rings and bracelets and necklaces of gold. When they looked heavenward to see what kind of large-winged creature was casting a shadow over them, he saw their gold painted faces, but no one who looked like Kayla. Besides, they all ran off screaming, looking for cover. He knew Kayla would be shaking her fist at him, cursing him for doing what he'd done to her.

Then he had another idea. The next girl he saw, he was swooping down and carrying her to the dragon fae's side of the river. Then again, that wouldn't work. He would have to manacle her in iron, or she could just transport away.

His blue scales blended in with the sky as he flew high above, but then they suddenly turned purple. He couldn't believe it and he swore under his breath.

He saw more activity in a farmer's market filled with plant stands of fruits and vegetables and flower stalls.

Then he saw the winged creature he'd fought with when he'd collected all of Kayla's gold, strolling through the market. The falcon fae really stood out. She was wearing her black leather clothing, long, black leather gloves, and thigh high black boots. Her dark brown hair was unusual too, the edges of her bangs sporting silver strands. Her brown spotted wings were folded against her back.

Standing with her, a girl was dressed in a purple corset and a blue-green colored pants-skirt, leather boots laced with the same blue-green color, her hair short, curly, and dark. He had thought Kayla might be with the falcon fae because she'd called her friend and was trying to get her locket back as well. He'd had it in mind that the falcon fae had attacked him, trying to recover the locket to return to her friend. But the girl with the falcon fae wasn't Kayla, and he was disappointed.

Both of them looked up. He was certain he would have a fight with the falcon fae, and he didn't want to. But he did want to know where Kayla was so he could talk with her, thank her for saving him, and learn more about her.

The other girl walking with the falcon fae gaped at him. She also wasn't afraid of him while everyone else was shouting in the farmer's market and ducking for cover. Some of the fae were running around with short swords, though, lucky for him, no one had crossbows.

He suspected if he swooped off toward the dragon fae territory, the falcon fae would follow him, if only to see if she could get her locket back. Then maybe she would take a message to Kayla for him.

He flew back to the dragon lands, not checking to see if she would follow, then landed, and shifted. He looked up then and saw her circling high above. He had to admit she had nice form if he wasn't still irritated with her for attacking him before.

"I'm looking for your friend Kayla. I need to speak with her."

"You should have thought of that before you sent the Dragon at Arms after her to throw her in the dungeon," she said, flapping her wings high above him, her arms folded across her waist.

"It wasn't like that."

"Tell me how it was then."

"I was asking to see her, and I made the slip that she was a golden fae. I was on pain medication. I didn't even know that I'd said what I did until Halloran told me. Tell her I want to speak with her."

"Why?"

"I want to apologize to her, and I want to talk to her about her locket."

"What of mine?"

"Are they magical?" he asked.

The falcon fae turned and began to fly away.

"Wait, all right. Let me talk to her and I'll make a deal with her."

"For her locket or both of ours?"

"Both. But I won't give them to her unless I'm able to speak with her first."

"What...what if you talk to me instead? And *I* make a deal with *you*."

"Who are you and what are you doing living with the golden fae?" Alton asked.

"I'm Sigrid and my people have always lived with the golden fae, though I am the last of my kind who live here now. And you are Alton, Dragon Thief."

He smiled at the title she had given him, but he wasn't speaking with her instead of Kayla. He had to personally apologize to Kayla and give her back her locket. She had saved his life, not the falcon fae.

"I thank you for the offer. But my duty is to Kayla."

"Your duty, is it? I will tell her." Then Sigrid flew off and disappeared beyond the tall pines.

He realized he hadn't told her a place or time he could meet Kayla. Cursing himself for not thinking of it sooner, he shifted and flew after the falcon fae, then had a thought. If he could keep out of sight, though as a dragon it was no small task, he could see where she went. If she ended up at a cottage somewhere, it might even be Kayla's. And then he could see her himself. Though he would probably wait until Sigrid left and Kayla came out of the cottage so he knew for sure it was hers. Well, or whoever else lived with her. She might have a ton of family living there. A father even, who would love to shoot him full of bolts. Maybe even a brother or two. Then again, she said she only lived with her mother.

Alton was determined to get this over with, learn what the locket looked like and return it so he wouldn't lose any more sleep over it. Which he couldn't believe was happening either. To *him*.

Instead of going to a cottage out in the country, Sigrid headed back to the farmer's market. He realized then that she had left her other friend behind and couldn't very well not return there to tell her what was going on. Though he wished she would just get on with business. He wished he could hide his fae aura. If he could, he would just shift and follow the girls and see if Sigrid told her other friend anything of value that would aid him in locating Kayla.

He landed behind a building and shifted, startling two wrens off a bird feeder, a blue fairy wren, its feathers a bright blue, and a variegated fairy wren, his head a mixture of blues, the rest of him in rust, black, blue, and various shades of brown. The fae had taken some of them with them to Australia eons ago, and called them simply fairy wrens, and the name stuck.

Alton kept out of sight as much as possible. But he couldn't follow them without being seen. The dark-haired girl that had been with her hurried to join Sigrid.

"What happened?"

"I couldn't catch up to him," Sigrid said.

Why would Sigrid lie to the other girl?

"Why would he come here? To find me?" the dark-haired girl asked.

From behind a wooden structure that served as a flower stall's wall, he tried to see the girl better. It couldn't be Kayla. But no one else in the golden fae kingdom might think he wished to see her.

Then another girl moved around the flower stall, doing as he was doing, eavesdropping. Except she saw him before he could duck behind the building. He could have vanished, but he still wanted to get a better look at the dark-haired girl.

This girl came around the flower stall wall, acting not in the least bit afraid of him as if she couldn't see that he was a dragon fae and that she should fear him. "What are you doing here?" she asked. "Have you come to return Kayla's locket?"

"You know her?" He couldn't have been more surprised.

"Yes. So if you're here, you must intend to return her locket."

"And apologize for what happened to her. I was heavily medicated and must have mentioned she was one of you. Well, one of the golden fae. I don't remember. Just that I was asking to see her."

"And I should believe you, why?" she asked.

"I wouldn't be here now, would I? She risked her life to save mine. I owe her at least that. I told that to the falcon fae, Sigrid. She was to bring word to Kayla that I want to meet her. But I didn't think to tell her when or where. We can meet on her side of the river where I met her before, tomorrow at noon?"

"If she can't make it?"

"Then if you could see me with a new time and place, I'll come again. I'm Alton, by the way, if you didn't already know."

"Oh, I know, all right. I'm Tanya, and Kayla's best friend."

"And Sigrid?"

"A new friend." Tanya didn't appear too happy about that, a little frown pinching her brows.

Alton took that as a good sign and decided to tell her what had occurred. "She wanted to strike a deal with me to get her locket back instead of me speaking with Kayla. Just a warning." He thought it was important to mention it just in case the falcon fae meant to double-cross Kayla or something.

Tanya's eyes widened, then narrowed. "What did she say *exactly*?"

He wasn't sure if Tanya didn't believe him or believed him and was angry that Sigrid tried to go behind Kayla's back on this.

"That I should talk with her instead of Kayla and that she would make a deal with me instead. Words to that effect."

"*Really.*"

"Ohmigodess," a woman screamed.

He'd been found out. "Tell her for me, will you?" Then he transported out of there, safer than flying out of the area as a dragon.

7

Tanya wondered what Sigrid was up to. If Sigrid had some hidden agenda, Tanya didn't want to let on she knew in front of her. Best to discuss it in private with Kayla and see what she wanted to do about it.

She hoped Alton was being honest with her. She didn't believe he had lied about what had happened concerning getting Kayla in trouble. Why come here and try to apologize and risk his own safety if he wasn't telling the truth? If this was all real, it was the best situation possible. He could bring Kayla's locket to her and apologize and then Kayla wouldn't have to chance exposing who she was by going to the dragon games. Tanya couldn't wait to talk to Kayla about it. And to tell her friend about Sigrid. Tanya had wanted to like her. To be her friend when she had none, but if she'd planned to betray Kayla? Forget that.

Tanya peered around the flower stall and saw Kayla and Sigrid walking toward the village, but Tanya was done with observing to see if anyone recognized Kayla. They hadn't. She'd asked a couple of guys and a girl who knew her if they recognized the new girl walking with Sigrid. No one had. Except they'd told Tanya if the new girl was Sigrid's friend to watch out.

If what the dragon fae had said was true, those who talked to Tanya were right to assume she and Kayla needed to be wary around Sigrid.

Tanya wondered what Kayla's mother would say about all the changes in Kayla's appearance. They hadn't bothered with the contact lenses, Kayla not wanting to wear them in her eyes. Kayla had always been a stick-in-the-mud about her styles. Tasha would probably be shocked and even maybe a little concerned. Tanya really hadn't thought that far ahead. All that had mattered was that Kayla got her locket back.

Before Tanya could transport to Kayla's house where she figured she would meet her later, Sigrid materialized before her, startling her. She gasped at her sudden appearance. "Where's Kayla?" Tanya asked, trying to cover how shaken she was.

"She's on her own for a bit to ensure no one recognizes her. If she's with me, people might be looking more at me and less at her. Why aren't you following her?"

Tanya didn't think Sigrid was just curious. She sounded like she knew something was wrong. "No one knows who she is. I've talked to several people. I figure she's all set to go." Now would be the time for Sigrid to say that she spoke with Alton, and they might have another resolution. Well, even before, when she was still encouraging Tanya to see if anyone knew Kayla.

"I would think you would want to be *very* sure Kayla would be safe when she goes to the games," Sigrid said.

So Alton had been right all along. Otherwise, why didn't Sigrid tell her there was a possibility Kayla and Alton could work things out?

"I talked to a woman who said you were speaking with a man with a dragon fae aura. What did he tell you?" Sigrid asked.

She knew. "He wants to apologize to Kayla and give her locket back." Tanya figured there was no sense in pretending she hadn't spoken to Alton now.

"And you weren't going to tell me?"

"I thought he already told you that and you would have spoken to Kayla about it." How could the girl twist things around to make Tanya look like the bad guy when *she* was the one withholding information in the first place!

"I see. You will not remember anything about the meeting with Alton." Sigrid blew green fairy dust in Tanya's face.

Tanya blinked the dust from her eyes and wondered where Kayla was since she wasn't with Sigrid now. "Where's Kayla? I thought she was with you."

"She's just walking around, seeing if anyone recognizes her. I was just checking on you to learn if you found anyone who knew who she was," Sigrid said.

"No. No one."

"Good. She's going to practice her dragon skills for the rest of the day. We'll go to the clearing by her cottage. Why don't you come with me and the two of us can observe her until then? I'm afraid people are looking at me too much because they're afraid of me, when we need them to just see her."

"Oh sure. Great idea." But Tanya kept feeling like she needed to do something. Yet whatever it was, it totally eluded her for now. Maybe she would recall what it was later.

KAYLA WAS glad no one who really knew her recognized her. She suspected no one who had met her in the dragon fae kingdom would either since they hadn't seen her more than once or twice. Now, she was eager to start her flying practice. She recalled what Brett had said to Ena and Alton about not being that good at his dragon flying skills yet and didn't think he could best Alton in the games. She suspected she would be a lot worse off than that because she was so completely new at it.

As soon as she rejoined Sigrid and Tanya in the woods on the outskirts of the village, Kayla asked Tanya if anything was the matter. She was frowning for one thing, instead of glad to see her. "No one recognized me, did they?"

Tanya shook her head and gave her a half smile.

Kayla knew Tanya well enough to recognize something wasn't right.

When they reached the clearing by Kayla's cottage, Tanya sat on the patio and waited for Kayla and Sigrid to fly. Kayla shifted and couldn't believe how beautiful she was. Well, not her face because she couldn't see it, but everything else. She loved the color and how protected she felt.

Even though Sigrid wasn't a dragon, she still flew as a falcon fae, and she showed Kayla tons of tricks to flying, soaring, gliding, and diving. The flame business was something Sigrid couldn't help her with though.

"I thought we would have a sort of sleepover," Sigrid finally said as Kayla shifted on the ground after finishing practice lessons.

Kayla had had a ball.

She was afraid they would talk all night. At least that was what she and Tanya normally did. But after the workout she'd had, she just wanted to take a shower, crawl into her own little bed, and fall asleep.

"Then we can start again tomorrow. You'll need to sign in tomorrow afternoon for the games and you'll be assigned to one of the barracks where the contestants are staying."

"Tomorrow?" Kayla never squeaked, but she bordered on it. She thought she had longer than that to practice with Sigrid. At least the flying part of the equation. She was still falling out of the sky when the wind shifted direction and she wasn't ready for it. She would look like a baby dragon kicked out of the nest.

"Yeah. I knew if I told you too soon, you would be all scared about it and not want to do it."

Kayla straightened. "Of course I'm ready for it."

"Good."

Tanya finally spoke up. "Are they all together?"

Both Kayla and Sigrid glanced at her, not sure what she was asking.

"You know. The guys and girls. Are they all rooming together?"

Kayla swung her head around to look at Sigrid since she seemed to have all the answers.

"How do I know? But probably not. Otherwise, they could end up with a bunch of little baby dragons," Sigrid said, and smiled.

"They may not let me compete. What if they have initial trials to get rid of all those who aren't ready for this?"

"Won't matter. You'll already be there. And you can learn when you can see Alton, get him off to the side and ask him for our lockets."

"I'll be totally unknown. Not of this dragon fae kingdom. Surely everyone knows everyone. So then I would have to be from another. And any of the contestants could know I'm not from theirs either."

"Then we make up one. You're a loner, on your own. That's why you're such a novice flyer. No adults or siblings to help you learn to fly or play with fire."

"Okay, sounds good. But what about preregistration. Wouldn't I be required to do that?"

"They have both onsite and preregistration. Unless you really don't want to participate in the games. And that's fine. But you might not see Alton until well after the games are over. That's cutting it really close to when you need to have your locket in your possession."

"And yours?"

"That goes without saying."

"How do you know so much about the dragon games?" Kayla asked.

"I sneaked in as a falcon once. You probably have heard I shift into one. No one paid me any attention. They just figured I was a real bird. No falcon fae anywhere around here."

TANYA HAD TOSSED and turned most of the night, trying to recall what had happened that she couldn't remember despite any amount of trying. She was glad that Kayla was so excited to leave and participate in the games, but apprehensive too.

And then an hour after Kayla left to face the dragons at the games, it came to Tanya all at once with full clarity. Alton had asked to meet with Kayla, and Tanya was supposed to tell her about the meeting. But then Sigrid had hit her with a handful of fairy dust, and Tanya had forgotten what had happened. Furious, Tanya wanted to ask Sigrid why, but Tanya was well aware Sigrid had abilities she didn't know anything about. She finally asked anyway, not able to keep quiet.

"Why did you stop Kayla from meeting Alton at her cottage?"

"She had one chance in a lifetime to make this happen," Sigrid told Tanya.

"Make *what* happen? It would have been so simple. He would have handed over the lockets, apologized, and that would have been the end of that."

"Right. But remember when I said I had gone there as a falcon to watch the games?"

"Yeah. So? What has that got to do with anything with regard to Kayla?"

"I fell in love with a dragon fae shifter. Forget it. I don't expect you to understand."

"Wait. You're thinking Kayla's going to fall for some *dragon*? Get real. She's a golden fae. *Not* a dragon. You're not a dragon either."

"Right. But sometimes love crosses boundaries, you know? She just has to hurry before—" Sigrid paused as if she had said too much.

"Before what?"

Sigrid let out her breath. "Before she turns back into a pumpkin."

"*What?*" Tanya just stared at the falcon fae, wondering just what Kayla had gotten herself into with trusting the witch.

"Haven't you ever heard of Cinderella? The human fairy tale? Their fairy tales show some of the most delightful tricks to play on people, you know. Some are worthy of being called fairy tales."

"The girl turned into a pumpkin?" Tanya couldn't believe it! Was that what would happen to her best friend? She had to warn her right away.

"No! The *carriage* turned into a pumpkin."

Tanya stared at her in disbelief, not knowing what in the world she was going on about. "What are you talking about? I don't mean about some stupid fairy tale. What about Kayla?"

"She *can't* stay there any longer than midnight of the final day of the games. If she does and I don't turn her back, she'll be a dragon shifter fae, for real."

"Are you nuts? Why didn't you just let him give her locket back to her!"

"You saw the love potion I make, right? Well sometimes people don't need it, but they need time to realize they're the right ones for each other. That wouldn't have happened if she hadn't participated in the games."

"I can't believe this. Un. Real." Tanya began to leave Sigrid's cottage, but Sigrid grabbed Tanya's arm.

"Don't interfere. *Please.* I know something about this. If you get involved, your actions could ruin it for them, and you would lose your valuable friendship also. Just give them a chance. Maybe when he sees her, he'll just turn the lockets over to her like he said he would, simple as that. But maybe something really special will happen instead."

Tanya worried nothing about this whole scenario was going to be simple, and it could be very bad—for Kayla. What would happen if she turned into a dragon shifter for real? Would the queen banish her? What about her mother?

"Okay, okay, okay. I know from your set jaw, you're all ready to go over there and rescue the fair maiden." Sigrid let out her breath in an exasperated way. "Listen. I know what I'm talking about in this instance. I want to tell you something that will hopefully convince you to leave well enough alone."

Tanya thought that nothing would ever convince her of that, and she was ready to go to the dragon fae kingdom herself, track Kayla down, and tell her the important thing Sigrid so conveniently had left out about this whole mess.

Until Sigrid told Tanya a secret that no one was ever to know.

KAYLA COULDN'T BELIEVE ALL the beautiful decorations all over the place, the flowers, plaques advertising the dragon games featuring dragons racing across the sky, shooting golden flames as if sword fighting with fire, dragons capturing flags from rooftops. Billboard posters showed off dragons who had won in previous years for various categories.

She was so enthusiastic, caught up in all the excitement that she barely remembered she was a golden fae, the dragon shifters' arch enemy. If she'd been thinking more golden fae-like, she would have thought about locating one of the dragon's piles of treasure while the dragons were busy playing games!

Then in a grassy clearing near a heavily wooded area, she saw tables set up with a banner sign hanging above them, declaring this was the registration area. Each table had a smaller sign indicating who handled what for preregistered dragons based on the alphabet. For those who hadn't preregistered, another set of tables were off to the side, and on-site registration was also done alphabetically.

Kayla took a moment to steady her rapid breathing before she walked toward one of the middle tables for names from J to M. She was halfway there when she remembered she was using the name Violet and had to detour to the end of the tables.

"Forgot your name in all the excitement?" a girl asked, smiling at Kayla as if she thought she was really funny.

With all the dragons converging in the area—Kayla never imagined just how many that would entail—she didn't think anyone would have noticed her faux pas.

The girl's burgundy hair in a mass of curls about her head made Kayla think of the redheaded Orphan Annie, only the color was wrong. She was about Kayla's age, wearing a ruffled black and pink skirt, black boots and a black fitted tank top. She had style. Kayla would give her that. Only she was pesky, and Kayla hoped she would go away. On the other hand, if it looked like this dragon fae could accept her as one of them and talk to her as if she belonged here, it could be a good thing.

"I'm undercover. I use all kinds of different aliases." Kayla continued to walk toward the registration table. The right one this time.

"Undercover, huh? In that get-up? It's too showy to be worn by someone undercover," she said, following along beside Kayla.

"See? It's working." Kayla glanced around at what the other dragon fae were wearing. Some were really subdued in browns and olive greens, understated, not showy in the least. But then would they wow the crowds with how truly spectacular they were as dragons?

"Why would you be here undercover?" the girl asked, as if playing along.

Kayla raised her brows.

The girl laughed and this time she seemed genuinely amused. "Oh yeah. You can't say because you're undercover. So where are you from? I know it has got to be a made-up place but humor me."

"Tenia."

The girl frowned. "Never heard of it. Are you here with any of your fellow dragon friends?"

"Nope."

"What's your name?"

"Violet. Yours?"

"Willow. Guess we're registering at the same table."

So far, so good, Kayla thought. She stood in line, waiting her turn, four others ahead of her. She glanced around at the other dragons, looking for anyone she knew—Ena, Brett, Halloran, Alton. No one yet. They might have come and gone already.

"Looking for someone in particular?" Willow asked.

"Nope. At least not that I could say."

Willow chuckled. "You are so good at this cover story. I would have forgotten it right away."

"Well, it's important to be in character because it could mean life or death otherwise." Which was really true.

Willow laughed again. "Woah sounds ominous. So when you find the fae you're after, what then?"

Kayla smiled at her.

"Oh, right, you can't tell me."

"Next," the woman said at the table and Kayla hurried to take a form and fill it out.

A few of the things on the entry form she had to fill in with her fabricated information: Name, Homeland, but a few things were true: Birth Date, Birthplace.

"Houston?" the fae asked.

"Yeah, my mother's mistake. She'd gotten tired of waiting for me to be born and so she traveled to Houston to her favorite ice cream shop and ordered her favorite ice cream. Strawberry topped with chocolate fudge and a strawberry on top. It might have been the fae travel there. She wasn't sure, but the next thing she knew she was having me, and they had to call the police and have her transported to a hospital. As soon as she had me, she took me right home. She said she was certain the hospital staff was completely confused about the whole thing. So I never lived there, but I was born there."

"Oh," the lady said.

"Yep."

"Here you are, dear." She handed Kayla a badge with a number and another form. "Just pick out the games you want to participate in. There will be a prequalification test to make sure you meet the minimum qualifications."

"I only just got my dragon abilities. What if I don't qualify in any of the events?" Kayla wore an expression that said she would be so disappointed if she didn't make it. In a way, she didn't want to qualify for anything. She hoped once she was registered, she could just hang around the contestants until she saw Alton and get this over with.

The woman tilted her head, looking a little curiously at Kayla, probably wondering why she hadn't had her abilities for very long.

Kayla shrugged. "We lived where dragons weren't favored. Mom never wanted me to shift. But then I wanted to come to the games and be around others that could shift whenever they liked. It feels great to be here."

The woman smiled warmly at her. "I'm so glad you're here. We have some beginner events for new dragons. We want to make sure everyone has a chance to participate in something and have fun."

"Thanks." Kayla was afraid to ask how old the contestants would be. She saw a few young fae running around the place, but at first thought they were with older siblings who were participating. How embarrassing would that be? To be shown up by a ten-year-old fae, or younger?

"Just sign up for your barracks over there and turn in your game form to that man at that table over there. A board with all the prequalification games will be listed with times and locations. You just need to be there on time. Once you're prequalified, a board will list names of those who made it and when the real event takes place. Be sure and list a good number of games that you can try so that if you don't prequalify in some, hopefully you will in others. But no matter what, have fun."

"Thanks." When Kayla turned to leave, she saw Willow eyeing her speculatively.

"See you around," Kayla said.

"Wait up. I'll go with you." Willow hurried to fill out her form and said, "I've been here for the last three years."

"Okay, then you know the ropes," the woman said.

Kayla didn't want to hang out with Willow, but what could she do? She would have to play along for a little bit. Willow was probably more like an expert at this, so that meant she wouldn't be in the games Kayla had to participate in at least.

"Thanks." Willow whipped around with her game form in hand and took Kayla by the arm. "You didn't tell me you were a novice. Then again, that might just be your cover. Pretend to be a real beginner and then watch the expert who is your real target."

Kayla smiled. The fae probably got a kick out of her story. Then she lost the smile. She wished she wasn't pretending to be such a phony. Sure, it was a fae way, but still, she was beginning to warm up to the annoying dragon, and she hated to have to lie to her. Then again, Willow knew she was hiding something.

"So which one is the girls' barracks?"

"The one to the right," Willow said.

Then a golden dragon near a refreshment stand caught her eye. Brett? An olive-green dragon moved in next to him, and Kayla was sure it was Ena and Brett then. The two of them kissed each other, their long dragon tongues curling around each other's in a friendly way. Kayla watched with fascination, unable to look away.

"What's the matter? Never been kissed by a dragon before?"

"No." Not that Kayla should have admitted it, but the truth was she'd never seen a dragon kissing another before.

Suddenly, a blue dragon materialized out of the blue sky high above, but as he drew closer to the ground, his scales shimmered into silver, then violet. The dragon had to be Alton. He was truly beautiful, and Kayla noticed then that others were watching his shifting color display.

"That's Alton." Willow folded her arms and stopped to watch as he landed on the ground and shifted. "He was supposed to be mated to Ena. That's her, the olive-green dragon over there. She got hung up on Brett, the golden dragon. He was human raised though."

"Are you from here?" Kayla asked.

"Nope."

"Are you with anyone here?"

"No. I came alone. My dragon clan is small, and no one is the age to really compete well any longer. They're either too old, too young, or just no longer interested."

Several dragons standing closer to Alton made jokes about his scales changing colors. "Are you gonna distract your opponent with changing the color of your scales?" a guy asked.

A girl punched him. "Hey, if you could do that, I would marry you in a heartbeat."

Kayla smiled.

"I dunno," Willow said to Kayla. "Can you imagine have dragonlings whose scales changed color constantly?"

"I think they're beautiful."

"Violet...don't tell me your scales are that color too?"

"They are. I love that shade of purple. It's a rich royal hue."

"The two of you would be a matching pair. Cute. Until his scales turned a different color again. Let's go get our barrack's assignment. We can sleep anywhere. I mean, girls with girls only. Boys with boys. But it's not alphabetized or anything. Then we need to sit down and decide which games we'll participate in. I'll help you if you need me to explain the various kinds of games. Have you even seen them before?"

"No."

"Okay, then I'll advise you as to which are the easiest and how to prequalify."

"Thanks. I appreciate that." Kayla glanced in Alton's direction, but he was headed for the preregistration table.

"He's kinda cute, isn't he? But he's still hung up on Ena."

8

Alton smelled lavender on the breeze and instantly thought of Kayla. He looked around to see if she was at the registration area, pretending to be a dragon fae again, but how could she when Halloran and others knew her by sight? And why wouldn't she have just met with him at her cottage like he said he would do instead of standing him up? He'd waited for hours, even thinking to leave the lockets on her porch, but was afraid someone else might steal them.

He continued to search the area here, but except for the people setting up the games, registering the dragons and such, everyone else that was here was dragon shifter fae. Not dragon fae. Not seeing any sign of Kayla, Alton headed to the preregistration table and got his number. He'd already filled out his game choice sheet. For the first time ever, though, he worried about whether he would prequalify for some of the more strenuous events. He couldn't believe how long it was taking for the injury from the bolt to heal. Now he knew something of how Brett must have felt when he had suffered wounds like this.

Alton considered the barracks and whether he wanted to stay there or at his castle. Resident dragons could do either, their choice.

His castle would have better accommodations and servants to cater to his every whim, but sometimes staying in the barracks offered him a way to learn more about his opponents. His heart wasn't really into any of this though. Not when he hadn't resolved things with Kayla.

That wasn't like him either. He was usually eager to win as many of the games as he could, extremely competitive, and wanted to be the winner to take all. He thought his disinterest this time had to do mostly with being wounded. At least he blamed it on that. He didn't want to think a golden fae was distracting him like this.

Olaf waved at him and hurried to join him. "Are you staying here?"

"I'm not sure. I was just going to see who was staying in the barracks this time." Alton considered the long, one-story building topped with a copper roof again.

"Not me. I prefer my own bed and meals over a noisy barracks. Because of your injury, I thought you would want to get more rest too."

"I do. In truth."

They saw Halloran approaching, dressed in his royal braided uniform, and he frowned at them. "Don't tell me you're even thinking of staying in the barracks." He'd always been above that, feeling he didn't need to know about his competition.

"Not me," Olaf said. He liked his creature comforts. "I can do just as well at the games without knowing more about who I'm going up against."

"Yeah, I agree." For this year, anyway, Alton thought. In years past, sometimes, sometimes not so much.

"Are you all right?" Halloran asked Alton.

He knew his friend was only concerned about him, but he hated that he wasn't acting his normally competitive self and it showed. "Yeah, I'm fine."

Olaf and Halloran exchanged glances, and Alton was certain they didn't believe him at all.

Then a girl wearing a blue corset and pants skirt with the gores in black so it had sort of a blue and black striped effect, caught his eye. Her hair was the same dark brown color, short and curly as the girl wore who was with the falcon fae at the farmer's market in the golden fae territory. And she'd been a golden fae!

Now she was a dragon fae again? No way could she be Kayla, yet...what if she was?

"I'm going to check out the barracks." Because the girl was close to there and he had to see her, smell her scent, listen to her voice, and be certain it wasn't her. Even if it wasn't, she had to be like Kayla, able to change her aura.

"I'll go with you," Olaf said.

"No!" Alton knew he spoke too quickly, too harshly. Both Halloran and Olaf were staring at him as if he had flipped out. "That's okay. I'll meet you at the fields for practice, Olaf, before the prequalification trials."

Olaf nodded. "Sure, see you there in...?"

"A half hour."

"All right. See you there."

Alton noticed then the girl was with another dragon fae, one with burgundy hair. He knew her for certain, had seen her at the games before for the last three years. Willow was nearly an expert, so he didn't know why she would hang out with a fae who was unknown to her. Had to be, if she was a golden fae who could hide her aura beneath another. Yet, what if the girl was truly a dragon fae shifter and had been just looking to steal from the golden fae?

He stalked toward the two girls. If the dark-haired girl was Kayla, she couldn't pretend she was a dragon shifter too. It was one thing to cloak an aura with another, as rare as that gift was, but to turn into a dragon also? He was intrigued beyond measure.

As soon as he was close enough, he suddenly had a brilliant idea and called out, "Kayla!"

OHMIGODDESS! Kayla turned around to see Alton striding toward her, and he knew her. How could he?

"Well," Willow said, folding her arms, smiling in a dark way. "Seems someone knows your real name. Or at least one of your other covers."

If Kayla hadn't turned, responding to the calling of her name, would she have fooled Alton into believing she wasn't the one he believed her to be?

Her heart was beating out of bounds, she was so concerned he would have her arrested. She thought of transporting right out of there. But she couldn't. She had to face him, try to get him to leave with her so they could talk, and she wouldn't have to do this. If he knew who she was, surely Halloran and the others would too.

"Excuse us," Alton said to Willow. "I need a word alone with—"

"Violet is her name," Willow said, smiling. "And she's my friend."

Kayla glanced at her, not believing the fae would stick up for her when she had to know she wasn't here under any kind of business but something shady.

Willow smiled back at her in a way that said she wanted to be friends, or something more maybe. Like partners in crime?

"And," Willow added conspiratorially as she leaned in to make the next comment in private to the two of them, "she's undercover."

That got a smirk from Alton. "I just bet she is. But we need to speak in private."

Before she could say a word of her own, Kayla felt his hand on her wrist, and then he pulled her into his arms and *kissed* her!

She was so shocked, she just gaped at him, didn't wriggle free, slap him, tell him off, or anything.

Then he winked, the cad!

Yet, she still didn't pull away like she should have. What was she waiting for? To see if he would try to transport her to a dungeon or something? He just stood there looking at her like they were courting, and he was in love.

Willow chuckled. "She has never been kissed by a dragon shifter before, she said."

Her comment made him smile darkly at Kayla again. "I suspect not. Not when anyone knows of my interest in her."

Kayla blushed, trying hard not to, knowing he was just saying so because of the role he was attempting to play.

Then he turned to Willow. "Not that I hadn't wanted to before, and if any others tried, they would have been in trouble."

"Well," Willow said. "I did say the two of you would be a matched pair—both violet-colored scales when yours are that color."

"*Really.*" Now Alton was looking at Kayla with a mixture of disbelief and curiosity. "Show me." And then he transported her someplace else.

When they landed, he was still holding her, and her whole body warmed with the way he wouldn't let go of her wrist. "Why didn't you see me at your cottage?" he asked, finally releasing her.

"What?" She thought he was taking her to the dungeon, but instead they were in the clearing where he and Olaf had been practicing before.

"I told your friend Tanya that I would bring the lockets, but I had to speak with you first. They are mixed in with my other treasure. I didn't know which to bring."

"What?" She couldn't believe he'd talked to Tanya about that. "When?"

"At the farmer's market."

Then she realized how he knew her. Not because she was easily recognizable, but because she had been wearing her golden fae aura at the farmers' market, and then in his realm, the dragon fae again. She hadn't thought about that. "You saw me with Sigrid then." Which was another giveaway since she'd been trying to get Sigrid's locket also and they had to be friends.

"I did. I told Sigrid I wished to speak with you concerning this earlier. She flew after me when I left the farmer's market. We spoke. Only she wanted to make a deal for the lockets instead."

Kayla closed her gaping mouth shut. "Sigrid had said she couldn't catch up to you."

"She lied. I waited for her right here to speak with her about you."

Why had Sigrid wanted to do such a thing? Because she was a witch! And Tanya? Her friend had acted strange, like she'd been pondering things and not really listening to their conversation that night when they had slept over at Sigrid's cottage. But that was also why Sigrid hadn't wanted her to stay at her own cottage that night, so she wouldn't run into Alton.

"Okay, wait, back up. You told Tanya you would meet me at my cottage?"

"Yes. And she was really eager to tell you. Then you never showed up, though I waited for hours."

"I'm sorry. I think Sigrid made Tanya forget that you spoke with her. Tanya would never have betrayed me."

"But Sigrid would?"

"Some call her a witch." Then Kayla realized what Alton was saying. "You're giving back my locket and Sigrid's?"

"I've changed my mind."

Now she was ready to slug him.

"So you've never been kissed by a dragon before. What brought that up?" Then Alton smiled. "Ena and Brett kissing?" Then the smile faded. "How were you going to pretend you could participate in the games? It's one thing to profess to be a dragon fae. Another to falsify you can be a dragon. Did you think to skip the practice and hang around until...well, what?"

"I didn't believe you told Halloran to arrest me. I had to know for sure, but I didn't believe it." At least she sure hoped she was right about this.

"I didn't. I wanted to apologize." He looked so sincere, she thought he was telling the truth.

"Okay, apology accepted. And I knew you wanted to give my locket back to me!"

"You're too interesting. I want to know more about you. Why is the locket so important to you?"

"I grow fields of lavender. Okay? Without it, they won't grow. That's who I am. The Lavender Fae. Everyone knows me that way, even if they don't know my real name."

"Kayla? Or Violet?"

She let out her breath in exasperation.

"Why has Willow hooked up with you? Does she know the truth?"

"No, but if she tells others that you met up with Kayla, and I'm using another name, someone might believe I'm the golden fae."

He nodded. "So what were you going to do about the prequalification trials?"

"I don't have to do them now because you're going to give me back the lockets."

He gave her the wickedest smile. "Even Sigrid's?"

"Yes. No telling what she would do to me if I didn't bring it back with me."

"Okay, so when do you have to have the locket back by?"

"A couple of days after the games."

He studied her hair for a moment, then reached out and touched it. "Will it go back to the way it was if you have Sigrid's locket?"

"No. I had it dyed and cut for real." And she wouldn't have had to do all of this if he'd just given her back her locket.

"I like it. But I liked the way you were before too."

"Why did you kiss me?"

"For saving me from the fae seers."

"A thank you wouldn't have been enough?"

Again, that dark dragon fae smile. "Not when you hadn't been kissed by a dragon before. Besides, I was protecting you from Willow. No telling what she would do once she learned you have an alias."

"I already told her I was undercover."

Alton chuckled.

The flapping sound of a dragon's wings as he approached made them turn and look skyward to see the brown dragon with the golden edged scales coming to join them. Her heart thundering, she was afraid she was about to be found out.

She hadn't ever heard a dragon making that much noise on an approach before. She wondered if he had done so to warn them that he was on his way. He was the same one who had been practicing with Alton before, she thought.

"If you can turn into a dragon, I would suggest you do so now." Alton moved her slightly behind himself as if to protect her.

She couldn't believe he would want to do so, not when he wouldn't give her locket back now. She wanted to wring Sigrid's neck for causing all this trouble, when Kayla could have been done with this and not had to gamble success with this sham.

"You have been keeping this one secret from us, eh, Alton," Olaf said, after he'd shifted. He quickly looked Kayla over as if trying to discern who she truly was. "He likes to keep all the female dragons to himself."

"All?" Kayla raised her brows at Alton.

"Not all," Alton said. "I leave one or two alone for the rest of you so that you don't get so jealous."

Conceited dragon.

"I don't know you," Olaf said.

"The feeling's mutual. I'd better get back to the registration area."

"No. We'll go together. Safer that way," Alton said.

Olaf eyed them both then. "Afraid she'll have suitors, Alton, that you can't fight off? I'm Olaf, by the way." He made a low bow with an elegant sweeping gesture of his arm as if he was standing before royalty.

"This is Violet," Alton quickly said. Was he afraid she hadn't remembered her alias?

"Did you want to join us in our practice then?" Olaf asked, not bothering to see if it was okay with Alton.

Really feeling like she needed to return to the registration, choose her games, and do the prequalification tests, she felt antsy. "If you're going to practice, I should just—"

"Watch or join us," Alton insisted.

Now she got the impression he really intended to protect her. Which she truly appreciated. She reached over, took hold of Alton's hand, and leaned in to kiss his cheek. She swore his cheeks turned a little red. Was it okay that he kissed her so suddenly, but not if she returned the favor? "All right."

"Which is it?" Alton asked, and she knew he was dying to see if she could turn into a dragon.

"I'll watch, thank you." She folded her arms and waited for them to begin practicing, wishing she could too, but not with experts like they were. She hadn't wanted him to see her try to fly or blow flames or any of what dragons did. She was certain any of the expert dragons wouldn't be hanging around the beginning gamers to see how they did, but instead intent on seeing how the other advanced dragons did in the trials.

"If you change your mind, join us any time, right, Alton?" Olaf asked.

"Yeah, sure."

Then Alton kissed her cheek back as if he was supposed to do that for his part of the charade, shifted—into a violet dragon and hissed out a smoky breath—then rose up into the sky, flapping his beautiful wings.

"He doesn't like that color," Olaf said. "But all the *girls* like it." Then he shifted and took off to join Alton.

Would Alton even notice if she left and returned to the registration area? Still, she loved watching them following each other in a ferris wheel formation, diving down and turning and heading for the sun.

She wondered what Olaf really thought of her. Had he heard of the golden fae who had saved Alton and Muriel's life? Did he wonder if she was the same girl then?

She assumed if she turned into a dragon, he wouldn't suspect she was a golden fae. At least she hoped he wouldn't. So she shifted. The dragons were so busy with their routines, though she noticed Alton was often maneuvering so that he could still keep an eye on her and make sure she didn't vanish, that while he was doing one of his upside-down turns, she thought he wouldn't see her change.

But both he and Olaf literally broke free from their routines, and flapping in place, stared at her as if she'd just grown several heads.

9

B y the gods, Alton couldn't believe it. Not only had Kayla shifted, but she looked like his matching mate, like birds of the same kind and color.

He kept reminding himself it was all an allusion. That the witch Sigrid had cast this spell over Kayla. But could Kayla really fly? Probably like Brett in the beginning. A novice.

Since Olaf had offered for her to join them, Alton flew down to land in front of her and shifted. "Come fly with us."

She shifted so she could answer him. "You are experts. I'm a beginner. I would waste your time."

Olaf was still hovering in place high in the sky, waiting for Alton to return.

"Come on. We'll do some really easy routines with you so you can get a feel for it. Nothing difficult."

The training from a real dragon would probably be better than one from a falcon fae.

"I don't know. I don't want you to get behind in your practice..."

"Come on. You don't have to do it for long. Just a couple of simple flying routines. If the falcon fae was showing you how to do this, she won't have taught you what you need to know. Falcons don't fly exactly like we do. And she probably couldn't help you with breathing fire either."

She had to agree wholeheartedly with him there. All Sigrid could do was nod, while Tanya had just smiled at the sight of her flying in the clouds, casting fireballs into the atmosphere.

"Okay, but I'm warning you, I'm a beginner, beginner." Like a one-day old dragonling only with a grown-up body.

Olaf landed on the ground in front of them.

"Don't I know it. Come on. Let's go," Alton said.

She was so unsure about this, but better to make a fool of herself, she figured, in front of just these two dragons, rather than all the dragons at the game site. In fact, maybe Alton would feel sorry for her and give her the lockets and send her home instead. Not that she liked the idea anyone had to feel sorry for her, but if she could get her locket back and that made it happen...

She did a little flying leap into the air and flapped her wings until she was airborne. She realized the guys were watching her from the ground still, arms folded across their chests, frowning. *Great.* She'd done it all wrong. But she didn't know a better way to take off than that.

The two guys talked to each other while she was in a holding pattern, waiting for them to do something. Olaf nodded, then Alton said, "I'm coming up. I'm going to show you some moves and Olaf's going to tell you what's going on or you might not understand."

She nodded.

"He's going to show you some basic moves. You need to feel the currents beneath your wings, work with them, not against them," Olaf said.

Easy for him to say. He'd been flying all his life.

When Sigrid had flown with her, it was one thing. She was smaller than any dragon, in human form with big wings, but hers hadn't been nearly as big as dragon wings. And she could talk to her as they were flying, guiding her in her moves. Now Kayla had to listen to Olaf down below and at the same time concentrate on what Alton was doing.

Alton flew around in a wide circle.

"No explanation there. Just follow him. He wants you to feel the air currents, get used to turning left. See how he angles his left wing down when he does it? Then he'll turn to the right and circle the same way. Just don't look at the ground when you're doing circles, or you could get dizzy."

And fall out of the sky? *Great.*

"Now you see how he's turning out of the circle? He wants you to practice a figure eight. One way and then the other. Do it as smoothly as you can." Olaf had to shout for her to hear him as she flew farther away until they were closer to where he was again.

She envisioned him having laryngitis when he returned to the game site. She wondered what he was thinking about, concerning this whole business with her. She wasn't from around here, hadn't ever been to the games, was clearly a beginner, yet here Alton was kissing her in front of everyone.

She felt her whole-body heat with mortification at the thought that more than just Willow had witnessed it. What if Halloran had? Or Ena and Brett? Would they suspect something was off with her too? Especially since she was certain they would know who Alton was seeing in a courtship way.

Alton suddenly was in her face, flapping his wings, hovering. What? Had she done something wrong?

Olaf wasn't saying anything, just watching the two of them.

Alton was stunning, his brown eyes watching her, his violet scales striking, even if he wasn't happy with them. She remembered what Olaf had said about him attracting females because of the color, and even the girl at the registration area had told her boyfriend if he'd been that color, she would have married him.

Then Kayla wondered if she looked like his sister instead of a mate. *Horrors.* Not that she wanted to look like his mate either.

What am I supposed to do? She wished Olaf would say something.

"You're doing great," Olaf finally said. "You're keeping your balance and holding your hover. That's really hard to do for a new dragon."

That's what she was doing? She thought this was easy. The circling and figure eights too. But she knew that it wasn't the turns so much as concentrating on the way the wind lifted her wings. That's what would get her into trouble.

Then Alton pulled away from her and did the weirdest thing. He flew up and down like an undulating serpent.

"That's to feel the current and do short dives and follow up with going up again, up and a little way forward and down, and so forth. It takes practice to be able to control shorter distance moves. It's much easier to fly a long distance, then dive down, then level out, then soar upward again. This teaches you more control while you're experimenting with the wind."

This was weird. She felt like she was going to be seasick. Then Alton turned and smiled at her in a dragon way. She realized just how many facial expressions a dragon could have too. They could raise brows and smile, frown, the whole gamut of expressions.

When he landed on the ground, she did too. Then both of them shifted.

"Good landing," Olaf said. "That's important too. Takeoffs and landings."

"How did I do on takeoff?"

"Like a pro," Alton said. And he sounded like he meant it.

Which made her feel so much better.

"Okay, now some practice with your fire," Alton said. "But I'll let Olaf show you, and I'll comment from down here."

She realized she really liked the way Alton showed her how to do things. He was infinitely patient. She braced for this next part because fire was so dangerous. She didn't want to catch anything on fire, though she knew the dragons were shielded from burns.

For a good half hour, maybe longer, she flew high above toward clouds that had formed a hole and she could no longer hear what Alton had to say, so she just followed Olaf's lead. He blew fire through the hole. And then before it closed up, she hurried to do so too. That was the trouble with clouds. The wind was moving them around so much, it was hard to use them as a target.

When they finally finished, they landed on the ground near Alton. "Well done," he said. "Now for your final lesson. It's time to practice smoking."

She frowned at him. Only when she was annoyed could she puff a bit of smoke. She didn't realize she could, until she huffed in her dragon form when she hadn't liked something Sigrid had told her.

"You breathe out smoke instead of fire." Alton showed her how he could form perfect rings of smoke, one after another.

"Showoff."

Then Olaf showed her how he could blow a smoke ring through a larger one.

She tried, but all she could do was blow a little billow of it, no rings. Nothing cute.

Both of the guys shook their heads. "Don't sign up for any of the smoking games," Alton said.

Which made her want to prove she could do it.

"We'd better get back and turn in her game sheet," Olaf said, and they both looked it over and marked the things she could try.

"I need to sign up for my barracks too."

"No. You'll stay with me," Alton said.

Her jaw dropped. In a castle? With the dragon fae? If her mother ever knew, she would have a heart attack.

Olaf chuckled. "Alton couldn't decide whether he wanted to stay in the comfort of his castle or the barracks where he could learn more about his competition. Looks like he has got another reason to stay at home now."

"What about you? Are you going to check out your competition?" Kayla asked.

"Not me. I never worry about it. I would much prefer my own bed to that of the bunk beds in the barracks. No one to carry out my wishes. The food is average. I love the games, hope I never tire of them, but I still want to enjoy my own accommodations."

"Have you ever won any of the competitions?"

"Several."

She glanced at Alton.

"More than his."

"But you win by checking out those who are competing against you. Will this handicap you?" she asked.

"Nope. I was seriously leaning toward staying home."

"He's hurting still from the bolt in his side, if he didn't tell you," Olaf said. "I already suggested he would get more rest being in his own bed at night."

Kayla stared at Alton in disbelief. "You're hurting still and you're out here helping me to improve my skills? And you're still competing in the games in the expert competitions?"

"He can't let it go. If he had two broken wings, he would still be flying." Olaf smirked.

"If I had two broken wings, I'm sure I would be at home resting. Are you ready to go?" Alton asked, sounding annoyed with his friend.

"Won't I be in trouble for not staying in the barracks?"

"I'll let them know where you'll be. And Willow also, since you've made friends with her, or she might be worried about you."

"Okay, thanks."

"Do you want to fly there? Get some more practice in that way?" Alton asked.

"Sure, that would be great." Though her wings ached from

using them, and when she shifted, her arms were sore from the exercise.

"See you at the first qualification test in a couple of hours?" Olaf asked Alton.

"Yeah, see you there."

The three of them shifted and then they flew back to the area where they were holding the registration, except that Alton broke away from Olaf and headed due east and Kayla quickly caught up to him. Not once did his scales change colors, and she wondered when they would again.

When she saw the castle ahead, she suspected it was his, no one else's. What a way to live as a dragon in a castle like that, the four main towers on the castle walls stretching to the heavens, the keep in the center covered in a copper roof that glistened in the sunlight.

She knew the jobs they took on could be dangerous, nothing like her planting lavender fields unless she burned herself with the weed wacker. Just like his mission to rescue the human and Muriel. She wondered what he was paid for his help in the venture. Shouldn't she have gotten paid too?

Yes. Alton should pay her back her jewelry. Maybe that was why he was bringing her here. So she could show him which was hers. Then again, would he even have the treasure here? Or hidden somewhere else?

As soon as they landed in the inner courtyard, they shifted, and men and women came out to greet him.

"My butler, Ferdinand."

The man bowed. He wore a navy-blue suit, and his hair was silver. "My pleasure, mistress." He bowed again, but his eyes glanced in Alton's direction as if questioning why she was brought here.

"Lydia is Cook. She makes astounding dishes."

The redheaded middle-aged woman smiled and curtseyed, her blue eyes also shifting to Alton.

"Please prepare the meal at once. We're headed back to the prequalification trials right after we eat."

"Right away, sir." She hurried off.

"These are my maids: Kitty, Belle, and Dorinda."

The ladies all curtseyed.

"And my man-at-arms, Solomon, who is in charge of all the soldiers under my command when we're not at battle."

"You have soldiers?"

"Yes, a garrison of them. I maintain them for my queen if she's in need of a force. Come, let's go inside and Kitty can show you to your quarters."

"Thanks. You really don't have to—"

"I do. For your protection."

"If you really want to protect me, why don't you just give me my locket, and I'll be on my way."

"You need to prove to yourself that you can do this. It can build character."

She snorted.

"You were fascinated by us practicing. I'm giving you the opportunity to have some fun with it. You would never be able to do this otherwise, would you?"

"No." And she had to agree she was having fun. After this, she would go back to being strictly a golden fae, working on her lavender gardens, and spreading the joy they would bring. She loved that too, but this was just pure fun for a change.

Alton showed Kayla his gardens while Cook prepared the meal. "Okay, you say Sigrid made you the way you are."

"Temporarily."

"You know she fought me for your locket. I couldn't have been more surprised when out of nowhere, this falcon comes and attacks me."

"For my locket? Are you sure? She never mentioned a thing

about it to me." Kayla glanced at the mermaid fountain and paused to watch the water flowing from her pitcher.

"Yes. Why would she want your locket?"

"To make me owe her? That's how she works. I don't know. She can't use my locket to make my lavender fields grow for her own benefit. I was gifted with the ability when I was born."

"Why would she want to make a deal with me to give her both lockets? I thought she was supposed to be your friend."

"She's an odd sort. She lives by herself, creates potions for all sort of things from encouraging people to love someone to even having a baby—according to Tanya. She says the queen's baby was the result of Sigrid's magic, but no one has said for certain. She also can cast all kinds of spells. As you can see with me. So why won't you just give me my locket?"

Alton took her hand and walked her through more of the gardens. "I don't want you to go home right away, now that you're here. I never knew anyone who wasn't a dragon who would continually imperil herself to come to the dragon fae territory. I have to admit you intrigue me."

"I'm not doing this to intrigue you, dragon. I'm doing this to get my locket back. It means everything to me. Didn't you hear the part I told you about how it makes my lavender plants grow? Without it, I would be banished from the kingdom."

Alton shook his head. "I can't imagine they would do that to you."

"Well, they can! What are you going to tell people about how you know me? Here I am someone unknown to everyone and then there you are kissing me in front of them."

"Smooth move, don't you agree?" Alton was smiling down at her warmly, not cockily, or she would have socked him.

"No, I don't. I think it's going to cause all kinds of speculation and all kinds of questions are going to be asked now."

"So we tell them the truth." He guided her into a maze of ever-green shrubs at least twelve feet tall.

She gazed up at the shrubs that stretched to the sky. It was amazing. "No way. Are you crazy? Don't you remember what happened the last time you told them I was a golden fae? Here I save your life and they want to throw me in the dungeon!"

"The truth in part, I should say. You saved my life a while back. Which you did. It has been like four or five days. And you and I haven't seen each other in a while. Some four or five days. We just connected. Which we did—over the locket."

"How was I supposed to have saved you?"

"Fae seers, like you did. Only that time you distracted the fae seers and the bolt missed me. So see? Almost the same story. Easier to remember that way."

"And why did no one else see me?"

"Most dragon shifters go on missions alone, unless there is a need for more of us to get involved. When anyone from the royal houses go missing, lots more of us are out looking for them."

"Okay, so if anyone asks how long ago we met?"

He smiled. "Couldn't have been too long ago or I would have kissed you before that."

"You are so conceited."

He laughed. "You don't remember the exact time."

"Did you recognize me when you saw me?" She still worried about that because he seemed to know right away who she was.

"You mean you're worried someone else might recognize you. I don't know. At the farmer's market when you saw me flying over-head, you didn't look to me like Kayla. But you weren't afraid of me, just like Sigrid wasn't and you *were* with her. Then when I returned, I overheard you and Sigrid talking and you had said the oddest thing, making it sound as though you were Kayla and not some other friend of Sigrid's." He stopped her and held both her hands. "I believe though once I saw you up close, smelled your sweet lavender scent, looked into your green eyes, and heard you speak, I would have known beyond a doubt it was you."

"What about the others who had seen me?"

"Brett, Ena? Maybe Muriel? They might know you. And Ryker, as observant as he is. But Halloran? Probably not. He didn't see you for hardly any length of time, did he?"

"No."

They heard footfalls, but Alton released only one of her hands. Was he really going to pretend they were courting so he could protect her? Even in front of his staff? Then again, she supposed that was a good idea if he thought one of them might turn her in if someone learned what she really was. She liked that he was. It made up some for him not giving her locket back. Yet, some part of her liked that he wanted to see her a while longer.

Ferdinand called out, "Supper is ready."

"Coming!" Alton smiled at Kayla. "That's the first time he has ever announced the meal from a distance. He must be afraid of interrupting us."

Kayla headed for the castle. "We'll have to let him know nothing was going on!"

When they sat down to eat, she marveled at the crystal water glasses and gold-edged dishes. She was used to her mother's plain green clay dishes and mugs, nothing fancy.

The food was much more extravagant than she and her mother ate also. Wild boar served with new red potatoes, gravy, small loaves of white bread, hearts of romaine lettuce, tomatoes, mushrooms, and red cabbage made into a salad, all fit for a king and queen. Or in this case, a wealthy dragon.

She suspected he always ate like this. That it wasn't anything special for her visit.

Two of the maids stood by watching them, as if waiting to serve them further.

"I'm fine, aren't you?" Kayla asked, not seeing the point of making the servants wait for more orders when she truly didn't believe they would need anything else.

Alton smiled at her, then motioned to the women that they could go. They inclined their heads, smiled at her, and then left.

"Thank you," she said to Alton.

"You are going to totally spoil my staff. Then what will I ever do with them?"

Kayla thought he was teasing about it.

After they finished eating, Alton asked, "Are you ready to go back to the registration area?"

The maids cleared away the dishes.

"Sure."

"No transporting. Let's fly. That will allow you to practice some more."

"What about people saying something about your scale pigment if we show up wearing the same color?"

"They're saying enough as it is. I'll just continue to ignore them like before."

"You sure it doesn't bother you?" She was certain it did as they walked out into the courtyard.

"No. Maybe we'll start a trend, only no one else but us would have our shade of scales." Then he frowned. "Why do you have that color? Surely you had a choice."

"It's the color of the lavender blossoms. A medium violet. I love that color above all else. Though I don't normally wear a lot of it in my wardrobe. For this, I wanted that one."

"I guess it makes sense. I wonder if she could change mine back to the way it was."

"Sky blue? Beautiful." Then she frowned at him before they shifted and flew off. "You don't think this has anything to do with Sigrid, do you? That she enchanted your scales so that you would continue to change colors until you returned her locket?"

Alton gaped at Kayla for a moment. "By the gods. What if she is the reason for this?"

Kayla raised her brows in question. "So do we take her locket back to her and ask her?"

"No. After the games are done, I'll show you my treasure, and you can tell me which lockets are the two of yours. I owe it to you, not to her."

"What if she doesn't change you back to the way you were before?"

"I'm getting used to it. Maybe not so much the violet color, but I think some of the others are pretty cool. It's made me somewhat of a celebrity around here." He looked a little worried, frowning a bit. "The time is approaching for you to prequalify for your games. Are you ready?"

"Yeah." Then they shifted and before they flew off, she noticed half of his staff came out to see them go. She wondered if they usually did that.

When they arrived at the registration area, she swore everyone stopped to look up at them. She supposed it was because of their unusual dragon scales and now not only was Alton that color, but he had brought someone along they didn't know whose scales were too.

The problem was that everyone continued to watch them when they shifted, and instead of just blending in with the dragon crowd, she stood out. Sigrid had thought it would help so that she wouldn't look like she was hiding, but truly, Kayla wouldn't have minded hiding a bit.

"Okay, I'll meet you right here after the trials. I would watch you, but I need to do my own."

"Thanks, Alton."

"Good luck." Then Alton kissed her again, and she couldn't believe it. The first was for show. Now what was it for? He smiled at her. "I've already shown everyone we're courting. I have to keep up the charade."

As much as her cheeks burned, she imagined she was red-faced. "Well, next time, I mean, if there was a next time—"

"There will be a next time," he assured her.

She shook her head. "Warn me, will you? So it looks like we're courting instead of that I don't know what's going on?"

He laughed and kissed her forehead. "I'll be back here in a couple of hours. Fly well."

When he left her, she felt very alone suddenly, and like who she really was. A golden fae who didn't belong.

"Hey, girl," Willow said, hurrying to join her. "Here I was telling you all about Alton and Ena and you already know him personally. So where did you go?"

"To practice with him and Olaf."

"Wow. You're kidding. They never take newbies with them to practice."

"I watched them practice too."

"I can't believe you're staying at Alton's castle. I sure wish someone like him would take an interest in me. And I can't believe the two of you have matching scales for now. Really cool. Who would ever have thought? Because I've never seen them before, I didn't believe anyone had them."

"So what games are you going to try to prequalify for?" Kayla asked, wondering what level she was.

"The blue games. The black are the expert. The green are easy. The yellow are the second level up. The blue are just below the expert. The red are right in the middle. I would have tried out for the black this year, but I figured I would end up practically killing myself when I'm not really at that level yet. I just like to push myself though."

Kayla looked at the fae lined up for the easy trials. They were all around eight to ten years of age.

"Oh, don't worry about how young they look. If you go for the next round, that's like eleven to sixteen experience level. Being you're brand new at this, you won't qualify at anything if you try to do one that's too hard for you."

"Then I can watch Alton," Kayla said.

"You don't want to participate?" Then Willow smiled. "Oh, I see, you have a major crush on each other, and you don't want to be apart from him for a moment. Or maybe you're just worried he'll be interested in a fae who's more of an expert gamer like him. I wouldn't worry about it. I haven't ever seen him interested in any girl besides Ena and now that she's unavailable, he's intrigued with you. He seems to prefer one girl at a time."

Like that would ever happen, given what Kayla really was.

10

"Alton, can I have a word with you?" Ena asked, racing to catch up to him.

Alton figured Olaf would be questioning him first about the mystery dragon. He should have known Ena would have seen him with Kayla and wondered who she was.

He stopped and waited for Ena to reach him. "I've got to get in line for this event," he said, motioning to the line a few feet away that was growing by the second.

She seized his arm and pulled him into the line. "Me too. Are you sure you're all right, enough to fly in the rigorous games you're signed up for? Olaf said he knew you were hurting when you were practicing some of the moves."

Alton was surprised she didn't mention Kayla. Maybe she *hadn't* seen her with him. "Minor pain. Nothing to be concerned with. Certainly nothing to keep me out of the games."

But then Ena glanced around, and he wondered if she was looking for Kayla. He was probably just being paranoid. He looked too though, to see if Kayla had moved up in the beginner's line yet. His was going slower because the experts had to do more of a routine. It was all based on skill, speed, endurance, and wits.

What shocked and concerned him was Kayla was standing in the line for the second level gamers, not the beginners. What was she doing?

"Who is she?" Ena suddenly asked.

He realized then Ena was looking at Kayla too. "A friend. Like you're a friend."

"I suspect she's more than that. No one knows her. I asked. She has never been to the games before. Yet, you know her? Intimately?"

"You're not jealous are you?" Alton knew Ena wasn't. He just wanted to change the subject. *Fast.*

"Olaf said she barely knows the basic skills of flying. Same with controlling her fire stream. None of us had seen a purple dragon before your scales turned that color and suddenly you have a friend who nobody knows who's wearing the same shade of color as you? Mere coincidence? Or something more?"

"I knew her from before," he said vaguely.

"You mean while you were trying to court me?" Ena now gave him the evil eye, which she shouldn't have, considering she had fallen for Brett.

"No. After you married Brett. Long after." Still, he didn't want her thinking he'd been seeing other girls when he'd wanted Ena to court him. Well, he'd seen other girls, flirted with them, like they'd flirted back, but he hadn't been interested in courting any of them. "We met, connected, and..." Alton saw Kayla take to the sky and fly through several hoops in the undulating maneuver he had taught her. He held his breath.

Ena turned to watch her when he stopped speaking abruptly. "Not so much of a beginner is she after all. Do you know what I think?"

Alton was certain Ena knew who Kayla was and he was ready to save her before anyone could incarcerate her in a dungeon.

∾

KAYLA WAS a bundle of nerves as she shifted and took off on her flight. She kept telling herself to do just what Alton had taught her, and she couldn't thank him enough for preparing her for this part of the qualification test. Five other dragons were also flying the same pattern she was at the same time. In a way, it was good because she felt the other dragons would take some of the attention from her. But it was also bad because she knew she wasn't just up here qualifying on her own against herself, but she was competing with the other dragons.

Which was silly, considering what she really was. Yet when it came to being competitive with others, she went all out. Then she took a deep breath. She wasn't competing with the others, she reminded herself. She was only doing this to prove to herself that she could.

So far, she seemed to be doing the sea serpent maneuver that meant going up and down correctly. It felt right. She'd only had one instance when the wind knocked her off balance, and she'd had a mini-panic attack. Or she should say she miscalculated using the air flow to her advantage. Next, she had to make a bunch of figure eights, long and wide, then hard turns and closer together. The long and wide ones weren't bad because she could take more time to get a feel of the wind under her wings. But the short ones were more hit and miss.

Then she had to do several tests that meant diving for objects in big baskets near the ground or hung from poles high above. This, she hadn't practiced for. She guessed they didn't do that in the beginner games, so Alton hadn't thought he needed to prepare her. She literally had to wing it. She was trying to estimate just how long her legs could stretch out to grasp an object, make sure the flag or other object, sometimes balls of various weights were firmly in her talons before she took off, then deposit the item in a big basket that was designated as hers at the end of the course. The purpose of the trials was to get to the end of this part of the game fastest, so that meant dropping the item at a faster pace and grabbing the next object.

Once she was done depositing all the objects in the basket, she had to retrieve each of them and return them to the places where she'd taken them from in order. It was a memory course, but also a way to set up the course for the next contestant. She hoped she remembered the order correctly, and tried to calm herself as she felt stressed to the max. If dragons could sweat, she would be sweating up a storm.

"I THINK magic is at play here. And I would be very careful if I were you," Ena warned Alton as they both kept their gazes on Kayla.

It was a little too late for that. "You know this because Brett has magical abilities?" Alton knew Sigrid had used her power to change Kayla. But if she did this to Kayla, he suspected she had done this to him too where his scales were constantly different colors.

"I know this because your scales keep changing color, at least they were. Then the mystery dragon shows up and you're both wearing the same color scales that didn't exist before."

"We don't know that for sure. The color may occur in some other part of the world."

"But it doesn't alter the fact yours keep swapping colors. Or do they now?"

"What do you mean?"

"Earlier today, your scales were silver, but when we returned here, you saw the girl and your scales turned purple. Has it happened before? I know you went with her and Olaf to the practice area by the river. When you did, what color were they? Did they change?"

Now that was something Alton hadn't thought of. He watched as Kayla dove to grab a flag before her opponent did. She fumbled with the flag with her talons, unused to judging how close she had to be to tackle objects. They hadn't practiced that maneuver because he thought she would be in the beginner trials, and they didn't do things like that. When he looked at the young kids in that line, he understood why she hadn't wanted to try out there. But he was afraid she was bound to fail.

"They've been this color when I haven't been around her." He thought. Unless he hadn't seen her at the time, and she *had* been nearby. Yet, it was true that every time he'd actually seen her, and he was in dragon form, his scales had turned that color. What if she was tied to his scale color then? But why? The locket! Had to be.

"It has got to be magic. I haven't seen Brett to learn what he thinks. He was picked to go early for the trial, queen's generosity, you know," Ena said.

Alton could tell Ena was proud of him. And he had to admit to himself that he was too. But he wouldn't admit that to Ena or anyone else.

"So how do you know her?" Ena asked again.

"She saved my life from fae seers." He thought their story was plausible.

Ena's eyes widened and she quickly turned to see Kayla going through a final loop. "That's the golden fae? Kayla?"

Great. He hadn't believed Ena would assume that she was the same girl who had saved him that time. But Ena knew him too well that he couldn't pretend she wasn't the same girl now. "You can't tell anyone."

"What is she doing here?" Ena's tone of voice was incredulous.

"I have her locket. She'd been watching Olaf and me flying one day in a practice session and lost the locket. It's somewhere in my piles of treasure."

"Well, give it back to her already. What are you waiting for?" Ena didn't give him a chance to answer. "I can't thank the golden fae enough for saving Muriel's life, but never had the chance to. Muriel keeps telling me how sorry she was when Halloran intended to lock Kayla up, and she didn't have a chance to thank her one last time again either." Then Ena frowned. "How in the world could a golden fae become a dragon?"

"A falcon fae who lives among them has powers. She's helping her so she can get her own locket back also."

Ena gaped at him. "How many lockets did you steal?"

He explained the whole situation and how he knew Kayla wanted to participate in the games. Afterward, he would give her the lockets and she would go home.

"Alton, what are you thinking? That's saying she doesn't kill herself in the games. And that my brother doesn't learn of this. He takes his position as Dragon at Arms very seriously. As he should."

"I agree." Alton knew Halloran as well as Ena did. "She was supposed to be in the beginning trials, not in the second level one." He didn't comment on the part about Halloran causing trouble for her.

"No one our age would want to be in the beginner class." Ena let out her breath and watched Kayla again. "So what was the kiss all about?"

Alton smiled at Ena. Was *she* jealous? "I wanted it to look like she knew someone, and no one would bother her." And he wanted to kiss her, to thank her for saving him. It seemed only the natural thing to do. Since Willow had said a dragon fae hadn't kissed Kayla —obviously since she was a golden fae—he wanted to be the one and only one to do so.

"Male suitors? You don't have to worry about that. None of

those in our expert class would want to court a girl who is just a beginner."

Alton raised a brow at Ena, remembering very well how Brett had turned into a dragon to both their surprise and was as new as they come.

"Brett was different. I got to know him as a person. First." Ena cast Alton a scornful look. "*And* he rescued me from my brother's dungeon, remember?"

Yeah, Alton remembered. If he had rescued her instead, would she have still fallen for the dragon/phantom fae? "There you go though. All she would need to do is rescue another guy and I would have to fight him."

Ena laughed. "She's not one of us. And when the magic is gone, she'll be what she truly is. She'll have to return to her own kind. She won't be welcome here."

"You won't tell anyone, will you?"

Ena scowled at him. "No. Of course not. Why would I do that after she saved Muriel? I'll let on I know her as your friend..."

"Violet. Thank you, Ena."

"You can thank Muriel. If she learns Kayla is here, Muriel will be so grateful and want to see her. But I think the best thing to do is keep her being here a secret from everyone. The fewer who know, the better. Speaking of which, here comes Olaf."

"I'm sure he's going to ask the very same questions."

"No doubt."

"Hey," Olaf said, joining them, smiling at Ena, and raising his brows at Alton. "So what's all this about with your new girlfriend?"

"She's an old friend," both Alton and Ena said at the same time, and Alton couldn't have appreciated Ena more for helping out. Though it did sound like the two of them were co-conspirators in some nefarious scheme.

Naturally, Olaf looked a little suspicious. "I believe I should have been in on the earlier conversation. I see I've missed out on what's going on entirely." Olaf glanced at the competition for the group where Kayla was coming in for a landing. "I thought she was trying out for the beginner games."

"Seems she loves to live dangerously," Ena said.

Then they saw Halloran coming to join them, and Alton straightened a bit. He prayed his friend hadn't seen him with Kayla and start all the questioning too. Both Ena and Olaf stiffened a bit. Alton wanted to tell them to relax and act normally or the whole charade would soon be uncovered.

"So," Halloran said, smiling at Alton, "I hear you have a new girlfriend."

11

After finishing the trials, Kayla landed on the ground, shifted, and went over to the big board to check out her score to see if she'd passed. She was third lowest from the bottom ranking, but it showed she had passed! The bottom two hadn't, but she saw the two dragon fae now standing in the beginner's line. She was glad they had a chance to try again. And they were much younger than her.

If she didn't go any further than this, she didn't mind. She was just so glad she had made it through the prequalification trials. She intended to see if Alton was flying yet. She would love to watch him in the trials. The expert ones were so much more extensive than what she had gone through. When she turned to look, she saw Ena, Alton, Olaf, and her worst nightmare, Halloran, Dragon at Arms, all watching her.

Her skin felt like she'd been dipped in the Arctic Ocean and left there to freeze. She straightened. For now, she was a dragon fae shifter. Her purple scales proved that. If Halloran thought to arrest her, what would the queen think? He was crazy?

Alternately, if he tried to arrest her, she could just transport home. She thought Alton might understand, and visit her with...

wait, he didn't know which of the jewelry was hers. Well, she could draw a picture of it for him.

The only way she could deal with Halloran was head on. She stalked straight for them. Halloran was looking stern. Ena appeared worried, her brows furrowing. Alton folded his arms across his chest and smiled darkly. Olaf appeared clueless.

She might be known as the Lavender Fae, which made her sound all sweet and innocent, but she had a dark side like the rest of the fae. And playing games was one of their fondest pastimes.

Abruptly, Willow hurried to join her, surprising her.

"Did you finish your trials?" Kayla asked her.

"Yes. Passed. What about you?"

"I made it. Bottom of the board, but I made it."

Willow smiled. "That's great. Then the others won't think you'll be much competition, and they won't know what they're in for when you prove you have what it takes to beat them."

"I'm just glad to be here."

"And seeing Alton?" Willow smiled in a devious way. "He's like a rose to the butterflies. They just can't stay away."

"We're just friends." Though she would be his worst enemy if he didn't give her back her locket at the end of the games.

"Uh-huh. I wish I could be his friend like that. As much as he likes the ladies, I've never seen him kiss one of them in public before. Not even Ena."

Yeah, but the only reason he kissed Kayla was he thought it would serve to protect her from the other dragons. Which she thoroughly appreciated.

As soon as she reached the dragon shifters, trying not to tremble and attempting to keep her heart from beating so spastically, so much for playing fae games—but there were five of them judging one golden fae and three of them knew for sure she was not what she appeared to be—she stopped in front of them and said, "I made it!"

She didn't expect Alton's next action—that he would move forward so quickly and pull her into his hot embrace and then kiss her again! And kiss her...and kiss...her.

It wasn't like it was before, hurried, worried, showing a brief claim to courtship. This one said he meant to kiss her longer, harder, showing her that he wanted this to be real, not just some faux display of affection. Didn't he?

Well, she wasn't going to be startled into inaction either, and she wrapped her arms around his neck and kissed him right back. His darkened eyes widened a bit, and she smiled up at him as she kissed him again. Two could play at this game. Yet, she'd never been kissed by any fae like this before, and she really didn't want it to end.

Everything else faded into the distance—the dragons qualifying for positions in the trials, the fae standing near them, and goddess knew what they were all thinking, or how they were reacting. Especially Mr. Dragon at Arms who so very nearly arrested her the last time she'd seen him. Or even Ena, who had to know Kayla was a total phony. And since Halloran was her brother, she would surely side with him.

But for this moment in time, nothing else mattered.

Then Halloran said, "I'm not sure I understand."

That was the understatement of the year, Kayla thought. She wasn't sure she did either.

"They're in love," Willow said, her hands over her heart, her gaze cast heavenward. "What else?"

What else indeed.

"Uh, the line has moved up without us," Ena said, hurrying to return to her place in line.

Olaf was smirking and motioned to the line. "Are you going to participate, Alton, or have you got better things to do?"

"Go," Kayla said. "I'll watch you." She smiled brightly at him, though she really did want to watch him. But she was afraid

Halloran was going to take her into questioning, and she thought the way Alton was still holding her hand, he thought so too, and he wanted to protect her more than participate in the games. Which really surprised her.

"Go, I'll be fine. Willow's staying with me." Kayla hoped that if she had another dragon shifter friend, Halloran would be even more confused.

"You can stay with me while I'm in line." Alton led her back to his place in line and ignored the way Halloran was staring after them.

But he wasn't Dragon at Arms for nothing. He rejoined them as Willow hung around with them.

"Shift," Halloran said to her in an authoritative I'm-in-charge way.

He must not have seen her flying or landing before she had shifted back to see the boards.

She folded her arms, irritated with him. How could she have qualified without being a dragon?

"She's qualified for the games, Halloran," Alton said, his words clipped. He wished Halloran would just drop the issue, but he knew he wouldn't.

Halloran cocked a brow. He was a couple of years older than any of the dragon shifters in the dragon fae territory because previous royalty had hunted their parents and other older dragons down. So he always thought he was in charge of the rest, even when he hadn't been officially.

"We can do this here or—" Halloran said, not to be thwarted.

"Oh, for heaven's sake." Kayla shifted into the dragon.

On her, the color suited her. Alton noticed then that other

dragon shifters glanced her way. Because of the novel color? Or because they were interested in her?

He let out his breath. *He* couldn't be interested in her. So why had the kiss made him want to have even more with her? Like a *real* courtship? She was lightness and spontaneity. She was sweet, yet not so innocent. Rather a mystery to be unraveled. He never cared if anyone watched him in the trials or in the end game, but with her announcement that she wanted to observe him, he wanted to prove to her just how good he could be.

It was madness. Tonight, after dinner, he was taking her straight to his piles of treasure, which was also something he would never have done, ever, in a million years. No one would dare try to steal from him, except maybe for one tempting golden fae, he thought.

Then she shifted back, and Alton gave Halloran a dagger of a look. Halloran's dark expression said he owed him an explanation, but for now, he was dropping the query. Now Alton would have to explain why he had told not only Ena that Kayla was a golden fae, but when he was under heavy duty pain killers too. Under the influence of the medicine, he could say he had been confused, but when he had told Ena that Kayla was a golden fae? That couldn't be explained away.

Halloran stalked off, and everyone watched him go.

Ena didn't say a word, just glanced at Kayla as if wondering how they were going to get away with the deception. Olaf was looking from one of them to the other, wondering what was going on. Willow was quiet and observing their behavior just as well.

Alton wrapped his arm around Kayla's shoulders and kept her close as if protecting her. He couldn't help it. She was here all because in the beginning she'd only been curious about him and Olaf practicing for the dragon games. Not to steal anyone's gold.

When the line moved up enough, Ena and Alton would have to go to qualify for the trials, leaving Olaf behind for the next group, but Alton was going to stay behind and let Olaf go first.

Ena said, "Go, Alton. I'll stay with her."

"Hey, you want to go to the viewing stands to watch the expert dragons?" Willow asked Kayla.

"She'll join you in a bit. I need to have a word with her," Ena said.

"Okay." Willow smiled, then left.

Alton was certain Willow was wondering why there was so much interest in Kayla. He hoped Ena wasn't going to tell Kayla she needed to go home.

"Go, Alton, or you'll miss your turn," Ena said, in her commanding tone.

He glanced at Kayla. She smiled reassuringly. "I'll be fine. See you when you're through."

He nodded, squeezed her hand, and took off with Olaf. They did have the routines they needed to do with a partner too.

"I can't believe you're dating a fae none of us have ever seen before. Except it seems Halloran knows her," Olaf said cheerfully to Alton as they got to the starting area.

"He thinks she's someone else." Alton glanced back at her, but Kayla was talking to Ena and not looking at him. He hoped Ena didn't give her a rough time. "Good luck, old man, on the trials."

"Yeah, you too. If you're hurting at all, back off. I don't want to have to rescue you when I'm trying to come in at a good spot in the trials. And when we're doing our routine together, well, just don't push it. I don't want to be the one responsible for you injuring yourself."

Alton snorted. Yet, it was something that *could* happen. He just hoped if something like that occurred, Kayla didn't see it.

As soon as Willow left them alone, Ena spoke low for Kayla's hearing only. They still had contestants behind them, none ahead of them though. Kayla really wanted to see Alton in the trials, though from this spot, she *could* see them. But she didn't want to be under interrogation at the same time.

"Okay, I know who you are," Ena said, "a friend."

Kayla shut her gaping mouth.

"You saved Muriel and for that she and I will be forever grateful to you. And"—Ena smiled warmly—"you've knocked Alton for a loop. Believe me that has never happened, ever. The entertainment has been vastly appreciated."

Kayla smiled, glad Ena hadn't been upset with her, but she knew the dragon fae shifter wasn't through.

"Since you're here and passing as"—Ena paused—"well, you're one of us, I would like to extend an invitation to my place for dinner tonight. I'm sure Alton wants you all to himself, but Muriel would like to thank you for saving her life."

Kayla couldn't believe it. She had been certain Ena was going to tell her to get out of here before her brother locked her up in the royal dungeon and threw away the key.

"What of your brother?"

"He will be a problem. There's no denying that. Will you come? Alton can come too, though he doesn't have to hug on you all night to protect you. You will be perfectly safe with us."

Delighted, Kayla laughed. "I would love to. Thank you." She had to admit she wouldn't mind the hugging too. Even though she knew once she had her locket back, it would be over between them. "Will your brother be there?" Kayla thought how tense things could be if he was.

"Not if I can help it, but if he learns you will be there, he might show up unannounced. I never know with him." Ena motioned to Alton as he flew across the sky. "He looks great, doesn't he? But if he hadn't been injured, he would be flying even faster, taking more daring turns. I can tell he's hurting, protecting his injury the best he can without straining himself too much. But he'll pass with flying colors still. He'll have to do better in the actual games." She turned to Kayla. "He needs to rest, not to practice every minute he's not in the games. He won't listen to any of us. Maybe you can make him listen to you."

"I'll try. Though I'm afraid he'll want to help me practice for the games too."

"That would be fine. The paces he'll put you through won't test his endurance like the ones he has to do for his own games."

"I'll certainly try." Kayla never imagined in her wildest dreams that she would be visiting with dragon fae shifters, considered a special guest even, and able to watch the dragon games. But not just that. She would be observing some that she even knew and would be rooting for them, which made it even more special. On top of that, she'd never envisioned she would actually be in the games herself. What an experience of a lifetime. Something she would cherish forever.

Suddenly, Brett stalked toward Ena, who quickly introduced her mate. He smiled warmly at Kayla, but she wondered if he would feel differently when he knew what a fraud she was. Would Ena tell him?

"This is Kayla, I mean, Violet, and she'll be having dinner with us tonight as our honored guest for saving Muriel's life."

Brett's eyes widened. Then he considered Kayla further, and she wondered what the matter was now.

"Magic?" he asked.

He knew. She nodded, feeling the earth crumble beneath her. Since he knew, he could tell everyone.

Ena took Brett's hand and kissed his cheek. "Brett is a wizard. He knows all about magic. I'll fill you in later, Brett. But mum's the word with you know who."

"Yeah, gotcha."

One of the game coordinators signaled that it was time for Ena and four more participants to move to their stations. "Will you stay with her until Alton returns?" Ena asked Brett.

"He doesn't need to," Kayla quickly said, not wanting him to feel obligated.

"I sure will. No problem at all. Do you want to go into the stands and watch Ena?"

"I would love to."

Brett moved her out of the line and toward the viewing stands but paused where it was relatively free of people. "So is the magic inherent or something else?"

"A falcon fae's magic." She explained a little about what had happened and how she was trying to get her locket back from Alton.

Brett shook his head. "That's where we differ. I would have given it right back to you. But it's hard for me to believe that anyone can use magic to change a fae into a dragon."

"Well, I'm a dragon, aren't I? I mean, not this very second, but whenever I want to be." That was obviously due to magic. "Do you know anything about Sigrid's magic?"

"No."

"Well, see? Just because you don't have that power, doesn't mean she can't do such a thing."

"I still have a lot of material to read and a lot to learn, but in my book, there's nothing about changing a fae into a dragon shifter."

"In *your* book. But in *her* book, she must have the spell for it. Or her ability was passed down from someone in her family or something."

Brett paused and considered Kayla thoughtfully. "Do your scales change color also?"

"No. Just Alton's."

"Since he met you?"

"Since he took my locket."

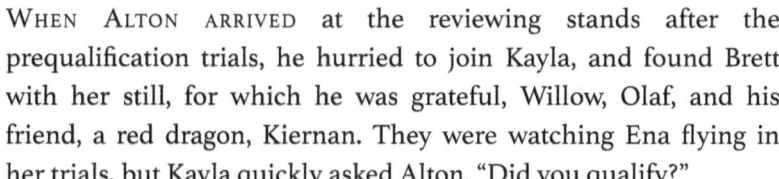

WHEN ALTON ARRIVED at the reviewing stands after the prequalification trials, he hurried to join Kayla, and found Brett with her still, for which he was grateful, Willow, Olaf, and his friend, a red dragon, Kiernan. They were watching Ena flying in her trials, but Kayla quickly asked Alton, "Did you qualify?"

"Naturally," he said, as if that was a no-brainer and smiled when she tilted her head to the side, folded her arms, and gave him a look that said it might not have been a sure thing. Feeling smug, he slipped his arm around her shoulders. Maybe she had worried about his injury giving him trouble. It had, but with the added incentive of her watching him, he'd gone all out to show off.

"I made it too," Olaf said. "What about you, Kiernan?"

"I flew at the same time Brett did. Passing scores in all events. But did you see that old granddaddy of a dragon flying in the trials? He must be forty-five at least."

It wasn't that he seemed so old, but because they had lost all the elders under an earlier king's rule, they weren't used to seeing older dragons. Halloran was twenty-two and the oldest among them.

"Granddaddy? My mother is thirty-eight. Don't ever let her hear you say that. And my friend's granddad is seventy-five and as young as they come," Kayla said, annoyed.

Everyone smiled at her.

"We're not used to anyone being older than Halloran," Alton said. "So how did the older dragon do? And what is his name?"

"Arne, meaning eagle. He beat us in strength and agility. He was actually amazing," Brett said. "Though he was so blue, I didn't see him some of the time as he matched the sky. Kind of like you, Alton, when your scales are that color. Even his eyes are blue, and they have a penetrating power behind them. As if he can read your every move."

Alton pondered that, not believing an older dragon could

best the younger dragons, but then again, maybe he wasn't as cocky as some of the younger ones. They had never been trained by the older ones, because they had died before they could really teach them much. So they'd learned from experimenting and with each other. It was the first time they'd even opened the games up to dragons located anywhere farther than about sixty miles.

"Just saying, we're going to really have to push it if we want to beat him," Kiernan said. "I've met Willow before. But...I haven't met you," he said to Kayla, curiosity in his expression.

Alton wondered if he'd heard something about what was going on with him and Kayla. Though even now, the way he was hugging her, Kiernan had to figure something was up. "She's my girlfriend, Violet." He'd never acted in such a way around any girl, including Ena. He kept telling himself he did so because he was protecting the golden fae from dragon shifters so they wouldn't learn the truth about her.

Kiernan was smiling a little, and Alton knew he was dying to know just what was going on with him and the mystery dragon shifter and who she *really* was.

When Ena joined them, she was smiling. "We all made it. Ready for dinner?"

Alton thought he and Kayla would be having a private dinner with Ena and Brett and her staff. Instead, Kiernan jumped at the chance to join them, and so did Willow. Alton wanted to immediately uninvite them, even if he wasn't the host for the dinner. Since Ena had made the comment in front of all of them, it was a little too late to do anything about it now.

When they arrived at Ena and Brett's castle, Ryker greeted them, his eyes widening to see Kayla. He quickly looked at Ena as if he thought she was making a big mistake, but he wisely didn't make a comment.

"This is Violet," Ena said. "She saved Muriel's life."

Muriel must have heard from one of the back rooms and ran down the hall to greet them. "You've come back!"

"Violet, yes," Ena said.

"Oh, oh, I wanted to thank you." Muriel gave Kayla a big hug.

Alton was glad to see that Muriel was so happy to get to thank Kayla and Kayla likewise was thrilled to see the maid.

"Lila is serving the meal now," Ryker said, casting a small smile at Kayla. "I'm glad to see you've returned."

"I wouldn't have missed it for the world."

"She's participating in the games," Ena said, escorting them to her dining room.

"Is she," Ryker said, making a statement, not asking a question and glancing in Kayla's direction as if trying to figure out how she had become a dragon fae so all of a sudden.

"She and Alton are courting," Ena said, motioning to the seats everyone was to take.

Ryker's eyes rounded and he quickly looked at Alton as if to see if he agreed with Ena.

"She's right." After Alton's telling Ryker to lock Kayla up because she would steal Ena and Brett's gold, he was certain the butler was confused, to stay the least.

They had barely served up the pork roast, potatoes, loaves of sourdough bread, and turnip greens, when Ryker had to answer the door and returned with Halloran.

Alton had this covered.

Halloran took his seat opposite Kayla and Alton, his gaze shifting from Alton to the golden fae, though she looked like a dragon fae based on her aura still.

"So I'm confused," Halloran said, placing a napkin on his lap. "You were Kayla, a golden fae, but now are Violet, a dragon fae?"

Before she could speak, or Alton could explain his mistake, Willow said, "She's undercover."

And that blew Alton's whole line of defense.

"Really," Halloran said, breaking off a piece of bread and buttering it. "Pray tell what you are undercover for?"

"I was teasing Willow." Kayla glanced in her direction and Willow smiled back.

"Why are you using two different names and two different auras?" Halloran asked.

"I do so because I can."

Halloran raised a brow. "Why did you pretend to be a golden fae in front of Alton then?"

"He caught me watching him and Olaf practicing for the games. Okay? I know some dragons don't like it when others try to learn their secret moves that they'll use in the games." Kayla shrugged and forked up a slice of pork. "When I saw him coming for me, I pretended to be a golden fae and ran off."

"You're practically a beginner. How could you use his maneuvers?"

"Like you said. I'm practically a beginner. I thought learning from a pro would help."

"And then you saved him in Texas and couldn't bring Muriel home at the same time? As a dragon, you could. Why couldn't you then?"

"I'd never tried to carry two people before. Because Alton was badly wounded, I had to hold him close. I think that's when we fell in love." She smiled at Alton.

"No," Alton said, not missing a chance to help the story along. "It was when she ran away. I knew then she was the one for me. Only I didn't catch her in time before she vanished."

Ena patted Brett's arm. "Just like with us."

"Not the same at all. *He* was your prisoner." Halloran studied Kayla for a moment, but she was eating some of her pork and ignoring him now. "Well, maybe something similar, if she hadn't gotten away from me."

"So what did I do wrong? You can't just throw any fae into the royal dungeon for no good reason, can you?" Kayla asked.

"Alton said you were a golden fae who planned to steal Ena and Brett's gold. That's the aura you were showing off when I saw you after you brought Muriel home. What was I to think? Why wouldn't you have been a dragon fae? Why would you vanish instead of showing off a dragon fae's aura, or turning into a dragon? And don't give me that bull about being undercover."

Willow's mouth gaped wide.

Kayla smiled. "You planned to arrest me and ask questions later when I had just saved two of your friends. Well, Alton. Not sure if Muriel is a friend. I had no intention of being bullied by you or anyone, so I left. Here, I'd helped out and I had no thanks from you. Not that I needed any, but I was just so surprised you would want to arrest me!"

"Alton had tried to have you arrested."

She smiled at Alton. "His mistake."

Alton finished his bread. "Yeah, an honest one to be sure."

"So you're marrying her now?" Halloran asked him.

Now *that* line of query put Alton on the spot. All this talk of love and courting and such, and they could never truly develop a relationship that deep because she wasn't even a dragon. How could he live in the golden fae territory if he wanted to marry her? He couldn't hide his dragon fae aura, nor would he want to. She couldn't live in the dragon fae territory either, not when she didn't have Sigrid's magic to maintain her dragon fae aura, and the dragon shifter ability, when everyone would think she was a dragon shifter.

His hesitation to comment made Kayla speak up instead. "Oh, well, you know how it is. He needs to meet my mother first. And, of course, with everything else going on, we haven't had time to do so."

"In the place you listed on your form?" Halloran asked.

She nodded.

"Can you change into other auras?" Halloran asked.

"Sure."

"Okay, let's see." Halloran wasn't going to be dissuaded from questioning Kayla all night, Alton could see.

"Enough, Halloran. We're having a nice dinner with Ena and Brett and to say thanks to Kayla for saving Muriel." Alton gave his friend a stern look, saying he didn't want to hear another thing from him regarding Kayla.

"Kayla now," Halloran said, a brow cocked.

Alton would never be able to keep it straight.

At Ena's castle, her servants often ate with her. Though they also served the meal and got up to get more food for them. Unless they felt they shouldn't intrude. In truth, they did at his castle also, but when he had guests, they preferred to eat after he and his guests had their meals. Especially when it looked like he was courting Kayla.

So for now, Muriel and the others were seated at the other end of the table, listening in on the whole discussion. Then Alton wondered where the prisoner was. He turned to Ena. "Where are Mark and Bryan? And that Hannah human?"

"Eating in the kitchen. They wanted to keep her company," Ena said, "trying to convince her that we're not so bad after all."

"Good luck with that," Halloran said. "If I had any say in it—"

"You don't." Ena sliced her brother a glower.

When it came to Ena's taking care of humans, she wouldn't let her brother say anything against them. It was her business to deal with.

He just shook his head.

"So," Kiernan said, "of all the experts signed up for the games, who do you think will win the gold?"

KAYLA HAD ENJOYED the dinner with Brett and Ena, and appreciated everyone for protecting her from Halloran, but she suspected he believed she was still a golden fae, not to be trusted, which was understandable because she was definitely here under false pretenses. He took Alton aside and spoke briefly to him after the meal ended. Kayla tried not to watch them, but she noticed Alton was frowning at Halloran and both looked back at her, which made her face heat with getting caught.

Then Halloran thanked Brett and Ena for a lovely meal, said good-bye to the rest of the guests, but only glanced in Kayla's direction with a warning look. She knew if she changed auras and was again a golden fae, he would arrest her, just on principle, and then question her without Alton and the others sticking up for her.

When the others wouldn't leave, though it appeared Brett and Ena wanted to have a word alone with them, Alton took Kayla's hand and said, "We're leaving. We have some business to take care of early in the morning before the games. Thanks again for the lovely meal."

"It was great," Kayla agreed. "Thanks again."

"And thank you," Muriel said, smiling at her.

Ena thanked her again also, for saving both Alton and Muriel, and added, "Sorry about my brother. He's a stickler for wanting everything to be perfectly normal. If there's any deviation of that, he wants to get to the bottom of it."

"I don't blame him, really," Kayla said. Though it annoyed her, she could understand his position. "That's his duty."

"It is," Ena agreed, "and he takes it to heart."

Then Alton nodded, and he and Kayla said their good-byes again and returned to his castle.

"Before the games begin tomorrow, I want to take you to where my treasure is," Alton said, taking her for another walk in the gardens before they retired for the night.

Kayla was surprised he would offer to take her this early,

instead of waiting for the games to end. "Will your gold be safe from me afterwards, do you think?" She thought he was only half joking that he was really planning to take her there. "Oh, you'll probably blindfold me."

"Good idea. I hadn't thought of it." He smiled down at her.

She suspected he really hadn't planned to blindfold her then. She appreciated that he trusted her enough to show her the location. Then she thought again and realized it would probably be guarded or have traps set for the unsuspecting so if she even thought of sneaking there on her own, she would be in real trouble. "I imagine it's well-guarded."

"It is."

She smiled. "So no blindfold really needed."

"You're right."

She laughed. "So who guards your treasure?" She loved seeing the stars and crescent moon sitting high above against the black night. The gardens smelled heavenly scent of roses, jasmine, and honeysuckle. She thought about how nice it would be if lavender scented the air too.

"When you have your locket back, maybe you could see if any of your lavender could grow here."

She was surprised he would suggest it. She thought he didn't mind taking her to the gardens because she loved gardening herself. "I could try. I thought you would wait until the games were over before you took me to find the lockets." She appreciated that he was willing to give them back and allow her the choice to leave or stay. She took his hand and smiled up at him as he returned the smile.

He squeezed her hand. "I want you to enjoy the games without worrying about the lockets. You can leave anytime you wish that way. If Halloran or anyone gives you trouble, you can just go. Not that I want that to happen, but just in case."

"You don't think I'll do so badly, or be too afraid to chance playing in the games, do you?"

"No. Not really."

"I've thoroughly had fun, you know. Trying out was scary, especially since we hadn't practiced some of the maneuvers, but I was glad I tried the next level of games that were more difficult. Sometimes challenging ourselves can make it even more worthwhile, whether we succeed or not. It's the effort we make that is so important. Not the win."

"I like the win." Alton sounded so serious, she was surprised to see him smiling down at her. "I'm glad you're enjoying them and being here. The beginners' games are tomorrow. We can go up to the mountains and get the lockets, then watch some of the games, or after we find the jewelry, you can practice some more."

"What if we practice on the way to the mountains?"

"We can do that."

"So is your treasure in a cave?"

"Yep. On Wolf Mountain. Have you ever been there?"

"Last summer. But I didn't find anything. No treasure or no..." She paused. She figured she would sound foolish if she let on she thought wolf fae really existed.

"No wolves?" Alton raised his brows in question.

She laughed. "I know it's silly. But forever, I've heard that fae wolf shifters live around that area, which was why it was called Wolf Mountain. Of course, I didn't find any sign of them."

"They're known to be elusive. Not like us dragon shifters who tend to be showier. It's hard not be when we fly against the sky for all to see. And we're big, not small and inconspicuous."

She closed her gaping mouth.

"Yes, they're real. They howl mostly at night to gather their pack or in the morning before they run."

"Where do they live? I mean, if they're fae shifters, they must live in some sort of buildings when they're fae."

"Cottages in the woods. Very much like yours, made of stones, some of wood, but covered in moss and ferns so that it looks like their surroundings."

"Are they winged? I've heard of both winged and wingless."

"They're both. Kind of like the fae and the winged fae, or the dragon fae and the dragon shifters. I wanted to ask you a question. Did Sigrid give you the ability to change into any other fae aura? Wolf even? Or are you only able to switch back and forth between dragon and golden fae?"

"I don't know. I would think only dragon fae because that's all I would need."

"Try to shift into something else."

She tried and couldn't. Her heart raced at the thought that she had been put on the spot by Halloran but she hadn't had the ability to change her aura to anything else.

"You can't," Alton said, taking a deep breath and letting it out.

"Yeah, I guess Sigrid figured I would only need to be able to do the one and nothing else."

"Good thing I spoke up then."

"Yeah. Nice save."

"You mentioned your mother. Where is your father?"

Kayla shook her head. "Mom said she met him when she was living near the hawk fae border. And, well, she didn't marry him."

"Oh. Any reason why not?"

"She would never talk about it. I think I was a mistake, but she would never say I was. If I said so, she would tell me that I was wrong. That she wanted me. She never married anyone else, so I think I put kind of a crimp in her social life. She sees family from time to time. She's visiting a sister right now, which is the reason I can get away with being gone. She thinks I'm with Tanya visiting a relative in the human world."

"I wondered about your family."

"I earn my own way from sales of my lavender products. So I'm pretty independent, but my mom and I are really close too."

"Have you ever wanted to meet your father?"

She had been curious about him, naturally. But since he had never tried to be part of her life, she didn't want to see him. "No. My mother always said it was my choice, but I figured it would upset her if I visited him. So I haven't bothered. He could have seen me instead, but he never bothered either."

"He's alive though, still, right?"

"Sure. According to my mom."

"My parents were murdered by an earlier dragon fae regime. I often wish they could have seen how I grew up—how prosperous I've been, all the high-risk missions I've successfully completed."

"And they probably would have said no to you going on them."

He laughed. "Probably. Just as your mom probably would have said no to you coming to rescue me and Muriel."

"Yeah, and not telling her anything about it."

"Or about me."

She sighed. "She would have a conniption if she knew what I was up to."

"What if I had one of my people broker a deal with you to sell your lavender to my queen? Maybe if we had money crossing the border between our territories, the royals would understand how it could benefit both sides," Alton said.

"I would have to ask Queen Avalon if she was agreeable."

"It might be a start."

"All right." Kayla loved the idea and that way she wouldn't have to sneak over to see Alton across the river, because she knew in her heart, she'd made a real friend, and she didn't want that friendship to end. Not with him, or with any of the other dragon fae or shifters that she'd made friends with.

"Did I get you into too much trouble by mentioning that we were getting married?" Kayla asked, raising a brow.

He laughed and headed back to the castle. "They will know it's all my fault when you tell me off and we call off the wedding."

When they reached her room, he kissed her again, as if they really were getting married and they hadn't had their faux fight yet.

And she kissed him right back, wishing with all heart they could be more than friends.

Early the next morning after eating some porridge topped with brown sugar and slivers of almonds, Kayla and Alton took off to the mountain chain where Wolf Mountain towered over all the other mountain peaks. It was snow-covered at the top, and a perpetual snow cloud clung to the peak, though the cloud would drop down lower in the winter months and persist.

She had never considered anything so beautiful, flying high above and even diving through the misty snowflakes, catching it briefly on her wings before she dove down again for the forest below. She still wasn't used to her wingspan and would sometimes clip twigs with her wings or knock off a shower of leaves. But she was getting better at it. And she loved how Alton took her to the top of a tree and made her land without putting her weight on top so that she looked like an ornament on a tree, her wings flapping gently to keep her stable.

Or to grab a pinecone from a tall, sturdy pine and set it high atop that same tree until the wind toppled the pinecone. Then she had to grab it before it landed on the ground. That was a trial in and of itself. No matter how many times she tried to grab a falling pinecone, she couldn't. Not with her talons. It was going too fast, or her reach wasn't right, or the wind had knocked it out of her grasp. She finally gave up and went for it on the tenth time with her dragon's beak. And caught it!

She hoped Alton wouldn't be laughing at her too much. She knew she should be able to catch the pinecone the other way, but it just seemed to be beyond her ability, at least for now. Yet, she didn't have much longer to get it right before being a dragon would soon be a thing of the past.

That disappointed her more than she wanted to let on. But what would be would be. She couldn't be something she wasn't, forever.

For now, she wanted to make the most of being a dragon though and enjoyed the sights from her high vantage point, seeing a couple of fae down below who waved at them. Or at Alton. Did they know him even when he was this color? Violet? Like her? Or maybe they were aware his scales had been changing color since he took her locket.

When they reached the cave on the south side of the mountain, she was filled with excitement—both of wanting to see the wolf shifter in person, and with seeing piles of dragon treasure. She would never have the opportunity to see such a thing ever again. She had to be the luckiest golden fae in the world.

Alton motioned for her to wait for him, then flew into the cave. After a minute, he walked onto the rock ledge in his fae form and said, "We're good. Come on down."

She couldn't slow her racing heart as she landed on the ledge beside him, feeling perfectly safe in her dragon form, but she shifted to show she wasn't afraid of the wolf or wolf fae, whichever form he or she would be in.

When she entered the cave filled with torchlight, she saw a beautiful fae, hardly noticing the ten-to-fifteen-foot piles of treasure to begin with. The fae herself was a treasure and made Kayla feel pale in comparison. Blond braided hair was curled up on top of her head, and she had the most beautiful green eyes that stared back at Kayla, as if trying to read her mind, or intimidate her, or something.

"This is Myla, and she is the guardian of my treasure."

"Can I see your wolf form?" Kayla asked eagerly, not bothering with niceties when she was too eager to see what Myla looked like as a wolf.

Myla smiled then as if amused Kayla would see her as a curiosity and not as one of the other wolf shifters probably saw her. When she shifted, she was just as beautiful, a gray and blond wolf with the same bright green eyes.

"Beautiful," Kayla said. "Oh, I mean both ways, really."

Myla shifted and smiled then with pleasure. Then she said to Alton, "Do you want me to give you some privacy? I can come back later."

"No, actually, have you noticed where I've piled my treasure lately?"

Kayla thought it was an odd question, but Myla nodded. "I always check to see what has been added so that I know if anything has been disturbed. On the furthest mountain of treasure, you piled the items you received from your queen for rescuing the fae seer, Mark. On the one near the waterfall, you deposited some gold when you were practicing for the games. And when you had to save a young man from being taken into servitude on a ship sailing around the world, you deposited your earnings on top of the jewelry. You've been practicing for the games so much, that's all you've been paid for recently." Myla motioned to the mountains. "If you don't get another job soon, you're going to be broke after paying me and the other wolves for their guarding services."

Alton smiled.

Kayla took it to mean that the wolf shifter was making a joke. This one didn't have wings. As much as Kayla loved the way Myla appeared in her very real looking wolf form, she wanted to see one with wings also. But she thought it might be too impolite to ask. Then again, she only had this one chance to come here. "Do any of the winged wolf fae come up here?"

"You wish to see one?" Myla asked.

"If it wouldn't be too much trouble."

"I'll get my friend Clarita and be right back." Myla glanced at Alton, making sure it was all right with him because she was supposed to be guarding his treasure.

"Yes, thanks, Myla, that would be great."

When Myla disappeared, Kayla asked, "Do the winged fae guard for you too?"

"Sometimes. I never know how they work out the schedule. Myla tends to be here more than anyone else. She has a younger brother and sister she cares for, so she can use the money. Let's go look for your lockets."

"She was kidding, wasn't she? About you running out of treasure soon?" Kayla looked at all the piles and thought it would take several lifetimes to spend all that much gold and other treasure. *Although*, as a golden fae, she couldn't help but admire anything and everything that was made of gold.

Alton laughed. "Yes. They don't believe in jewels or jewelry. Which makes them perfect for guarding the treasure. When I proposed bringing the treasure here in the first place, I thought I might have a lot of opposition. Fear that others would invade their territory, looking to steal the treasure. But they love guarding it and the money it brings in. And they haven't really had too much trouble." He climbed to the top of the pile and though some of the jewels and coins began to roll downhill, he managed to stay on top and began sifting through the coins. "Come on up."

Kayla turned into a dragon and landed on top, then shifted.

With her additional weight, more of the coins began to move down the pile. "What do you use in payment? Part of the treasure, right?"

"Yes. The treasure means nothing to them, but they use it to barter for goods they do need."

That worried her. What if he had paid the wolves with her locket, and they had used it to barter with someone else?

"I'm not finding it," she said, feeling panicked.

He kept showing her other lockets, but none that were the right ones.

"What if you paid some of your guard wolves or even someone else from your treasure? Your staff? Your food bill? Something else?"

Alton paused, his brows furrowed. "I don't think so."

But he didn't sound sure of it. "Would Myla know?"

"Would Myla know what?" the girl asked, walking into the cave with a winged wolf.

The wolf was white, her wings a shimmery pale mix of colors. "Oh, she's beautiful," Kayla said, forgetting for a moment all about her locket.

Myla laughed. "I'm sure he loves hearing you say so."

The winged fae shifted and he was a fae without wings, blond-haired, blue eyes, smiling, even though Kayla had called him a beautiful girl.

"Where are your wings?" Kayla couldn't believe he would have them in his wolf form and not in his fae form.

They suddenly appeared and were just like the ones he wore as a wolf. "I'm old enough to hide them when I want. Myla said you wanted to see a winged wolf, so I obliged. But I can hide them on my wolf form also."

"But you don't have wings, do you, Myla?" Why else would she have had to get another wolf who had wings if that were the case?

"No. Clarita was busy. This is Trey."

"Oh, yes, of course. That's what had confused me."

"What were you wondering if I'd known about?" Myla asked.

Alton went back to digging through the pile of treasure, a slight mist from the waterfall spilling into the cave but far enough from the treasure so as not to get it wet. "If I'd given a gold locket and one that was bronze in payment for any services lately."

"You mean the ones you just deposited recently?"

"Yeah," Alton said.

"Well, though things haven't been disturbed, I meant that no one had stolen anything. As to paying folks, then yes, you've given us payment and to some others, I'm certain."

Kayla described the lockets, but Myla shook her head. "I couldn't be sure. I think most of us take gold or silver coins. And we normally wouldn't take the treasure at the top of the mountain, but near the bottom where it's easier to reach."

"From which pile?" Alton asked, still searching for Kayla's jewelry.

"Any of them," Myla said.

Kayla hadn't give up either, but she wasn't so self-assured now that he would have the lockets still. And she was irritated at Sigrid too. What if Alton had retrieved them sooner before too many others were digging in the piles of treasure for payment of services?

"Is it a family heirloom?" Myla asked, joining them to help.

"It's something that is part of who we are when we're first born. I'm a lavender grower. It's tied into my ability to grow lavender fields. Once I come of age in a few days, the magic will be infused within me and whether I have the locket with me or not, I will still carry the magic with me."

"So without it," Myla said, "you will lose your ability?"

"Worse. I'll be cast out from the golden fae society. The queen loves the lavender flowers for everything, a dye for her clothes even."

"I can't imagine anything so absurd. I mean, that they would cast you out for your inability to grow a flower."

"You must have something you treasure," Kayla said, trying to show how important it was to her.

"The forests, the lakes and rivers, the mountains. That's what we care about. Many of us have tree farms and sell to those who are trying to landscape or reforest their lands."

Kayla noticed that Trey was busy going through another pile of treasure, from the top. "This is the one where Myla said Alton dropped the treasure," Kayla said to him.

"You think she is always here? I was here the one day, and I distinctly remember him dropping the treasure over here. On this pile," Trey said.

Kayla was so hoping Trey was right. She shifted into a dragon, flew over to that pile, and landed on top, trying to avoid knocking him off, then shifted again.

"Your scales are the same as Alton's now," Trey said, smiling at her.

"Because of the locket," she said. "Once I have mine and the bronze one, he should be back to normal."

"Disappointing," Myla said. "I like not knowing what color he'll be when he shows up. Then I can growl at him until he shifts and proves he's who he's supposed to be."

Kayla would have laughed, but she was too concerned that her locket was gone for good. She assumed, as wolves, they could smell Alton's scent and know it was him. She found several lockets here, but none that were either hers or Sigrid's.

Then Alton held up a locket and said, "I found yours! It smells of lavender. This has got to be it."

Kayla transported to the pile and joined Alton. Thrilled beyond measure, she saw that it was hers. She couldn't have been happier. "That's it." She reached for it, but he shook his head and instead, he placed it over her head. She wrapped her arms around him and gave him a big kiss. "Thank you. And thanks to both of you for looking for it also."

"But you still need the other?" Myla asked, brow raised, a smile settling on her lips.

Kayla didn't think she was smiling about the locket, but about Alton kissing her and vice versa.

"Yes. I can't go home without it." That was the problem. She had to find Sigrid's too, or she didn't know what the falcon fae would do to her. Besides, she'd promised. And the fae must have had the same urgency to get hers back as Kayla did.

But as long as they searched, which was several hours, all on the same pile of treasure because Alton had found hers there, they found no sign of it. Kayla glanced at the waterfall cascading next to the other entrance of the cave and scrambled down to the bottom of the mountain of treasure, making the coins and carafes and such, slide down with her in a tinkling mass. Then she rushed over the stone floor to peer down into the waterfall.

"What if somehow it fell off the pile and landed down there?" She motioned to the crystal-clear pool of water at the bottom of the falls, ferns tucked into rock crevices making it a beautiful little hideaway.

"I would think that would be impossible. There's no gold anywhere near there," Alton said, joining her.

"We've looked at several feet of the top layers of the treasure and not found it. Who have you paid for services recently?" Myla asked.

"I only take coins," Trey said. "So does Myla. But Canton likes jewelry. I think he has a secret fae girlfriend who isn't a wolf."

"But everything goes through me," Alton said.

"Right," Myla said. "We would never take anything from you. So he must have asked you for jewelry in the past when he was guarding."

"And Simon?"

"I don't know what he likes in payment," Trey said. "I can go ask."

"Please. We'll go and see Canton. Then if nothing pans out, we'll transport home to see my butler and learn if he has taken any jewelry for paying the staff or for supplies." Alton rubbed Kayla's arm. "We'll find it."

She sure hoped so because if they didn't, she wasn't sure what would happen next.

She was glad he wanted to transport because she was getting tired, flying as a dragon. But she wondered if he was worn out because of his injury. "Good idea."

They transported to a path in the woods that led to a stone house and saw a black wolf, who shifted when he saw them. He was wearing black trousers and a black muscle shirt. Kayla thought he could be riding a human's motorcycle and suit the part. But she couldn't believe she was seeing all these wolves in different colors and how beautiful they were.

"I hear you're looking for me," he said, casting a glance in Kayla's direction. "I'm Simon, by the way."

"Yeah, I need to locate a locket I might have given someone that is important to the owner. Any help in locating it, or if I gave it in payment, I'll generously pay something else instead," Alton said.

"What did it look like?"

"It had the engraving of a falcon on it. Do you take payment in some form other than coin? I don't always pay you; my assistant does. So I'm hoping if I've given it away, I can substitute something else for it."

"I don't recall anything like that. Is it gold? Silver?"

"Bronze," Alton said.

"I'm not interested in bronze. It's not as valuable. I would check with Canton, if I were you."

"All right. That's where we were headed. Thanks, Simon," Alton said.

"You're welcome. Is she your girlfriend?"

"Yeah."

Simon smiled at her broadly. "Too bad I didn't see her first."

"Hey, later." Alton rushed Kayla along to the house in the woods and Kayla wondered if Alton worried she might be interested in the wolf fae now. She did find them fascinating. But Alton even more so.

When they reached a stone cottage, they heard laughter inside.

"Maybe his girlfriend is with him," Kayla whispered.

"Or not, if he's trying to keep her secret."

They made their way to the front doorstep and Alton knocked, calling out, "It's me, Alton. I need to talk to you about a payment that was made on my behalf."

A redheaded guy opened the door and looked from Alton to Kayla. "Yeah?"

"I'm looking for a falcon locket, bronze, that might have been used to pay someone who was guarding the treasure."

Canton raised his hands in a gesture of can't-help-you-there.

"I'll make it worth your while if it was given to you, triple the payment. It just belongs to someone when it shouldn't have been given away. It was my mistake."

"Who says I might have it?"

"No one. My assistant might have taken it with some other treasure and used it to pay for merchandise, for all I know."

"I...don't know."

"We understand you have a girlfriend who might like jewelry."

"Wolves aren't into jewelry," Canton said slyly.

"We understand she's not a wolf."

"Alton's a dragon shifter, Canton, not a wolf," the girl said out of view, but she was getting closer as she walked down the hall to join them. "What difference does it make if he knows we're seeing each other?"

Before Kayla even saw the girl, she knew her at once. Helena, the blue-eyed, blond who captured all the guys' eyes, who she'd seen at the farmer's market with two other guys. Now she had even captured the attention of a wolf?

Kayla quickly transported back to the woods before Helena saw her and wondered what she was doing wearing a dragon fae aura and chumming around with a dragon shifter at the same time.

13

Alton wasn't sure why Kayla hastily disappeared, until he saw Canton's girlfriend—a golden fae. He suspected Kayla knew who she was from the sound of her voice.

"So do you have a bronze falcon locket?" Alton asked, trying to keep the heat from his voice. He realized that though he cared a lot about Kayla, he still didn't care for all the golden fae kind.

The girl slipped her arm around Canton's waist. "I thought when a dragon fae paid for services, he wouldn't be asking for the payment back."

She was adorned in all gold. Alton didn't believe she would want anything that wasn't gold, and her boyfriend would know that.

"Thank you for your time," Alton said to Canton, ignoring the girl. "If you hear of anyone who might have received the locket in payment, let me know and I'll make it worth your while and pay whoever has it also."

"Sure thing." Canton was sincere sounding. He worked for him, so Alton was certain he would get in touch with him right away if he did discover who had it.

"So Canton can give me more gold," the girl said, tightening her hold on Canton.

Alton had thought Canton was more alpha than that. He wondered if he'd made a mistake in allowing him to stand guard over his treasure. "I've got to go. See you later."

"Good luck," Canton said.

Alton headed outside and shut the door behind him. He didn't see Kayla anywhere. He hurried into the woods, hoping she would be around here somewhere, just staying out of sight and waiting for him.

Then he saw a wolf appear nearby, a black wolf. Simon shifted. "She told me to tell you she returned to your castle to ask your personal assistant if he paid anyone with the locket."

"Thanks. I'm headed that way then. If anyone learns about its location, please let me know."

"Will do."

Then Alton returned to his keep and found Kayla questioning his whole staff about the locket. He was glad they were fully cooperating, probably figuring that he was courting her, so it was what he would want to do. Which he did.

"Helena wanted gold only, right?" Kayla asked Alton.

"The golden fae? Yes. How far have you gotten here?"

"Ferdinand has told me that he paid the whole staff and the bills this week, right after you must have deposited my gold on top of your treasure."

"Any lockets used in payment?" Alton asked Ferdinand. He was his butler, but also his personal assistant who managed all the finances.

"Most everyone wants payment in coins because the value is more of a known factor. But two of your guards asked for some jewelry, because they have sweethearts," Ferdinand said, his brows pinched together in a frown.

Alton knew Ferdinand didn't like having to question anyone about the payments they had received. It was theirs to do with whatever they liked. They had earned it. But this was too important to ignore.

"Have them meet with me in my office, would you?"

"Yes, sir." Ferdinand stalked out the door.

"The rest of you are dismissed."

Everyone but one of the maids left.

"Yes, Dorinda?" Alton asked, hopeful she knew something of the matter when no one else seemed to.

"I know who got it."

"The locket?" Alton couldn't have been more thrilled.

"George Fitzwilliam, the boot merchant. We all thought the locket was boring. Bronze, not as valuable as the gold or coins Ferdinand was handing out. Ferdinand had been annoyed that he'd grabbed it up in his haste when he'd taken some of the items to pay for things. Rather than return it, he took it with him wherever he went to offer it in payment. And, curious, I asked if he had to return it to your treasure pile. He said no, the boot merchant accepted it, was eager even."

"Why didn't Ferdinand tell us that?"

"I suspect he's sending the soldiers into speak with you, then running into the village to see if he can ask the boot merchant if he has got it still. Ferdinand thinks the world of you, sir. He wouldn't want to lose his position here for anything. I'm sure he's afraid the locket is more valuable than anything and that's why George was so eager to have it."

"He wouldn't lose his position. It was my mistake, not his. Ask the soldiers if they know of the locket. Kayla, uhm, Violet and I are going to see the bootmaker." He turned to Kayla and took her hand. "We're going to get it back. I promise."

She didn't look like she trusted that they would, as worried as she appeared. And he couldn't be certain either.

KAYLA DIDN'T THINK she'd ever been on this much of a wild goose chase before over anything. But she was still hopeful that someone had the locket, the bootmaker in particular, and that he hadn't given it to anyone else. Did he know who it belonged to? And thought to ransom it to Sigrid? She wondered how that would turn out if the merchant threatened Sigrid and she used her magic on him.

When they arrived at the bootmaker's shop, the sign in the window said the shop was closed, but then Ferdinand exited the shop and his eyes widened to see Alton and Kayla watching him.

"I'm so sorry. I guess you know why I'm here. I thought I could get it from Mr. Fitzwilliam. But he says he doesn't have the locket." Ferdinand looked downcast and Kayla felt bad for him.

"You are not losing your position over this, Ferdinand, but you should have told me. I'll speak with him." One of his staff members might not have the influence that a dragon could. Alton opened the door and walked in with Kayla.

The bootmaker's black eyes widened. "I don't have the locket," George quickly said, his voice raspy. "I already told your man."

"Okay, so where is it?"

"I don't know."

"You lost it? You thought it was something important. You were eager to receive it in payment. Why? If it's that important, how could you lose it?" Alton sounded incredulous.

"She came in here to buy boots, okay?"

"Who?" Kayla asked.

"Sigrid. The falcon fae. The locket's owner. I meant to send it back to her, not knowing how you ended up with it, but I was certain she would want it back. She always wore it."

"She came here often?" Kayla asked, shocked.

"She...had a crush on a dragon shifter. She came here for the games last year and then she followed him in here to look at boots. So she didn't look so conspicuous, which was hard not to do when she has wings, so she bought a pair of boots. She loved them so much, she bought another pair before she returned home after the games. I noticed the necklace and asked if it was an heirloom, and she said it was."

"So how did you lose it?" Alton asked.

"I had it in my hand, and I either dropped it on the floor when I was getting some different size boots out for someone, and then a shopper took it, or I dropped it in a boot and the new owner just kept it."

"Do you have receipts for all the boots that were bought around that time?" Alton knew he did. The man kept meticulous records.

"I do." He pulled out his records and showed them to Alton.

"Did you check with any of these people?"

"No. I really was busy about that time, resoling boots, selling new boots. Everyone wanted new ones for the games this year, just like last year. So I forgot about it, quite frankly. I looked around several times, underneath the racks, and in the boots that were left. I kept thinking I would run across it. I just didn't think of contacting anyone who had bought boots. Well, and I've been too busy."

"Do you mind if we contact the buyers? I know three of them are locals. But the other three?" Alton pointed out the names.

"Uh, yeah, they're participants in the game. I only know they were taking part in it, but nothing else. They must be staying in the barracks."

"Okay, thanks. We'll talk to them."

"I'm so sorry. I should have...well, I don't know. Your advisor was trying to get rid of it as payment, and I didn't think you would be interested in it at all. I just thought I would return it to her. Do a good deed, you know."

Kayla wondered if there was more to the situation than that. Did he know the falcon fae had all kinds of abilities? Did he hope if he turned it over to her, she would do something good for him in return?

"Tell Ferdinand if you see him before I do, to reimburse you for the lost necklace. You still need to be reimbursed for your goods."

"Thank you."

Then Alton took Kayla outside.

"Who are the three dragons you know that had bought the boots?" Kayla asked, not having seen the list.

"Ena, but she would have given it back to the bootmaker. Kiernan, not sure. I'll ask him. And...Halloran."

"Oh, great."

Alton smiled at her. "I'll ask him."

"They'll probably be at the games, won't they?"

"Yeah. Oh, I meant to give you back your other necklaces, bracelets, and rings."

"They don't mean half as much to me as my locket does. And Sigrid's locket. I'm ready to go to the games if you are." All she cared about right now was finding the other locket.

WHEN KAYLA and Alton arrived at the games site, they found the beginners all taking part in the trials and the winners of the first round had been posted. Some of the higher-level dragons were watching them.

"Faster!" "You can do it!" "Go for it!"

Kayla thought it was nice that they weren't making condescending remarks to those in the beginners' trials, but instead were encouraging them.

Then she and Alton saw Ena and Olaf near the viewing stands for the expert flyers. Brett and Kiernan were watching the beginners. "I'll talk to Ena," Kayla said.

"Okay, I'll check with Kiernan."

Kayla joined Ena and Olaf and told them the news.

"I'm so glad you found your locket," Ena said. "I'll pop into the castle and check inside my boots. After I tried them on, I put them in a box and haven't worn them yet. I planned to wear them tomorrow for the trials."

"Okay, thanks."

They saw Halloran headed their way, and Ena grabbed Kayla's hand. "Why don't you come with me?"

Before Kayla could say yes or no, she was standing at the front door of Ena's castle.

"Sorry for the abrupt transport and no warning." Ena opened the door. "I didn't want to leave you with Olaf to deal with my brother if he decided to hassle you further."

"Thanks, Ena. You don't know how much that means to me."

"I've known my brother forever, so I completely understand."

Ena took her up to her room, and it was so lavish, just astonishing: everything gold gilt painted, a huge bed with gold embroidered navy curtains surrounding it, gold tassels pulling them back. Just what a golden fae would love.

Ena pulled out a box from a closet and opened it up. Lovely black leather boots were sitting in it. Kayla practically held her breath when Ena pulled one out, turned it upside down, and shook it. Kayla knew finding the locket in one of them would be too easy.

"So have you shifted into the dragon since you found your locket?" Ena asked, pulling out the other boot.

"No."

"I'm wondering if Alton's scales will still be violet when he's near you. Or if they'll continue to change until the falcon's locket is returned to her."

"I don't know. Maybe." Kayla wished now that they had shifted just to see what difference it would make.

"Nothing here," Ena said, sounding disappointed.

Kayla was too. "Okay, so your brother also bought a new pair of boots that day." Kayla hoped maybe he had the locket then. Surely as a Dragon at Arms though, he would have returned it to Mr. Fitzwilliam if he had discovered it.

"All right, let's go talk to him then," Ena said cheerfully.

"What if he doesn't want to tell us if he has got it?"

"I'll know if he does or doesn't. I'm sure he wouldn't keep it if he found it. What would he need it for?"

Still, Kayla was hopeful that he had it so that she could return it to Sigrid. They left Ena's castle and transported back to the games where they saw Halloran speaking with Olaf, and they quickly joined him.

"Have you worn your new boots yet?" Ena asked Halloran.

"Couple of times."

"You didn't happen to find a locket in one of the boots, did you?"

Halloran folded his arms, glanced at Kayla and saw her locket, then turned his attention back to Ena. "What's this all about?"

"Just that the bootmaker lost a locket in his shop and the only other place it could have been was if he'd dropped it into a boot that he'd sold at the time. You were in the store when I was, so I knew you had bought a pair. Alton's checking with someone else. Three are here at the games."

"It's Alton's mission then? He's getting paid for it?" Halloran sounded suspicious.

"His obligation, he feels. He wants to make it right since the locket was part of his payment for merchandise."

"But Alton didn't lose it." Halloran appeared as though he figured something else was going on. "So why should he feel obligated to pay for something the bootmaker lost? More than that, what is the locket's importance?"

"It belongs to a falcon fae," Kayla said, her brows raised, waiting for Halloran to challenge her. "She's a friend of mine."

"So *that's* why you're here. To get it back. Yet Alton is the one paying for the locket."

"He took it from her."

Halloran smiled. "I see. I was beginning to worry that Alton was losing his common sense. Good. So why does he feel obligated now to return it to her?" He raised his hand in a universal sign to stop and not answer the question. "I know the answer. You have gotten under his scales, and he is doing it as a favor to you. Maybe there is something more to his liking you than just protecting you for saving his life. I still don't know how you could change auras and suddenly have a dragon shifter ability. Unless"—Halloran glanced off to see Brett headed their way—"it has something to do with magic."

"Sure it does," Kayla said. "I think anyone who can shift, even the wolves, makes them magical."

Halloran greeted Brett with a question right off. "Can magic be used to turn a fae, any fae, into a dragon shifter?"

"If you're asking if I used magic to turn myself into a dragon shifter, no, and it can't be done."

"What if someone else had the magic that could do so?" Halloran persisted.

"How long have you been questioning what I am?" Brett asked, sounding surprised.

"Not you. Her." Halloran motioned to Kayla.

"In my opinion, no. There is no magic that can turn a fae into any kind of shifter. They have to be born with the genetics to make it happen."

"In your opinion."

"In my *expert* opinion."

Halloran smiled a little.

Willow waved at Kayla from a distance and ran to where they were standing. "Kayla, there was an older dragon asking all about you because he saw we were friends."

"Who?" Kayla couldn't imagine anyone would be asking about her, unless it was some of Alton's close friends, and they wanted to know who she really was.

"He's a blue dragon and he's older. Maybe forties? He was flying in the expert trials. I noticed him because he looks a little like one of my uncles, and I thought he had shown up for the games after all when he said he wasn't entering. Anyway, he said you caught his eye because of your beautiful scale color. I told him you were Violet, or Kayla, depending on which alias you were using at the time. He was confused. I told him it was a joke. His name was Arne."

"The dragon who did so well when Kiernan and I were flying," Brett said.

"Yeah. He came out with the highest score. I looked," Willow said. "Anyway, he wanted to know who the violet dragon was who had been with you. When I told him Alton, he wanted to know all about him. Then he said he wanted to meet Violet."

"Why?" Kayla wondered if the dragon knew what a fraud she was and wanted to expose her.

Willow shrugged. "He said he would meet you at the barracks in a few minutes."

Kayla glanced around for any sign of Alton but didn't see him anywhere. He probably was questioning the three contestants about their new boots and if they'd discovered a locket.

"I'll go with you," Willow said. "Since Alton doesn't seem to be around at the moment."

Ena opened her mouth to speak, when Halloran intervened. "I've got this. All right, Ena? I promise I'm not going to throw Kayla in the dungeon."

"If she tells me you're questioning her further..." Ena folded her arms and tilted her chin up as if she intended to take Halloran to task if he hassled Kayla any longer.

Halloran only smiled and escorted Kayla across the field to the barracks.

"Thanks," Kayla said, not that she didn't worry about the questions she thought Halloran would ask her again, but she was a little nervous about what the blue dragon wanted with her.

"You probably wonder why I offered to stay with you," Halloran said.

"You want to question me more."

Halloran chuckled. "I would like some straight answers. But truthfully, I want to know what Arne's interest is in you. Maybe *he* will shed more light on who you are."

"I doubt it. I don't know the dragon." Kayla looked at the men and women standing near the barracks talking, but she didn't have a clue which was...no, a man with blond hair and penetrating green eyes was watching them approach. Before they reached him, she saw Alton headed for them, and she thought he might be concerned about her being alone with Halloran.

"Kayla? Or is it Violet?" the man asked.

"Kayla. And you're Arne?"

"No. That's my brother. He's off talking to one of his competition, and will be here in a second. I'm Sid. Uncle Sid. *Your* uncle."

Kayla felt her legs give out, but thankfully, Halloran grabbed her arm to steady her.

Alton reached her then, pulled her into his arms, and held her close. "What's going on?" he asked, practically growling.

"Looks like some of Kayla's family showed up for the games," Halloran said. "Only she doesn't even know them."

"Yeah, sorry about that. I'll let your father tell you all about it, but I wanted to tell you that I'm your uncle too," Sid said.

"You're...you're a dragon," she said, her thoughts reeling from the news, and realized belatedly she shouldn't have said that. Not when *she* was supposed to be a dragon.

"Just like you are." Sid glanced at a man approaching them who looked similar, except his eyes were bluer, his hair just as blond, and he was a little taller. "You were right, Arne. Her mother hasn't told her."

"How can that be? You're..." Kayla paused. "Can we take this discussion somewhere else?" She'd already said way too much in front of Halloran, but she had to learn if what the men said was true. Her father and his brother were dragon shifters.

Which meant she was too.

14

————

"I agree. Let's talk where it's less crowded," Arne said to Kayla.

"I'm going with you." Alton still had his arm around her waist.

She felt so lightheaded, she was glad for it.

His brows furrowing deeply, Arne didn't look happy about Alton going with them, but finally just nodded.

"We can go to the clearing where I practice flying with Kayla," Alton said.

"Are you sure you don't want me to go too?" Halloran asked Alton.

"No," everyone said at the same time.

He just smiled as if he knew that was the answer he would get.

"We can go there then. Lead the way." Arne shifted into a dragon, and he was big, his form imposing, a little frightening.

Then Alton kissed Kayla's cheek, to her surprise. Was he still playing his courting role to the hilt in front of Halloran? It appeared he no longer needed to. Not when she was part dragon shifter. She still couldn't believe that she was.

But when she tried to shift, she couldn't. Her lips parted in surprise, but she didn't want Halloran to learn she couldn't shift.

Had Arne lied about being her father? She was so confused; she didn't know what to think.

Then her Uncle Sid said, "I see you're wearing Tasha's locket."

"The one my mother gave to me, yes."

"Why don't you remove it and slip it into your pocket. Or I can keep it safe for you."

No way was she ever letting go of it. But something about the way he said the words, as if her mother had been devious about gifting the locket to her angered her, that he would even suggest it. Yet, she wasn't shifting. Could the locket be the cause? She didn't believe it, but she pulled it off and slipped it into her pocket, buttoned it, and tried to shift. And it happened. At once, she was a violet dragon, and she felt an incredible amount of relief. And annoyance too. Her mother had kept her from shifting all these years?

She didn't think Halloran would attempt to arrest her with two big dragon shifters who said they were related to her, watching over her. Not to mention he would have had a fight with Alton, if she hadn't been able to shift.

Then Alton shifted and kissed her again, but as a dragon this time. He smiled at her, showing off his wickedly beautiful teeth, and she smiled at him, though she hadn't seen what her own dragon teeth would like. She imagined hers were just as wicked to look at. His long snout nuzzled hers, their long tongues did a little dance together and then he smiled again. Wow, she could really get used to this.

Then Alton took off, and she flew to catch up to him, and realized he was just as violet as her still. If she wore the locket, would he be blue scaled again? She still hadn't tried that. Had the locket truly prevented her from turning into a dragon? From shifting all these years? If so, she couldn't help being furious with her mother. How could she do this to her? Lie to her?

Then again, how could Kayla have hidden her aura if she had

shifted into a dragon in the golden fae kingdom? If she wanted to grow her lavender, she would have to wear the locket. But if she wanted to be a dragon, she would have to remove it. When she came of age, would she have to choose between the two?

Why couldn't she be both?

They finally reached the clearing, set down, and shifted. She had a million questions for her father, even though it seemed so weird calling him that since she hadn't met him before. Except, she did feel a strange sense of family, even with Sid.

"Before you ask anything of me, let me explain what happened," Arne said.

"Okay."

"Your mother and I were in love. We still are."

"How could you be? You haven't once seen her!"

"Many times. Every time Tasha left you with her parents so she could see her sister? She was seeing me. But we knew it would be hardest on you. She knew before you were even born, it would be your calling to create gardens of lavender."

"But the locket has kept me from turning into a dragon all these years?"

"Yes. Your ability has been...suppressed. For your own good. She couldn't be sure what would happen if the royals learned you were a dragon shifter. Most likely, force you and your mother out."

"But then we could have lived with you." None of it made any sense. Why couldn't they have lived with her dad all this time, if her mother and he loved each other that much?

"When you come of age, wear the locket, and—"

"And I'll never be a dragon shifter again?" Her eyes filled with tears at the thought. She had the most extraordinary gift, the best of both worlds, and she didn't want to give either up.

"The magic from the locket will be infused with your very being. You'll always be able to grow lavender wherever you go."

"What if she wants to be with me?" Alton said. "We're getting married. She wants to be a dragon shifter too." He wrapped his arm around her waist again, his challenging gaze switching from her father to Kayla, his look softening.

She wanted to say that they had been joking, hadn't they? He wanted to be with her for real? Even if she was also a golden fae?

"Don't we?" Alton said, his voice firm, not truly asking her a question to see if she agreed.

"Do you even know that if I wore the locket when I come of age, I would be able to shift into a dragon again?" Wait, had Sigrid not been the one to make this happen? But why hadn't Kayla been able to turn into a dragon before? When she had lost her locket to begin with?

The issues continued to bombard her, everything she knew coming into question.

"Do you honestly know, Father, if I wore the locket when I came of age, I would ruin my chance to become a dragon shifter again?"

He smiled a hint at hearing her call him father and shook his head. "That's the problem with real life. We never know what the future truly holds. You plan your whole life out, and something occurs that knocks the whole plan out of whack."

"Like you loving my mom?" Kayla hastily brushed away the tears trailing down her cheeks. She didn't want to make choices like that. Be near her mother, or never be able to see her again? Be with her mother, and not be able to see Alton or her father again?

"Yes. We didn't plan on falling in love. It just happened. She tried to steal some of my gold. She said it was because she was riveted by my beauty and wanted to catch my attention. I said it was because she was a golden fae and couldn't resist my treasure."

Kayla smiled, never having known that side of her mother's personality.

"We had the best time together, Kayla. But then her parents needed her home. Your grandparents and great grandparents were elderly, and Tasha's sister already had two boys and a girl she was raising, and she couldn't help out all the time. Then you came along, and Tasha had to think of you, and she still had to take care of her aging parents."

"But then they died."

"Only this past year."

"Was she not going to let me have a choice? A say in what I wanted to be?"

"Remember that plan I was speaking about? About how they can be tossed out in a heartbeat because of unforeseen circumstances?" Her father looked at Alton.

He only smiled back like this had been *his* plan all along.

"We were going to celebrate your big coming out a little early. Only the next thing we know, you're off saving dragon fae and dragon fae shifters, something that is *my* kind of work. You're falling head over heels for a dragon shifter. And you're participating in the dragon games, something that no golden fae could ever do. What made all that happen? Your curiosity about the dragons practicing for the games. Why do you think you kept searching for the mushrooms on their side of the river?"

"Because Mom..." Kayla's heartbeat ratcheted up a few notches. "Mom loved them."

"They're the same as the ones in your own backyard forest."

"She wanted me to get caught by the dragon fae?"

"She wanted you to see them, to be curious about them, to get to know them. Which you have done. I wouldn't have suggested it. But I would have been on hand had they arrested you. They would have heard my angry roar, and I would have proved to everyone you were a dragon fae with every right to be there."

"But...but Sigrid, the falcon fae, she turned me into a dragon."

"No. Her mother made the locket for your mother, infused it with the magic that would keep you from shifting. To protect you. Sigrid must have known this. Once you weren't wearing the locket, she suggested she could turn you. That way you didn't have to deal with the shock of the truth—that you are a dragon shifter. And a golden fae."

Kayla thought back to what Brett had told her. "Brett, who also knows of magic, said no one could change a fae into a shifter unless he was already a shifter."

"I wouldn't know for certain, but it seems plausible. He didn't know about his dragon shifter ability either."

"And my aura?"

"You have had the ability to be either aura for as long as you've lived, only again, the locket suppressed your dragon aura. You have to choose which one you wish to wear, and so why would you choose to be a dragon, if it's not something you ever thought you could be?"

Kayla realized her dad made perfect sense. "So if I had wanted to fly across the river, or turn into a dragon when Alton caught me that one day, I could have just called upon the ability to shift before I ever spoke to Sigrid." She cast Alton a smug smile. If only she had turned into a dragon when he had taken her to the beach beyond No Man's Land. What a surprise he would have had.

He was smiling back at her, probably imagining the same thing.

"Exactly. You had to believe you could do it. First."

"So now where do we go from here?" Kayla was so bewildered. She didn't want to be denied the chance to see her mother or grow her lavender for the queen even. But she didn't want to give up being a dragon fae either. She was excited about being one actually and doing the kinds of jobs her father and Alton did. Maybe not all the time, but in the winter when her gardens weren't growing. It would be great! Though she loved the cottage where she stayed with her mother, the idea she could live in a castle made her smile. Would she have to have her own piles of treasure somewhere else, or would Alton let her add her treasure to his in the cave, if they should marry?

"Okay, so you want to participate in the games, right?" her father asked.

"I do."

"All right. I think it would be a good idea if we get some practice in. And I might even be able to show Alton some moves he hasn't thought of also."

She thought the world of her dad for offering because Alton would be in direct competition with him at the games and her dad didn't seem to mind.

After they shifted, her father showed her how to fly in great arches, how to land on the smallest of objects, how to grasp pinecones, drop them, and grab them in midair. Maybe she'd just needed more practice or maybe something her father had said had finally clicked with her. She really was having fun with this.

Then he showed Alton how to do a dragon roll in the sky, spewing fire at the same time. The maneuver was more spectacular than anything she had ever witnessed. She sat on the boulder in the middle of the clearing and watched the two of them practicing until Alton had the maneuver down pat. Maybe not quite the same as her father's form, but she loved the way Alton had perfected his in his own manner.

As soon as they landed on the ground beside the boulder, they shifted and Alton asked her father, "Are you staying at the barracks?"

"I am."

"Will you stay with us at my castle instead?"

"I would have suggested it, if you hadn't." Now he was being a protective father, which she appreciated.

Alton smiled. "I have a whole staff that ensures your daughter is in perfect hands. But I would be honored."

"Would it be too much of an inconvenience if my wife comes also?"

Kayla closed her gaping mouth. Her father had said he loved

her mother, but he had married a dragon fae instead? She could have screamed, she was so mad.

"I think it's time we all were together," Arne continued.

"My mother?" Kayla asked, still thinking he meant he had a wife who wasn't her mother and maybe some kids too that would be half siblings.

"Of course. Who else do you think I meant? We talked about it, and Sigrid has cloaked her fae aura."

"But I thought you said Sigrid hadn't done that with me. That she couldn't."

"Not that she couldn't, but that she didn't need to."

"Oh. Mom would watch me flying in the games? She wouldn't mind seeing me as a dragon?"

"She already has and was about to expire right on the spot when she saw you trying out for the second level trials. She is so proud of you and has been trying her hardest to stay out of your view when you've been around. Though she couldn't believe it was you at first. She said you've done something different with your hair."

"Uh, yeah, to disguise who I really was." Kayla couldn't believe that her mother had been watching her all along. "Why didn't she let me know?"

"Because she didn't want to ruin it for you. She wanted you to participate without the knowledge that the two of us have been watching out for your welfare once you decided to try out for the games."

"I was worried all along that Halloran would have me arrested!"

Her dad shook his head. "No chance at that. Like I said, I would have taken care of the matter promptly."

Now she would be doubly worried about "performing" well with both her parents there. "Did she know I'd lost my locket?"

"We learned of it from Tanya. She has been so concerned about you. We assured her we were keeping you safe."

Tanya. Kayla let out her breath, glad her friend knew what was going on even if she hadn't.

"What about Kayla's Uncle Sid, my brother? Can he stay with us also? I would like for Kayla to get to know him better," Kayla's dad said to Alton.

"Yeah, sure," Alton said.

"Let's go pick up your mom, shall we? So we can tell her the good news? I'm used to living in a castle. Staying in noisy barracks is not for me."

She was glad she wasn't staying there either.

Arne asked Alton, "You aren't pushing your game too much after your recent injury, are you?"

Alton shook his head. "I can do this."

"All right. I just don't want my future son-in-law, if Kayla wishes to marry you, to kill himself during the games. It's not worth it. Believe me, I know. I've been there, done that."

"I'll be fine. Thank you, sir."

Kayla couldn't believe it when she and her father and Alton flew back to the game site and found her mother visiting with Ena and Brett. Thankfully, her mother must have known they were okay to talk to, or she had been careful about what she had said to them. Then again, they would know she was a golden fae if they knew she was Kayla's mother.

Ena smiled brightly at Kayla. "We've been keeping your mother company, delighted to meet her. We would invite all of you for dinner, but I suspect you'll be having dinner at your place tonight, Alton."

"Yeah. We have some matters to discuss."

Kayla hugged her mom, and they both had tears in their eyes. Her mother touched her short hair and smiled. "Beautiful."

Kayla was glad her mother wasn't disappointed in her, and she couldn't wait to ask just how she had gone about stealing treasure from a great dragon shifter, Arne, Kayla's father.

I⊤ WAS one thing to pretend marriage, quite another to make it come true. But Alton had never felt the way he did about Kayla for any other girl, even when he thought Kayla wasn't a true dragon shifter. Knowing she was half, made him happier than he could ever be because they could fly together, be together, and not be separated like Kayla's mother and father had been. He wondered if the situation with her parents being apart would change now that Kayla knew what she was, and that Tasha no longer had to take care of Kayla's grandparents.

They ate a feast of crab and shrimp, rice, and greens fit for a wedding while Kayla drilled her mother about stealing her father's treasure. Kayla was so happy, and Alton was too. But he knew she had to make a decision still about growing her lavender and staying in the golden fae territory or being a dragon shifter and staying with him. He was glad her Uncle Sid had come along too, though he was quietly listening the whole time.

"Arne was off partying with Sid, and everyone knew what a fierce dragon he was. Except I could see he had a soft spot when others couldn't. I had seen him in a mixed crowd of fae, and he had seen me. I don't think he saw me as his enemy. I think he just liked all the gold I was wearing, wishing it could sit on his pile of treasure too."

Tasha had blond hair like Kayla, but her eyes were more amber. When she smiled or when she frowned, he could see how much Kayla and her mother looked alike.

"Ha!" Arne said. "*She* was the treasure. And she had such a devilish look about her, I suspected she wanted to test my resolve. Sure, I went out partying, but I followed her when she went to find my treasure. She must have been watching me for weeks, trying to learn where it was in the first place. And then she finally located it, though I made it difficult enough so that we had time to get to know each other."

"Believe me, all he could do was talk about the golden fae. I thought he was just going through a phase." Sid shook his head. "If so, he's still going through it."

That reminded Alton of how he was torn between giving Kayla's locket back or keeping it for a while longer so he could get to know her better.

"Then what happened?" Kayla asked.

"I found her staring in wonderment at the piles of gold."

"He had a dozen of them, mountains of gold. He really worked hard to make all that money. Plus, he was the only one in the area, so he had lots of business. Sid had his own territory farther west. I just stared at all the gold, overwhelmed. I couldn't even decide on any one piece, just stood there eyeing all of it. I heard him arrive, the sound of the flapping of his wings before he settled on the cave floor, but I ignored him."

"She *laughed* when she heard me. I truly believe she wanted to get caught," Arne said.

"But she didn't steal anything," Kayla said, sounding disappointed.

"Oh, she did. She stole my heart. She finally saw a ring, and rescued it from the pile, turned, and faced me and said, 'With this ring, I wed you, great dragon shifter.'"

"Did I say great? I don't remember that part," her mother said, smiling broadly at him.

The others laughed.

"Yes. I remember it well."

"You took a ring from Dad's treasure to give to him?" Kayla asked. "That's precious."

"That's why I loved her so much. She was daring and fun to be with. And then we wed. We had been together for only six months when news reached your mother that your grandmother was dying.

Shortly after that, her father fell ill. Tasha learned she was pregnant, yet she couldn't tell anyone who the father was or that she was married to a dragon shifter. So we saw each other when we could. We hoped the day would finally come when we could share our story with you and anyone else who cared to learn of it, and we could be together again."

"What will happen if I don't wear the locket when I come of age, Mother?" Kayla asked.

"We don't know. None of us do. I think in your heart, you already know the path you'll take. And we are happy for you, whatever you decide," her mother said.

"What about you?" Kayla asked.

"Oh," her mother said, smiling, "I can finally live with the great dragon shifter and enjoy all those piles of gold. No lilac gardeners are in the area, and the castle is just to the south of here, so we will be together. If you live here, we can see each other as quickly as the dragon flies. We don't have to worry whether we'll be accepted there either."

"Father said you would have told me about being a dragon shifter before I made the decision to remain as a golden fae or not."

"Yes, but you might not have believed any of it until your dad could be here to prove it to you. I didn't realize you'd lost your locket and everything that had followed. Not until your dad told me you were participating in the games. And then I had to see Sigrid so I could be there with you and your father."

"Now the pressure will really be on," Kayla said.

"No. You've never been a dragon before. You can't be expected to be an expert overnight. Just enjoy the games," her mother said.

"What about the cottage?"

"If you decide you don't wish to wed Alton and you want to continue to take care of your lavender gardens, the cottage is yours. Otherwise, Tanya would love to live there. Or, you can live with us and plant your gardens where we are."

Alton had been taking everything in, glad things were working out for the family, but he had a question for her dad. "So, you taught me a grand maneuver and if I wanted to use it in the games, it might appear as though I've found where you've been practicing and copied you."

"You made enough changes to the maneuver to call it your own. Maybe those who watch us will think I copied you." Her dad smiled at him.

"No. I would have used it before. It's sheer genius."

Arne laughed. "You'd better marry Alton, Kayla. I don't think anyone could be right for the job otherwise."

She smiled and looked delighted her parents were happy she was courting Alton. But then she frowned, turning her attention to him. "Ohmigoddess, in all the excitement, I forgot about Sigrid's locket. Did you learn anything from the three dragons who had purchased new boots?"

"All of them said the same thing. They didn't find anything in their boots."

"What are we going to do about it?" Kayla asked. "If I don't bring it back to her in payment for her—wait, she didn't do anything for me that I hadn't already done for myself. Still, I want to return it."

"We can't always keep our promises, even as much as we want to," her mother said. "I learned that the hard way when I couldn't stay with your father as I had intended."

"We can look for it in the shop, see if maybe Mr. Fitzwilliam missed seeing it. Maybe it's underneath one of the display stands," Alton said.

"Okay, but my trials are tomorrow. I want to help look for the locket though."

"We'll watch you in the games tomorrow," her mother said. "We wouldn't miss it for the world."

"Right afterward, we can check out the shop," Alton assured

Kayla. And he prayed they would find it still in the shop. How many times had he looked for something and couldn't find it, but another pair of eyes could?

IN THE MIDDLE of the night when Alton was sound asleep, someone knocked on his bedchamber door, jarring him awake. "Yes?"

"It's me, Kayla," she said in a low voice.

He hurried out of bed and threw on a robe to see her. Was she worried about the games tomorrow? Or something else?

"What's wrong, Kayla?" He drew her into the study, but she started to pace and didn't sit down.

"Halloran didn't say no."

"About?"

"About having the locket! He changed the subject. I can't remember all that was said, but I was running it through my mind, unable to sleep, and Ena asked him if he had the locket. He didn't say no. He asked why it was important and made all kinds of other comments."

"It doesn't mean he has it. He could very well have asked the questions, which is typical of him, and forgotten to answer the question Ena had put to him."

"Maybe." Kayla paused. "Okay, here's a really far-out notion. Who was the dragon fae that Sigrid had the crush on? None of us even thought to ask Mr. Fitzwilliam who she had been following into the store."

"Yeah, I agree, that's far out."

She frowned at Alton. "It is. But what if it was Halloran and what if he didn't say he didn't have the locket because he didn't want to lie to Ena? Or if he did, he knew she would see through his lie because she knows him so well? He's your best friend, right?" Kayla persisted.

"Yes, which is why I don't want to go to his keep in the middle of the morning to bother him about this."

"Well, *I'm* not his best friend and it won't bother me to do it."

"And get yourself arrested." Alton sighed. "All right. Meet me downstairs. I'll be right down."

"Thank you."

"You might not thank me if he throws both of us in the dungeon for waking him at this hour for disturbing the peace. *His* peace."

"If he has got Sigrid's locket, it would serve him right."

15

Alton hated waking his friend, who wasn't a morning person in the least. Alton woke Halloran's butler, and the man stated he would not disturb Halloran—that Alton had the honors if he so chose. Kayla waited down below in the foyer, while Alton went upstairs and knocked on Halloran's bedchamber door.

"The world better be at war for anyone to wake me at this ungoddess hour," Halloran growled, but he didn't come to the door right away.

Alton was afraid he'd gone back to sleep. "Halloran, it's me. I have to ask you a question."

"Then ask already and go away."

"Do you have the falcon fae's locket? Sigrid's?"

Silence followed.

Alton quickly came to several conclusions about the silence. Halloran had it and was trying to think of a way to dispute it or come up with a reason why he was keeping it. He had gone back to sleep. Or he was so annoyed Alton would wake him to ask such a question, that he wasn't about to answer him.

Suddenly, the door jerked open. Alton hadn't expected that and jumped a little. Halloran's eyes were narrowed, and he was frowning as if he had been woken to fight in a war. "Yes. Now go away."

Alton's jaw dropped. Kayla had been right. "Sigrid has a crush on you?" Not that Halloran's having the locket had anything to do with that, but Alton wondered if Halloran was the one Mr. Fitzwilliam had been referring to when he said Sigrid had liked one of the dragons.

Halloran grunted.

"Give it to me so I can let Kayla have it so that she can return it to her friend."

"What will you pay me for it?"

Alton folded his arms. "It belongs to her. I took it from her when she tried to take Kayla's locket from me."

"I've heard Sigrid was being devious about the whole situation. Why would you want to give it back to her?"

"Because I took it and Kayla promised."

"You know the truth. Now leave me to sleep."

"Halloran—"

Halloran closed the door in his face and the bolt slid across.

Furious with him, Alton didn't know what to do about it. He transported downstairs to tell Kayla what had happened, but she was gone, and the butler said, "She left, sir. She heard what was said as loud as Halloran was growling about it."

Alton frowned. "She didn't say where she was going?"

"No, sir. She just said, 'Fine.' And then she left."

Alton knew it wasn't fine with her. Did she intend to return later and steal it from Halloran? If she did, she could be in real trouble. He returned to his keep, but when he knocked on her bedchamber door, there was no answer. Concerned, he opened the door and called into the dark room, "Kayla?"

No answer still. He turned on a light and went to the bed where the curtains were closed, expecting her to be lying there, arms folded, her face a mask of fury. The bed was empty.

"Kayla!" he said in exasperation. Where would she have gone? To see Sigrid? To tell her who had the locket but wouldn't give it up? He figured that was as good a bet as any.

KAYLA KNOCKED on Sigrid's door, having to do this, even though she would need to be at the games in just a couple of hours. She wanted Sigrid to know where her locket was, just in case they had trouble getting it back from Halloran.

Sigrid came to the door, raised her brows at Kayla, then left the door standing open while she retreated to the kitchen. "What's wrong?"

"Sorry for coming so early, but we finally discovered where your locket is." Kayla shut the door behind her.

"I see you have yours back." Sigrid made them some tea.

"Yes. But long story short, Halloran has got yours. We just learned of it, but he's not giving it back."

"What are you going to do about it?"

"Sigrid, why didn't you tell me that I'm a dragon shifter besides being a golden fae?"

"My mother swore me to secrecy, once I overheard your mother talking to mine about making the locket more powerful. I couldn't let you go on thinking you were only a golden fae when you were clearly interested in the dragons. And then one in particular."

"Why did you try to steal the locket from Alton?"

"To hide it away. I wanted to make sure it stayed safe, but that you had a chance to really get to know Alton. It didn't work, and he stole my locket instead."

"And that was the reason you helped me 'become a dragon.'"

Sigrid smiled. "I thought that was genius, didn't you?"

Kayla smiled. "Yeah. It was very clever of you. What of the transporting?"

"It was tied in with the locket. I had to give you the ability to transport on your own."

Kayla felt the gold necklace in her pocket. "So I can't transport if I don't wear the locket?"

"Once you come of age, you'll be able to do so without it." Sigrid brought over the tray of tea. "That comes naturally."

Kayla let out her breath with relief.

"You have doubts whether you're going to wear the locket when you come of age?"

"I care for Alton, and I might lose my dragon shifter abilities if I choose the golden fae abilities over that. What will you lose if you don't have your locket back on time?"

"Can I tell you a secret?"

Kayla nodded. "Of course."

"The deadline has passed. I have come of age, and I can fae transport again."

Kayla felt terrible about it. "Ohmigoddess. I've failed you."

"You and Tanya have been my friends when no one else wanted to be. You were willing to face danger to get both our lockets back. Not just yours. You can't know how much I've wanted to have friends when everyone has avoided me or put me down because of what I can do."

"What have you lost because I didn't get your locket back to you in time?" Kayla didn't think the loss of Sigrid's abilities was worth that.

"I have lost nothing and gained everything. Invite me to watch the trials. I will get my locket back."

"It's done," Kayla said. "Wait, come stay with us at Alton's castle. I'm sure he won't mind having you. And let's ask Tanya too."

"Ask Tanya what?" Tanya asked, coming out of the guestroom, rubbing her eyes.

"You're here."

"Yeah, having a sleepover."

A knock at the door made them all turn to look at it.

"Alton, I'm guessing," Sigrid said.

While Kayla went to get the door, Sigrid explained to Tanya what was going on.

As soon as Kayla opened the door and saw a tired looking dragon, she said, "Alton." She was worried then that he would be upset with her for taking off without a word to him.

"I hoped I would find you here," he said.

She took his hand and led him into the cottage, and she introduced him, as if they didn't all know who he was. "I asked if they would come and stay with us at your keep, if that's all right with you. Then they can watch the games." Not that she wanted them to see how poorly she could do, but she wanted her friends there who she thought would enjoy the games as much as she did.

"Of course. You're both welcome to stay with us for as long as you like."

"After the games, I'll be returning home," Kayla said. Alton looked astonished, but she shook her head. "We need to court longer. What if I found another dragon who suited me more?"

"You wouldn't." Then he smiled at Sigrid and Tanya. "Come join us." Then he pulled Kayla into his arms and transported her back to his castle. He pressed his mouth against hers as they traveled in a void of blackness, and she held him tight and kissed him back.

"You are so sure of yourself."

He laughed. "That's because I know you love me."

As soon as they reached his keep, he roused Ferdinand to let his staff know they were having two more guests, important friends of Kayla's. His butler quickly got hold of a couple of the maids to prepare the rooms. "Go to bed, Kayla. I'll greet the ladies and let them know where their rooms are, but if you don't get more sleep, you'll be too groggy to perform well at the games," Alton said.

She didn't care. All she cared about was that her friends were here, her family was here, and Alton was the dragon of her heart.

AT THE GAMES the next morning, Kayla was a nervous wreck, trying not to think about her turn. Because she had come in with the lowest of passable scores at the prequalification trials, she and the others who were at the bottom of the ranking went last. To get her nervousness under control, she would have liked to have stayed away, but if someone fell out at the last minute, she might be substituted, so she had to watch all the contestants participate. Since the first had done best, they looked like they were ready for the next level in the games.

She was certain she wouldn't do half as well, though she would give it her best shot. Her mother's words to her, "no matter what, have fun," stuck with Kayla, though in the beginning, she was just going through her paces, trying so hard not to make a mistake. Every lesson she had been taught kept coming up in her thoughts as she hoped she did all this right. She didn't hope to win, but just to make the best score that she could. Next year, after a year of practicing, watch out!

While she flew the course where she was supposed to pick up different weighted objects from a beach ball to a bowling ball, she thought she was doing really well. She was moving much faster than she had during the prequalification trials. She hadn't missed grabbing the objects from the baskets or tops of pillars like the first time she went to grasp them, which helped her speed considerably. Before, she had been trying to play catch up with the other dragons during the whole trial. During the real game, she was doing much better. She knew it all had to do with Alton's, Olaf's, and her father's lessons.

Her mother had cautioned her about taking unnecessary

risks, which she had expected. Then her father and Alton had worried about her too. She reminded them this was only one level up from the beginners. They reminded her it wasn't the beginners' game, and she was as new as they come. But she could tell both Alton and her father were proud of her for giving it a try.

She had picked up half of the objects she needed to finish this game, when a high gust of wind coming out of nowhere knocked her off-balance, and she did a roll to compensate for her mistake. Not to gain her speed, but in a fun way, reacting to her blunder. She hadn't done one before, only watched her father and Alton doing them over and over again, and she had no idea if she'd done it right. Or if it might even disqualify her. It also slowed her down so that she was playing catch up again. She told herself not to panic. She would make even more mistakes if she freaked: lose the object, fumble with it, pass the next place she had to set the object on in her attempt to make up her time.

It didn't help that her family and Alton were watching her. Nor that all her new friends and old were too, silently wishing her the best because during the actual games, everyone in the stands had to be absolutely quiet so the contestants weren't distracted. The experts would have no problem with it. But for those in the other games, it could make a difference in their performance, she suspected. She could just imagine people shouting for their favorites and instead of paying attention to what she was doing, she would be listening to see if she could hear Alton's voice above all the rest.

For now, she was trying to catch up to the olive-green dragon to her right, and the emerald green dragon to her left. She couldn't watch the other dragons' progress since they were too far away. Because of her speed—though she'd nearly compensated for being behind—she overshot her eleventh drop basket. She did a flip, so annoyed with herself, she hadn't realized she'd done anything so wild until after she had done it, hoping again the judges wouldn't disqualify her.

She dropped the item into the basket, but she was too high, and it bounced! *Right* out of the basket. She swooped down and grabbed it, twisting around with the use of her tail until she was over the basket, closer this time, stretching her legs out, and dropped it again.

She hovered for a second, worried the ball would just hop right back out of its own accord, but this time, it stayed put. Hovering in place made her more behind than before. She dove after the other dragons who were already at their baskets, and she was certain she would never catch up this time. She remembered her mother's words to have fun. And so she did. She didn't do what she was supposed to do, the regular routine for speed and agility. She experimented with some of the moves her father had taught Alton, and some he'd shown her, slowing her down even more—twists and turns and loops.

She picked up the pace and thought about her lavender fields, growing them, breathing in their intoxicating scent, drinking the calming tea made from the flowers, and was at peace. She couldn't win at this rate because she was too far behind. But she realized there would always be next year, and she could do practice sessions with Alton and her father and Olaf, if he wanted to work with her further, and maybe next year or the next, she would have an unbeatable score.

She finally finished replacing the objects in their original places and hurried back to end the game. She was done, glad to have participated, but glad it was nearly over, and hated being the last one in. The other dragons must have left already, yet everyone observing seemed to still be in the stands.

She dropped down before the judge's table, did a dragon's version of a bow, then shifted and saw all the smiles on their faces.

Well, she might not have been the fastest, most accurate dragon in the competition, but she hoped she'd made it fun for the judges to watch too.

Then she headed for the stands, wondering why no one was leaving. That's when she saw the other dragons heading in. The two green ones, a brown one, and a red. She paused, staring at them in disbelief. How in the world had she gotten ahead of them?

Her family and friends quickly surrounded her, giving her hugs, and just shaking their heads.

Her mom was grinning. "I think you were the only dragon participating who had fun. And it showed."

"It's not all about how fast you move, but how you play the game," Alton said. "Even if the judges didn't like that you deviated from the course, you made up for it by coming in first in speed and using advanced techniques to make fun of your mistakes so that it looked like you had done it on purpose! Brilliant, really."

She laughed. "I could have only done it because of watching you and my dad and Olaf, and all the help you gave me."

"You look so unstressed at the end. What were you thinking about?" her mother asked.

"My lavender fields." Kayla thought Alton looked a little disappointed that she had not been thinking of him. She took his hand and squeezed. "But before that, I was thinking how much I wanted to have fun, just like you told me to do, Mom. And of course all about the teachings that Alton and my father and Olaf had shared with me that helped me to make it fun."

Ena disappeared, then came back and gave her another big hug. "I just checked the boards and you're in first place!"

Kayla knees weakened, and her eyes filled with tears, though they were happy tears. "No, I goofed up so many times."

"You made up for it," Alton said, "in a way that only you could."

Then Kayla saw Halloran standing off to the side watching them, arms folded, and he was wearing a smirk. Before anyone could know what she was about to do, she transported to where he was and poked him in the chest with her finger. "Give Sigrid's locket back to her."

Halloran smiled, but she wasn't the only one watching him, waiting to see what he would do. Kayla was surprised Sigrid didn't take him to task.

"Come on, Sigrid. We have some business to take care of." Halloran was dangling her locket from his hand.

"Aren't you afraid I'll put you under my spell?" Sigrid asked, walking toward him, a wicked smile in place.

Halloran had to be the dragon Sigrid had the crush on. But then she saw Kiernan and smiled at him.

Kiernan? He had been in the boot shop buying boots that day also.

"See ya later, girlfriends," Sigrid said to Kayla and Tanya.

Kayla didn't know what to think, but she suspected Sigrid could take care of Halloran and the situation with her locket better than she could.

Alton joined Kayla. "Looks to me like something else is going on behind the scenes."

"With Halloran or"—Kayla glanced in Kiernan's direction, while he was watching Sigrid and Halloran walk off toward the forest—"him?"

Alton chuckled under his breath. "Who knows. Tonight, we feast about your success. We can watch to see how Willow does in her games, the day after tomorrow. Your father said he would show both Olaf and me more maneuvers tomorrow."

"We'll watch. I picked up a lot by watching you this last time."

"Okay, works for me. I think I do better when I know you're watching."

She smiled, loving that he felt that way, but she couldn't help wondering what was really going on with the falcon fae.

16

The next day, the guys practiced for hours, even Kayla's Uncle Sid, while the ladies made a picnic lunch and served it at noon. Kayla wasn't certain who would win in the competition for the top slot in the expert games as much as all the guys seemed to do well. When the games continued the next day for Willow's class, they were all there to watch her and congratulate her afterward. She had come in second place and couldn't have been more thrilled.

She didn't seem to mind at all that she had come in second and finally told Kayla the reason why. "If I had come in first, I would be up against you in the final game."

"What?" Kayla gaped at her. "*What* final game? The experts go tomorrow, and I thought that was it."

"Nope. They have one final game. All first-place winners, no matter what their level, are pitted against each other. The game is weighted so that the experts still have to take on the expert tasks, and so forth. Any mistakes in the final game can cost the participant his place in the final bid for power. Although you will still be in the hall of fame for this year's games as a first-place winner in your category."

No way could Kayla win, she didn't think, if she had to play the games without making any mistakes. She sighed. Oh, well, like with anything, she would do the best she could. She hoped she didn't fail too miserably.

ALTON WAS NOT ready for this. Not with the way he had practiced before the games. He had stretched his muscles way too much after injuring himself, and now he was afraid he wouldn't do that well. Yet, everything was riding on his performing well. Not only did he want to impress Kayla, but he wanted to ensure that her family saw him as a perfectly eligible mate for her. He was always really competitive, but this time, he didn't care about winning as much as pleasing them.

"Alton," Kayla said, kissing his cheek before he had to go, "I love you."

He expected her to tell him not to push too hard or to wish him well, or anything other than that. He hadn't had anyone tell him that since his mother died, and yet this was not the same as a mother's love, and all his aches and pains seemed to fade away.

"What happened to checking out the other dragons first? Courting me longer? Staying at your mother's cottage?" He smiled down at her, not meaning it at all, but he still had to tease her.

"Oh, I can do that, of course. But I wanted to tell you I loved you first, just so you know."

He couldn't help the tears that filled his eyes, and he cupped her face and kissed her mouth. Then he dragged her into his arms and hugged her tight. "I love you right back, Kayla."

And when he released her as one of the men running the games called his name again, he saw her eyes were just as misty as his were.

"Break a leg," she said.

"Only humans would think that was a good luck saying."

"I think the fae started it."

He laughed, squeezed her hand, and hurried off to do this. And turned into a purple dragon. He guessed whatever spell Kayla had over him, not Sigrid, had sealed his fate.

Brett had gone against Kiernan, Olaf, and some others. Olaf won in that round. Alton wondered if it had been due to Kayla's dad's teachings. After that, her Uncle Sid, Ena, and Halloran had been up against several others. Sid had come out on top and beat Halloran by a point. This time, Arne, Alton, and the remaining dragons were pitted against each other. Then they would do the routines requiring a partner.

Alton thought he was doing great. No mistakes so far, and his speed and agility were good. But he was aching something fierce when he did the roll. Suddenly, a sharp pain shrieked through the area where the bolt had struck him, making him lose his balance, his concentration, and his ability to fly.

Screams from the spectators filled the air, but just as soon as Alton fell, Kayla knew it wasn't part of his routine, shifted, and went to his rescue. The other participants this round were busy completing their routines and didn't see the disaster unfolding.

Olaf, too, knew his friend was in trouble, and shifted, then flew off to help Alton. Kayla was worried sick about Alton's injury, but she was also concerned how this would impact on how he viewed himself in front of his friends, her family, and most of all her. He should know they all loved him no matter what.

Brett and Ena had quickly come to his aid as well, talons on his tail, legs, Kayla's arms around his neck as she flapped her wings like the rest of them, hauling him off to his castle. He was dead to the world.

As soon as they reached his castle, Ferdinand rushed out. "What has happened?"

"He overexerted himself in the practice sessions. He hasn't

healed enough," Ena said, after she had shifted, and the others carried the dragon inside. "Alton, wake up. Shift so it's easier to get you to your room."

His eyes opened and he stared at her, at Kayla still in her dragon form, at the mural of dragons flying across the tall ceiling in his keep. He groaned, shifted, and they nearly dropped him. "Don't tell me I passed out at the games."

Kayla shifted, kissed his cheek, and found it hot. "He's running a fever. Get a healer."

His maid, Doreen, was already headed out the door.

Kiernan, Olaf, Halloran, and Uncle Sid were suddenly there, helping to carry Alton to his room. Kayla pulled his bedcovers aside, and then took off his boots and socks before she pulled the covers over him.

They heard everyone else downstairs after that—Willow, Tanya, Kayla's mother and father, and Sigrid returning too.

"Isn't anyone watching the games?" Alton asked, as Kayla ran a wet cloth over his brow, one of his maids standing nearby with a wash basin.

"They're over, old man," Halloran said. "Didn't I tell you that you should sit this one out?"

"How did I do?" Alton asked, and Kayla cringed to hear anyone say that he had been disqualified.

Everyone chuckled.

Arne said, "Spectacularly. That was a maneuver I never thought anyone could perform so well during a game."

Alton laughed. "Bad huh?"

"Yeah," Halloran said, "but I told you so. Next time you'll listen to me. Even so, you had the sympathy of a couple of judges."

Alton reached for Kayla's hand and squeezed it. "At least I won't be flying against you."

"Why didn't anyone tell me I would have to fly in another game against all the other first place winners?" Then Kayla frowned. "Who won in that last round?"

"Your father won in the last round and two points higher than his brother," her mother said, rubbing Arne's arm, smiling.

"Oh, great. I just meet my father and now I have to compete against him."

"No, not against me." Arne patted her shoulder. "Against yourself, but you do what you have to do. You'll do fine. It doesn't matter how well you do, just that you do your best."

"Don't you go doing poorly just so I won't feel bad," Kayla said.

"You could have in my case," Alton said. "I wouldn't have minded."

Everyone laughed again.

And then the healer was there, ushering everyone out of the room, except for Kayla and the maid.

"How bad is he?"

"He needs to rest. He haoos been training constantly, Doreen said. He never should have been on such a schedule. I hadn't even okayed his being in the games!" the doctor said.

Kayla frowned at Alton.

He shrugged, winced, and let out his breath. "How could I not when I had to impress so many?"

"Me. Only me. And you already did that when you helped Ena and Brett rescue Mark and the maid. If you hadn't taken a bolt, I probably wouldn't have had time to rescue Muriel. I could have been the one injured instead."

"Did you ever learn what happened between Halloran and Sigrid?"

"No. But she's wearing her locket again."

"He needs to rest," the physician said. "And though I would insist he not go to watch the last of the games tomorrow, I know he would disobey me because you will be in them." He sighed. "Good luck tomorrow, and I'll be on hand in case you need my further assistance. The medicine should help. Make sure he drinks plenty of fluids, but most of all, make sure he rests."

"Thanks, Doctor." Now Kayla really felt guilty about waking Alton in the middle of the night to learn if Halloran had Sigrid's locket. They'd been busy ever after that, and he definitely hadn't had time to rest, especially as much as he'd been pushing himself to do well in the practice sessions with her father.

Once Alton was asleep, she joined the others downstairs, Ferdinand already having given the orders to prepare a feast.

She saw Sigrid sitting between Halloran and Kiernan and she again wondered if one of them was the one Sigrid had the crush on, or someone else they didn't know. Someone new to the games. And how did Sigrid get Halloran to give up her locket?

That night, Kayla couldn't sleep. Not only was she worried about the games, she was concerned about Alton sitting in on them to watch her participate. She wished she could ask Sigrid or even the doctor to give Alton something that would make him sleep well through the games so he would feel better by the time she returned. She was certain he would be upset with her, so she skipped that notion.

~

THE NEXT DAY came before Kayla was fully awake or ready. She was glad to see Alton eating, though he still looked a little flushed.

"Are you sure you don't want to stay home and wait for me? It would take the pressure off me." She smiled at him.

He laughed. "No way. I have to see you and your father competing in the final games."

Despite Alton's objections, the doctor sat next to him in the reviewing stands, ready to take care of him in a medical emergency. And all his friends and hers and her family sat around him as if he might die on the spot if they weren't seated near him. She cherished all of them for the way they were taking care of him.

Her father said to her before they flew in the last of the games, "Think of your lavender gardens. It worked before. Remember all that I taught you. And take care. Don't kill yourself in the games. Alton needs you."

Just as much as she needed him. "Good luck, Dad. If anyone can win, it's you."

"I already won when I caught your mom admiring my treasure, and she brought home another treasure worth more than all the jewels in the world."

"Thanks, Dad." Kayla gave him a hug, and then waited for the bell to ring. Then she saw Willow in line, and she couldn't have been more surprised.

Willow smiled at her and shrugged. "The guy who came in first partied too much last night. He's sicker than a dog this morning, even though he wanted to fly no matter what. They gave him a sobriety test and he flew into a tree." She smiled again. "So I guess we're competing, or not, but I want to wish you the best of luck."

"You too, Willow. Thanks for being my friend."

"Same here. You're the most interesting friend I've ever had."

"Thanks, I think."

They both laughed, then shifted, and the bell rang. Kayla jumped a little, and then she and the others were off. Since each of the courses was based on the level of ability, the two junior courses were shorter. As long as she and the beginner didn't make any major mistakes, they would be done sooner than the three other participants in the more advanced games. She was at least glad for that.

She considered what her father had said about thinking of her lavender fields as a way to relax and get through this. Instead, she thought of Alton and how she and he could go on missions together and add piles of gold in the cave where the wolf shifters guarded it.

Gold. And more of it. It wasn't that she was greedy, but she was just wired that way. Between being a golden fae and a dragon shifter, she loved the idea. More than that, she loved the notion she would be with Alton. And she was glad her mother would be with her father.

Before she realized it, she was halfway through the course. She hadn't made any mistakes yet. At least she didn't think she had. Thrilled she was doing so well, she didn't feel she was in competition with anyone. Though she did have the thought that she and her dad made up two-fifths of the competitors. Forty percent were pretty good odds.

She began thinking of her lavender garden and how she could try growing it at the castle gardens instead.

"She's a golden fae! Not a dragon fae!" someone in the stands shouted.

Kayla lost her concentration at once, dropping the heavier ball, missing the basket, figuring Halloran was going to attempt to arrest her. If he could catch her. But then her heart nearly stopped when she saw the person pointing at her mother, not at Kayla. Ohmigoddess!

Uncle Sid socked the man in the nose. And a fight broke out.

One of the judges shouted, "Continue the games. Halloran, arrest that man!"

Which man? Uncle Sid for assaulting the other? And then her mother, once they realized she was truly a golden fae?

Kayla swooped down and caught the dropped ball, placed it where it belonged, and finished the rest of her games, not caring whether she won anything at all. All she cared about was her mother. She was certain her father would feel the same way. When she ended the games, she quickly bowed to the judges, shifted, and hurried for the stands. Halloran was gone. So was the man who had made the outburst.

Uncle Sid had his arm protectively wrapped around Kayla's mother's shoulders. She breathed a sigh of relief. Alton was holding her mother's hand, smiling. When he saw Kayla, he quickly rose, looked dizzy, pale, teetered a bit, and she hurried to pull him down on the seat again so he wouldn't collapse.

They were quiet. She knew she'd lost because she'd dropped the ball. The guy in the beginners' group came in after she did, even though his course was shorter than hers. She wondered if she made a mistake and missed returning something to its place. The next contestant returned, then Willow, and finally her father.

There was a long pause as Willow and Kayla's father joined them while the judges discussed the matter. Halloran returned to the stands and smiled at Kayla and inclined his head toward her mother.

Kayla couldn't believe it. He had to know her mother was truly a golden fae, just like Kayla had been when Halloran had first met her. Now he was ready to cover for her mother?

"Despite the interruption in the games, our winner today," the judge said, "is Arne of Dresden. He wins the treasure, but all our first-place winners will have a place of honor also and will receive a locket of gold."

Kayla jumped up from the bench and hugged her dad before her mother could. "We know what you need to be doing from now on. Teaching the rest of us your techniques."

"I would be happy to. The chest of treasure I will give to you as a dowry, Kayla."

"You mean it goes to my husband when I marry?"

Alton chuckled. "It can all be yours, as the start of your own pile of treasure."

"You mean I don't get to share in yours?" she asked, teasing him.

"All of mine is all of yours."

"Okay, but really, I only want the gold. You can have all the rest."

He groaned, and she knew he wasn't feeling well still as warm as he was. She meant to take him right back to his bed as he stood and pulled her close, kissing her forehead. "I didn't think I would ever say this to anyone, but I'm happy to give up all my gold to you, if it makes you happy."

"I knew you were the one for me when I told you I planned to steal all your gold, and you challenged me to do so."

"Tomorrow is your big day, Kayla," her mother said.

Kayla nodded. "I want to go home tomorrow, but I'll stay with Alton tonight."

Flushed from the fever, Alton said, "I'm going with you tomorrow."

"If you're feeling better."

"I will be."

She didn't think he really believed that but wanted to come no matter what. Her family, Tanya, Sigrid, and Alton returned to his castle. Though he requested a feast in honor of Kayla's father and also for Kayla for their success at the games, Alton didn't eat much. She suspected he just wasn't feeling well enough. She made him go to bed early. Instead of visiting with her family, she stayed with him, talking until he fell asleep.

THE NEXT DAY, the whole lot of them went to Kayla and her mom's cottage. Sigrid had given all the dragons golden fae auras so they would blend in if anyone showed up and found all the dragon fae there.

Kayla considered her lavender gardens, still dormant, and her mother's lilac gardens also. She sighed, feeling bad to leave them behind.

"I'm taking my gardens with me," her mother said. "Arne's staff is moving them today before the queen learns of it."

That gave Kayla an idea. She glanced in Alton's direction and smiled. He laughed and bowed. "Whatever your heart desires."

"You have always taken care of your gardens. What if the magic only makes it easier, or better, but even without it, you would be able to produce a fair amount?" her mother asked.

"So what do we do?" Kayla was excited about the prospect. She would do anything, work even harder if she could keep her gardens, and yet still be a dragon shifter.

"I'm making beef ribs, baked potatoes, and a salad, and lavender tea," her mother said.

"And I made a lavender cake for the party." Sigrid smiled.

"Yeah, and I made lavender bread," Tanya said.

"Do you really want me to have my staff move your fields of flowers?" Alton asked.

"Yes. I do, more than anything else in the world."

"Okay. I have plenty of room for them. I will be right back."

"Thank you, Alton."

"Thank you, for making the choice to stay with me."

They kissed, and then he finally released her, noting her father and Uncle Sid were watching them, looking like a protective family. Kayla's mom had already gone inside with Tanya and Sigrid to make the meal. "I'll be right back."

Alton couldn't have been gladder she had chosen him, and he would do everything he could to make her happy. He transported home, still feeling under the weather, his fever coming and going and right now it was in full force. But he wouldn't have given up the chance to help celebrate Kayla's coming out.

Not only did he solicit his soldiers to help move her plants, Alton found Willow there, getting ready to return to her own home, but she wanted to say goodbye to Kayla first. He invited her also to attend Kayla's coming-out celebration.

"Oh, wow, I so want to be her best friend. She truly was under-cover! That is so cool."

"Let's get Ena and Brett too."

As soon as Halloran arrived, he was going to ask Ena and Brett to come celebrate with them. Halloran was there, and Alton had to invite him too, though he wasn't sure how receptive his friend would be about venturing into the golden fae territory. Alton had forgotten he was wearing the golden fae aura when he arrived at Ena and Brett's castle, until Mark commented on it.

"Sigrid, the falcon fae, gave me the spell." Alton quickly changed his aura back to dragon fae, surprised that no one else had mentioned it before this. He supposed his own staff guessed what was going on. "She can do the same for all of you while you come to the party."

"Let's go. We'll bring more food, my cook, and the rest of my staff to help out and to celebrate. They love Kayla for saving Muriel's life," Ena said.

"Me too," Mark said. Then his face reddened. "I mean, I want to go too because Muriel is a friend and so is Kayla for saving her."

"Me too," Bryan said, hurrying to join them, Hannah, the other fae seer in tow.

"Not me. I've seen enough fae to last a lifetime," the human girl grouched, scowling.

"She doesn't really mean it." Mark gave her a dark look to watch her words while she was around the fae.

"Lock her up," Ena said. "She doesn't need to be at the party with us if she's going to be a pill about it."

And then in a huge mass, the dragon fae arrived at the cottage to see Kayla, half of Alton's soldiers digging up the plants and preparing to move them, while the other half of his men remained at Alton's castle and were digging holes for the plants' new home.

Likewise, Arne's men had come to remove Kayla's mother's plants. It was sad in a way, though the plants weren't blossoming quite yet anyway, so it was a good time to move them. But he was certain that Kayla, and her mother even, would miss their cottage lifestyle among the flowers. Kayla would have tons of help and so would her mother, in their new gardens. They wouldn't have to do it all themselves. He just hoped that her mother was right, and Kayla could still grow her flowers successfully.

He wanted to ask her when the plants would begin to flower, but he was letting her visit with all the ladies inside right now. He thought maybe she and her mother couldn't watch their gardens being dug up.

But then they heard horses off in the distance, and Alton quickly went inside to tell Sigrid she needed to hide all the dragon faes' aura.

Sigrid came outside and saw all the men. "Are you kidding me? No way. I don't have the power to offer that much fae magic to everyone."

"It's too late anyway." Alton saw the streamers of the lead soldier, his braided uniform revealing he was part of the royal house. "I think we're in for some trouble."

The ladies all joined them, and Kayla gasped. "The queen is coming. She'll see we're digging up the fields. Not to mention that all these dragon fae are here."

"Even if we had them leave before she got here, she would still see the mess the gardens are in and know we are moving them," her mother said.

"Then we make a stand, though I don't want Alton and Dad's soldiers to fight them," Kayla said.

"We make a deal," Alton said. "A bargain that we will continue to sell the lavender and lilac to the queen and anyone else in the realm."

"Sounds good to me," Sigrid said.

"Why didn't anyone tell us to bring a sword instead of shovels," Mark grumbled.

Everyone was watching the queen's procession. She must have had around twenty courtiers with her and another ten soldiers.

They paused about a quarter of a mile away, and a man rode forth.

"That's Easton, her advisor," Tasha said.

"The queen is visibly outraged that you have brought all these dragon fae here to uproot your gardens when she came to congratulate your daughter on coming of age," Easton said to Tasha as he grew closer to them, his shoulder-length gray hair blowing in the breeze.

"My husband is a dragon shifter fae," Tasha said, her words spoken proudly. "My daughter is both dragon shifter and golden fae. We will continue to sell our flower products if the queen wishes it. But I have lived long enough away from my husband, and my daughter will be marrying the dragon shifter you see here." She motioned to Alton, who inclined his head.

"We will have to have a peace treaty between our people before that can happen," Easton said, frowning.

"I would put in a good word with the queen," Halloran said. "I am Dragon at Arms."

"And I would as well," Brett said, since the queen appreciated him for saving her life.

Easton bowed his head a little, then turned his horse and galloped back to the queen with the news.

"She is often fair-minded," Tasha said. "Hopefully, we can come to terms."

"If not, our queen and our people will be delighted to buy your flower goods," Alton said.

"Well, I'll just have to skip across the river and buy from you then." Sigrid sounded as though the idea really appealed to her.

"Me too." Tanya gave Kayla a hug. "I will miss being so close to you."

"Nonsense. You can fae transport anytime to the castle and stay with us. And I can come back to visit you here also."

Easton rode back to them. "The queen is agreeable. As long as there are no tariffs imposed on the products, she will wait to see the peace agreement that you can get your queen to agree to. Good day."

When he rode off, Kayla said, "She's not going to like that we're not paying taxes to her." Then she turned to her mother and father. "Dad has a castle nearby?"

Tasha laughed and gave her a hug. "Yes, and it was going to be a surprise for when you came of age."

They watched the queen and her entourage ride back to her castle, no congratulations to Kayla. "She probably wouldn't have liked hearing I came in first place on the dragon trials in my category either."

They all laughed.

Alton hoped they could have peace between their people, trade for many things, not just Kayla and her mother's flowers. It would be good even for the dragon shifters to take on quests that the queen or her people needed them to. As long as no golden fae tried to steal from the dragon shifters, present company excluded, and no dragon shifters tried to steal from the golden fae, again present company excluded, he thought it could work.

All that aside, he knew being with Kayla was the best thing ever as he wrapped his arms around her, and they watched her fields being moved to the castle grounds, the start of a new and wondrous beginning.

"I love you," Kayla said, looking up at Alton. "Now that I can't wear my locket, I feel naked. I will have to find another."

"The gold locket you received for first place?"

"No," she kept his arms locked around her and watched them digging up her plants. "I will have to see what else you have in all that beautiful treasure of yours."

Alton laughed. "I knew it. So when are you going to start bringing in more gold too?"

"I'm ready."

He really wasn't ready to take her with him on any missions where she could be the one injured by fae seers shooting bolts. "Tonight...," Alton said.

"She is staying with us," Arne said, sounding like a strict father. "And you may call on her anytime you wish."

"I have to take care of my gardens," she said.

"And you can, all day long. But at night?" her father said.

"Then that means we go for a fast courtship." Alton winked at her, but he meant what he said. He truly wanted to be with her, always.

Kayla smiled at Alton. "First, I pick up all the gold I want to wear."

"As a dragon shifter, we don't display our gold."

"As a golden fae, we do. Then, I have to pick out a ring for you. So everyone knows you are mine."

"Out of my own treasure?" He lifted a brow.

She shrugged. "It worked for my mom with my dad. And then..."

"We get married."

EPILOGUE

Kayla really planned to enjoy a courtship with Alton for a few weeks at least. That lasted two days. They were hopelessly in love, and she had come of age, after all.

Adorned in all her gold and proud to be a golden fae with her dragon fae aura, she and Alton had married in grand style, a peace treaty between their peoples negotiated, and the only issue that remained? If she could see any flowers growing in her lavender fields.

She was looking again, Alton feeling great now, and he came out to find her. "We have a mission. I thought I would take you on any that I was notified of so you could learn how it's done. Though, all are so different from each other, whoever knows?" He paused and crouched before a plant. "Kayla!"

She was already headed back toward him, ready to go on the mission when he began eyeing a plant. Hope renewed, she ran toward him and when she reached the plant, she saw the beginnings of life.

"You have done it!" Alton said.

"We have done it!" Because without Alton being there, having his people move the plants and plant them again, she could never have done it. The locket her mother had given her was tucked away in a gold box on the chest in their bedchamber.

He grabbed her up in his arms and twirled her around, then stopped and kissed her. "I believe I have a real gold mine in you."

She laughed. "But I have all your mountains of treasure." Though the real treasure was the love they had for each other. "What is the mission?"

"A golden fae has stolen some of my...our treasure," Alton said.

"A golden fae?" She couldn't believe it! "The flowers will be here when we get back. Let's be dragons."

ACKNOWLEDGMENTS

Thanks to the following fae who gave me all kinds of fabulous ideas for the Golden Fae story: Erin Wolf, Lisa Moody, Melodie Luckett, Elizabeth Patti, Ashley Smith, Michelle Graham, April Kirkland, Mary Bannian, Aprille Shadowspeak, Tamara Henson, and Terri White!

ABOUT THE AUTHOR

USA Today bestselling and award-winning author **Terry Spear** has written over a hundred paranormal romance novels, young adult, and medieval Highland historical romances. Her first werewolf romance, *Heart of the Wolf,* was named a 2008 *Publishers Weekly*'s Best Book of the Year, and her subsequent titles have garnered high praise and hit the *USA Today* bestseller list. A retired officer of the U.S. Army Reserves, Terry lives in Spring, Texas, where she is working on her next werewolf romance, shapeshifting jaguars, cougar shifters, vampires, hot Highlanders, and having fun with her young adult novels, helping with her granddaughter and grandson and raising two havanese.

For more information, please visit her website at: www.terryspear.com,

Blog: https://terryspearbooks.blog/

Follow her for new releases and book deals: www.bookbub.com/authors/terry-spear

Twitter: @TerrySpear.

Facebook: http://www.facebook.com/terry.spear.

ALSO BY TERRY SPEAR

Adult Titles

Romantic Suspense: Deadly Fortunes, In the Dead of the Night, Relative Danger, Bound by Danger

***

The Highlanders Series: His Wild Highland Lass (novella), Vexing the Highlander (novella), Winning the Highlander's Heart, The Accidental Highland Hero, Highland Rake, Taming the Wild Highlander, The Highlander, Her Highland Hero, The Viking's Highland Lass, My Highlander

Other historical romances: Lady Caroline & the Egotistical Earl, A Ghost of a Chance at Love

***

Heart of the Wolf Series: Heart of the Wolf, Destiny of the Wolf, To Tempt the Wolf, Legend of the White Wolf, Seduced by the Wolf, Wolf Fever, Heart of the Highland Wolf, Dreaming of the Wolf, A SEAL in Wolf's Clothing, A Howl for a Highlander, A Highland Werewolf Wedding, A SEAL Wolf Christmas, Silence of the Wolf, Hero of a Highland Wolf, A Highland Wolf Christmas; SEAL Wolf Hunting; A Silver Wolf Christmas, SEAL Wolf in Too Deep, Alpha Wolf Need Not Apply, Between a Wolf and a Hard Place, SEAL Wolf Undercover, Dreaming of a White Wolf Christmas, Flight of the White Wolf, All's Fair in Love and Wolf, A Billionaire Wolf for Christmas, SEAL Wolf Surrender, Silver Town Wolf: Home for the Holidays, Night of the Billionaire Wolf, You Had Me at Wolf, Joy to the Wolves, The Wolf Wore Plaid, Jingle Bell Wolf, The Best of Both Wolves, While the Wolf's Away, Christmas Wolf Surprise, Wolf Takes the

Lead, Wolf on the Wild Side, Her Wolf for the Holidays, A Good Wolf is Hard to Find (2024), Dreaming of a Highland Wolf (2024), Mated for Christmas (2024)

SEAL Wolves: To Tempt the Wolf, A SEAL in Wolf's Clothing, A SEAL Wolf Christmas; SEAL Wolf Hunting, A SEAL Wolf in Too Deep, SEAL Wolf Undercover, SEAL Wolf Surrender

Silver Town Wolves: Destiny of the Wolf, Wolf Fever, Dreaming of the Wolf, Silence of the Wolf; A Silver Wolf Christmas, Between a Wolf and a Hard Place, Home for the Holidays, Jingle Bell Wolf

Wolff Family Lodge Wolves: You Had Me at Wolf, Wolf on the Wild Side, A Good Wolf is Hard to Find

Highland Wolves: Heart of the Highland Wolf, A Howl for a Highlander, A Highland Werewolf Wedding, Hero of a Highland Wolf, A Highland Wolf Christmas, The Wolf Wore Plaid, Her Wolf for the Holidays, Dreaming of a Highland Wolf

Billionaire Wolf Series: A Billionaire in Wolf's Clothing, A Billionaire Wolf for Christmas, Night of the Billionaire Wolf, Wolf Takes the Lead

White Wolf Series: Legend of the White Wolf, Dreaming of a White Wolf Christmas, Flight of the White Wolf, While the Wolf's Away, Mated for Christmas

Red Wolf Series: Seduced by the Wolf, Joy to the Wolves, The Best of Both Wolves, Christmas Wolf Surprise

Wolf Novellas: Day of the Wolf, Seal Wolf Pursuit, Wolf to the Rescue, Night of the Wolf, United Shifter Force

***

Heart of the Jaguar Series: Savage Hunger, Jaguar Fever, Jaguar Hunt, Jaguar Pride, A Very Jaguar Christmas, You Had Me at Jaguar, The Witch and the Jaguar, Dawn of the Jaguar

***

Heart of the Cougar Series: Cougar's Mate, Call of the Cougar, Taming the Wild Cougar, Covert Cougar Christmas, a novella, Double Cougar Trouble, Cougar Undercover, Cougar Magic, Cougar Halloween Mischief, Falling for the Cougar, Cougar Christmas Calamity, Catch the Cougar (Halloween Novella), You Had Me at Cougar, Saving the White Cougar, Big Cat Magic

***

White Bear Series: Loving the White Bear, Claiming the White Bear, Bear of a Halloween

Grizzly Bear Series: Bear in Mind

***

Wolves of Old: Wolf Pack

Vampire romances: Killing the Bloodlust, Deadly Liaisons, Huntress for Hire, Forbidden Love, Deadly Liaisons, Vampire Redemption, Primal Desire, Huntress Unleashed

Vampire Novellas: The Siren's Lure, Vampiric Calling, Seducing the Huntress

***

Comedy Romance: Exchanging Grooms, Marriage, Las Vegas Style

***

Science Fiction: Galaxy Warrior

Young Adult Titles

The World of Fae:

The Dark Fae

The Deadly Fae

The Winged Fae

The Ancient Fae

Dragon Fae

Hawk Fae

Phantom Fae

Golden Fae

Falcon Fae

Woodland Fae

Angel Fae

***

The World of Elf:

The Shadow Elf

The Darkland Elf

Warrior Elf

***

Blood Moon Series:

Kiss of the Vampire

Bite of the Vampire

Night of the Vampire

The Vampire Chronicles Series:

The Vampire in My Dreams

Demon Guardian Series:

The Trouble with Demons

Demon Trouble, Too

Demon Hunter

Non-Series for Now:

Ghostly Liaisons

The Beast Within

Courtly Masquerade

Deidre's Secret

The Magic of Inherian:

The Scepter of Salvation

The Mage of Monrovia

Emerald Isle of Mists